THE
BIRTHDAY
REUNION

BOOKS BY CLAIRE SEEBER

THE
BIRTHDAY
REUNION

CLAIRE SEEBER

bookouture

Published by Bookouture in 2023

An imprint of Storyfire Ltd.
Carmelite House
50 Victoria Embankment
London EC4Y 0DZ

www.bookouture.com

ISBN: 978-1-80314-946-2
eBook ISBN: 978-1-80314-945-5

For Bridget Shepherd and all my female friends, both now and then. Thank you.

PS No long-lost birthday parties though, maybe!

And if a house be divided against itself, that house cannot stand.

PROLOGUE

Best friends forever, or so I thought. That's how it was meant to be.

When we first met, we promised to have each other's backs – not stab each other *in* the back.

But on this sweltering Mediterranean morning, trying frantically to catch my breath under the purest, bluest sky; fighting to balance on the rocks I've just clambered up so desperately, my sweaty feet and hands scratched and bleeding, it's clear that someone didn't get the memo.

The view across golden sands and turquoise sea might be as gorgeous as *Vogue*'s travel pages, but the ruined thing on the edge of the water makes my stomach heave.

Less than fifty metres away, sprawled in the middle of this tropical beauty spot, motionless as a floppy giant starfish, gentle waves lapping at the upturned soles, is a body.

By the looks of it, a very dead one, face down in the hot sand, ugly and destroyed, a thick black knife handle protruding from its spine like a bulging shark fin.

And even as I try to process the nightmare I'm gazing at, the sun beating its burning rays on the frazzling skin, my stomach

churning with nausea; as I just about manage to contain my first
retch, I think – there's something wrong with the picture, fresh
corpse or not.

I just can't quite work out what. Yet.

But I will. I have to.

Before it gets us all.

Police is my frantic thought as I start to scramble the other way
down the rocks.

We need the police immediately; we need official help – but
we can't get off the bloody island. We can't even call for help, as
we can't make our phones work; they haven't worked for days.

We're almost at the stage of using smoke signals. Literally –
a bonfire was lit last night in desperation, to no avail.

Unless one of us swims to the mainland – and no one has
dared even suggest it after the boating disaster – we are well and
truly trapped.

And as the corpse gently sizzles in the heat and I scrape my
grazed knees on the rocks again as I try to get away, that book I
read at school, *Lord of the Flies*, floods my head – the mad chaos
of it, the frantic fight for survival – and the image of a human
head pinioned on a stick blurs into my imagination.

Fighting nausea, I hear a sob.

It takes me a few seconds to realise it's my own.

Over the rocks now, I begin to run, and all I can do is pray
it's towards safety this time.

To safety – and not straight into the arms of the killer.

ONE
SIMONE
MARCH 2022

And So It Begins...

I hear the post arrive before I see it, heralded as ever by our crazy mutt barking at the letters that plop heavily onto the mat, footsteps receding quickly.

'Shut *up*, Nell!' I drag the dog away from the door before the postman complains again; already not our biggest fan. 'You'll get us all in trouble.'

Boring bills in brown envelopes, a gardening magazine I splashed out on for my husband's birthday, hoping he'd take the hint, if he ever had any time. 'Bit middle-aged,' he'd said, winking at me, and he's never opened it.

A postcard from my in-laws, from their annual boating holiday in the Lakes.

'Deck shoes don't make you a real sailor,' Jodie whispered the first time I met them, when she was still around. 'Or posh. Just saying.'

'Don't be mean,' I muttered with a shiver of discomfort. 'They'll be my family soon.'

'Bad luck.' She grinned, filling our glasses. 'I give you five years tops.' She must have seen my face though. 'Joking, babe, *obviously!*'

Well, she was wrong, wasn't she? I think fiercely, pushing the memory away and swiping up the mail. I'm still here, twenty years on, still married, still late for an Easter fair meeting at my son's school.

But in amongst the usual letters, I'm holding something different today, I realise slowly.

A thick cream envelope, A5, with gold edging. Heavy and expensive-looking.

And on the grainy front, my name, picked out in swirly gold type.

Something about it sends shivers down my spine.

I dump the lot in the wonky heart-shaped letter rack our daughter made in DT at school last year, almost tripping over my husband's battered Reeboks abandoned halfway across the hall runner.

Reeboks for show and not for exercise, of course. Lazy Mike.

That expensive envelope's probably just an offer from a fancy catalogue, or the launch of that new French bistro on the high street, I tell myself, kicking the trainers to the side.

But at the kitchen door, I find myself pausing, the dog at my heels.

I go back and gingerly slide the envelope from the pile, carrying it to the kitchen, where Mason's left his packed lunch on the side, yet again.

Normally I'd worry about him missing a meal, but I'm distracted by my stomach plunging like a fairground ride.

I switch the kettle on, then hold the envelope up to the patio doors.

It's way too plush to be a marketing ploy, I know that really.

It's an invitation, I can see now: probably to a wedding. Maybe one of Mike's colleagues from his old firm...

'Just open it,' I murmur to the dog, panting at my feet, tongue lolling in hope. 'Right?'

She blinks in response.

But I don't open it. I push it away and just sit, the kettle long since boiled, my eyes lighting on the biscuit tin. For a few seconds, I consider eating my feelings – a weird mix of dread and excitement churning in my stomach.

It's the name on the front. It's my name, sure, but it's also a nickname I haven't heard in years. *Dilly* – short for my surname, Dillane.

A nickname no one uses apart from—

My phone pings, and I jump like a guilty child.

Hannah, her text just five stark words:

I knew she'd be back.

TWO
VICKY

When I slide the card out of the posh envelope and see it for the first time in all its pink, gold and black glory, I actually laugh.

JODIE'S 40!

You're exclusively invited to *the* Do of the Decade!

Thursday 9–Monday 13 June 2022

Infinity pools, hot tubs, massages at midday!

Champagne and mocktails at sunset!

AMAZING memories to make & most importantly:

Elite Company to Die For & All for Free!

~~Pumpkins Carriages~~ Airplanes at dawn

The Party in Paradise won't be the same without YOU!

Call this number for all the details

We Promise You a Weekend to Never Forget

05666 999 911

'Something funny?' My new waitress grins as she plonks the groaning tray down beside my stack of messy accounts.

'Oh yeah.' I turn the invite over in my hand. 'Completely hilarious.'

'I bet it's not as good as the fact that table five want three more Mango Magics,' the girl stage-whispers. 'And the blender's just blown up.'

'Again?' I sigh. Nothing's really prepared me for being responsible for literally everything in the café. Small business owner? Small earner, more like. I shove the bills under the ledger.

''Fraid so.' She dumps the dirty cups in the sink and cocks her pretty bleached head at the glossy card lying there. 'So? Something good?'

'Not really, no.' I'm not sure how I feel about it, to be honest. 'Just a silly party.'

'Ooh, I love a party.' She empties milk into a jug. 'Can't beat a really good boogie, don't you reckon?'

'Well...' I consider her words. When was the last time I actually boogied? Lord only knows. 'Yeah, I guess I was the same at your age, flower.' Wow, I sound ancient. When did I get this old? 'I mean, I still do like a party, of course, if it's with the right crowd.'

But I think sadly of my social life these days, the highlight of which is usually a night in with Dave, his low-alcohol beer and a Chinese takeaway, watching yet another one of those depressing Nordic crime box-sets he favours, or maybe the snooker if I'm *really* lucky.

My phone buzzes in my bag.

Yes, I got one too, I type quickly. *Madness begins again.*

Because sure as eggs is eggs, as my mum would say, any birthday party of Jodie's is sure to be trouble.

There's a very good reason I haven't spoken to her in years. A good reason why I won't go to the party.

Especially one that, as the invite declares, is taking place in Paradise.

Paradise Lost, more likely.

Paradise – or Hell?

THREE
HANNAH

I don't even read it.

I don't have to. I know what it is by just glancing at it – at the glittery, ostentatious invitation that's meant to be smart but just looks tacky. It's so *her*.

Words peep from the open envelope, something about partying in Paradise, and I drop it straight into the waste-paper bin as if it's burning hot.

It's made my heart speed up, just seeing her name in the daft curly print, and I suddenly feel like shouting or crying or punching the wall, really, *really* hard.

But I don't want to scare my mum, so I do none of those things.

Instead, I pull the card back out of the bin and let myself out into our box of a garden. I pace once around it, very fast. Then I walk around again, this time slowly. Walking makes no difference to the feelings churning in my gut though.

I still hate just the thought of her.

It's freezing and grey out here, barely any leaves on the trees on the other side of the ugly wall. Spring hasn't sprung yet. I can't remember the last time I went somewhere hot and exotic, or lay in the sun on a lounger. Despite the fact that here, on paper, is the perfect opportunity to do just that – and maybe even for free – the truth is, frankly, I'd rather poke my own eyes out.

Yeah, that seems preferable to attending any sort of do hosted by that... that *witch*.

My breathing has sped up again, and I try to slow it down.

I imagine the others getting their invites; my best friends. *Remaining* best friends. What might they want to do?

With a stab of anxiety, I know they won't necessarily feel the same as me.

Simone is constantly fluctuating these days between fear for her children and boredom. She loves her kids so much, but despite her protests, I know she struggles with constant domesticity, with a feeling of failure.

It hasn't been as easy, maybe, as she hoped.

And Vicky is Vicky, and we all know she used to love to party almost as much as Jodie did.

So I also know my next job will probably be persuading them to keep away too – for their own sanity and safety.

'Hannah?' My mother's wavering voice drifts through the back door, and I come to with a start.

'I'm here, Mum,' I call back, aware of a sudden shooting pain in my hand. 'Just a sec.'

Looking down, I realise I've been clutching the stiff card so hard, it's left red marks across my palm.

To match all the other scars Jodie left me with.

FOUR
VICKY
THURSDAY, 9 JUNE

Gatwick Airport

I'm returning the glasses to the airport bar when the monitor blinks to say our flight's just been delayed by half an hour.

Never keen on flying, I always need one strong drink before boarding. The fact that I've started early means the gin I've just downed softens the blow of the delay a bit – but then being delayed probably isn't a bad thing, given what we're about to embark on.

In fact, I'm surprised we've got here at all.

I order a couple more (warm) gins – they've run out of ice apparently – and head to the table we just vacated, speeding up slightly to beat a grey-haired, frosty-looking couple with a pot of tea.

As I plonk my tray down with an apologetic smile seconds before they can, Simone appears in the entrance. I wave vigorously.

Frowning, she negotiates her way through a large, loud stag party, on at least their fifth pint by the looks of it.

And it's still only 11 a.m.

'Expecting company?' Simone seems confused as she arrives back at the table. 'Thought we were headed to the gate?'

'You can keep me company any time.' A well-built Brummie winks at me, swaying a little too close as he toasts me with his pint.

'You're all right, thanks, mate,' I mutter, turning away. 'We've got another half-hour till we board apparently, so I just thought...' I gesture at the drinks. 'While we wait.'

'Fair enough.' Simone delves in her bulging Boots carrier bag. 'Aha.' She locates a bottle of factor 50. 'You always burn, Vick, so...'

'Aw, thanks, Mum,' I deadpan, but this is what I love about my oldest friend. She's nothing if not maternal, my lovely Simone, and she knows me so well. Sometimes I'd like her to be my real mum. 'No, that's great, thanks, mate.' I reach for my own bag on the back of the chair. 'What do I owe you?'

'Oh, call it quits.' Simone nods at her gin and tonic. 'But, um, seriously – who's that other one for?'

'I was thirsty,' I quip, but the three drinks on the tray suddenly seem really sad: an incomplete family. 'Old habits die hard, I guess.'

'I guess.' Simone sighs as I rummage through my bag. It's obvious we're both thinking of Hannah. 'Did you see Jodie's interview last week? Extolling the virtues of rehab. Very Amy Winehouse.'

'That's odd.' My search isn't turning up my purse. I check my jacket pockets. 'Must have left it on the bar.'

But when I ask at the bar, the barman says nothing's been handed in. 'Sorry, love.'

'Are you sure?' I'm normally careful; I hate misplacing things – and this isn't a good thing to lose at the best of times. 'I was only just here paying—'

'Vick!' Simone's voice is urgent across the frosty grey heads. 'Our flight's final boarding.'

Rushing back to the table, I crouch to look under it: nothing except old crisps and a single flip-flop.

'Oh God.' Panic rises in my gullet. 'It must have been nicked.'

'It has to be here if you just had it.' Simone's gathering her own things; she hates being late. 'Check your pockets again. We need to hurry.'

The rowdy stag party are teetering on the verge of real aggression, arguing about some rugby game. One of them bangs into me as I stand again.

'Sorry.' He leers down at me, and I glower back. Perhaps *he* took my purse for a joke.

'Hey,' I begin, 'have you seen my—' But the barman interrupts me.

''Scuse.' He's holding something up. 'This yours?'

'Oh God, thank you!' The wash of relief I feel seeing my bright pink purse is visceral. 'Was it on the bar after all?'

'No.' He passes it over with a weird defensive air. 'Some young woman just handed it in. Said she found it in the ladies' loo.'

'Really?' I look around. 'Who?'

He points, but all I glimpse is a swish of a chiffon skirt as a figure leaves the bar, baseball cap over her hair.

'Hey, wait a minute,' I call, but she's already disappeared.

'C'mon.' Simone has my wheelie case, and I grab it.

'Thanks,' I say, hurrying to the exit. 'Hey!' I call again, but the figure is headed in the opposite direction to our gate.

'I don't think our flight *was* delayed, you know.' Simone sounds flustered as she rechecks the monitor. 'It says the gate's closing. C'mon!'

'I'm sure it was.' I trot after her. 'Oh – I forgot my scarf! You go on.'

As Simone pauses to put her phone away, I nip back into the bar.

At the table, I see the tray and the drink meant for Hannah – who to my dismay hasn't come. She refused to join us on 'pain of death' – her words, and she's always been a woman of her word.

Briefly I contemplate drinking the gin, but I resist, as a great wave of sadness washes over me that she's not here.

FIVE
SIMONE
MARCH

I'd been seriously doubtful about the trip since Vicky had first called.

'Look, I know what you're thinking, but why don't we just bite the bullet and go?' she said. 'Have a laugh?'

The truth was, I'd been struggling on and off since Mum finally died a few years ago. Then, just as I was emerging from the doldrums, our ten-year-old son, Mason, was diagnosed with severe dyslexia. I mainly felt relief that we could start to help him now, but his distress was worsened by school bullies, who took every chance to make him feel stupid.

It culminated in a horrible playground fight, after which I wrote an enraged piece about bullying, consequences and restorative justice techniques for the school newsletter.

It was the first time I'd written anything apart from a shopping list for years, and so no one was more surprised than me when it elicited a phone call from the deputy head.

'I saw your article. Brilliant suggestions.'

'Thank you.' I couldn't deny the warm glow I felt at his words.

'I wonder if you'd come to the teaching conference in

London next month. To talk about bullying from a parental point of view.'

'That's very kind, but I can't,' I said automatically. 'My husband's away with work.'

It was a lie, but that phone call had ignited a spark in me; the remnant of a long-dead ambition buried after the horrible death of my friendship with Jodie – buried along with other dreams. To move to New York, to fly a plane or run an ultra-marathon through the Sahara. Basically anything the least bit exciting or out of the ordinary.

The dreams I'd always felt my life with Jodie had annihilated.

But that phone call made me think twice about seeing her again.

She'd ruined things for me professionally once, so perhaps now she owed me. Perhaps she could actually help me...

So I invited Vicky and Hannah round for supper to discuss the party; to debate whether it was worth even trying to see Jodie.

Maybe it *was* time to let bygones be bygones. After all, we'd all once loved her so much.

But I should have known it wouldn't be that easy. Nothing that involved Jodie was *ever* easy – that was the truth we'd discovered too late first time round.

That freezing March evening, sitting round my kitchen table with red wine and a big dish of chilli, for all my ambivalence about going to Ibiza, I could never have imagined we'd all be taking our lives in our hands if we agreed to go to the 'Do of the Decade'.

How stupid and naïve were we?

SIX
VICKY

I *had* kind of made up my mind by the time we met at Simone's, even if the others hadn't.

But I didn't want to go to Ibiza alone, so I needed to persuade them.

And honestly, things had been so bad recently with Dave, my long-term partner, I needed to get away, and I wanted female company. I was done with grumpy, moody men claiming they were too depressed to work, with me paying for everything.

In her big cosy kitchen, an old Blur LP scratching along quietly on Mike's ancient record player, Simone cooked a big pot of chilli and a sticky toffee pudding. Hannah's favourites, designed unsubtly to cheer her up – and maybe to persuade her to come, if we were honest.

She'd been having a rubbish time recently – her life was pretty miserable with those awful parents – so I plied her with her favourite red wine, inasmuch as you can ever ply Hannah with alcohol.

Which is to say, not much at all.

'Thanks, but I can't get plastered these days,' she kept

repeating, distracted by her phone. 'And I have to be on the ball to cycle to the station.'

'Get a cab?' Simone went to top up Hannah's glass – still almost full. 'Or Mike can drop you when he gets back. You go out so seldom, Han.'

'Ah, I don't mind.' But she looked tired and deflated, I thought. The shadows under her big eyes were more pronounced than usual, her face almost gaunt. 'And I don't want to be any trouble.'

'Ask Jeff to take over for a night.' I hoped she wasn't getting ill. 'You look done in, hon.'

'He's in Brussels for work.' She put her hand over the glass to stop Simone pouring. 'And he's so busy right now. It's not fair.'

Hannah's older brother was nothing if not useless. He lived in London, and was always busy with work or his young family, leaving Hannah to care for their elderly parents almost single-handedly. Fair play, though, he'd offered to pay for a smart nursing home a few months back – except Hannah wouldn't hear of it.

'Over my dead body,' she always said when the subject came up, and at first, I used to retort, 'It probably will be, the way you push yourself,' biting back the idea that if only the cantankerous old pair *would* leave this earth, she'd get her life back. 'I owe them.'

Owe them what though? A life of servitude?

But even I'd given up trying to convince her.

Softly spoken and gentle she might be, but I knew Hannah had always retained a core of steel – along with a moral code stronger than Atlas. If she didn't want to do something, she definitely wouldn't.

Case in point being Jodie's fortieth.

Although, to be honest, Hannah probably had less to be

upset with Jodie about than anyone else did. Apart from having known her longest, she'd got off most lightly. Sort of.

And as I felt Simone waver that cold evening in March, growing keener on the idea of going, the two of us had tried our best.

But Hannah wasn't having any of it, to the point where it started to annoy me.

SEVEN
SIMONE

Sitting in my kitchen, we'd all pussyfooted around the party.

We chatted about Hannah's job, and her parents, a dour Catholic couple I'd never warmed to, both now verging on senility. We toasted Vicky's brave new venture, the Garden Café, for which she'd remortgaged herself to the hilt; and we talked a bit about my children.

But I'm always painfully aware that other people's kids aren't very interesting, especially if you don't have any yourself. And despite the fact that my two oldest friends were great godparents to Mason and Tiger, I felt too ashamed to admit my recent struggles.

Meanwhile, the further through the wine we got, the louder Vicky became. Hannah kept checking her phone, almost compulsively, until I wanted to say, 'Put it away, for God's sake!' She reminded me of Tiger, glued to her screen at all times now she was a teenager.

Feeling tense as I mixed the custard, I braced myself to mention the party.

'Right, girls.' Vicky topped up our glasses again. 'I bet you both fancy a weekend in the sun?' She'd beaten me to it.

'What?' Hannah's head snapped up. 'Where?'

'Jodie's fortieth?' Vicky met her eye with a defiant grin. 'Don't we deserve some fun?'

'You're joking, right?' Hannah stood up so abruptly, her chair fell over, making us all jump. 'You can't mean it.'

'Why can't I?' Calmly Vicky finished her drink. Having originally declared 'I have no intention of celebrating that cow's big day, Ibiza or not', she was doing a typical Vicky – changing her mind and expecting us all to follow suit.

'Because you promised.' The friction in the room buzzed like the white noise on an untuned radio. Hannah stood staring and speechless, clenching and unclenching her fists.

'Oh, come *on*, Han,' Vicky pleaded. 'Don't be such a drama queen.'

'Vick!' I stood and righted the chair. 'That's a bit rich.'

'But we swore.' Hannah's voice was barely above a whisper, but it cut deep. 'We *all* did. We promised each other back then, back when...' There was a long pause. 'Back when, you know. She wrote those things.'

How could I forget? How could any of us?

'She's right.' The back of the chair suddenly felt like a shield as I sensed Hannah's angst. 'We *did* swear. We all swore we'd never go near Jodie again.'

Gingerly I took Hannah's arm and guided her to sit. She was trembling, I realised, but also rigid.

'We made a promise,' she whispered, eyes saucer-like.

Honestly, it shot me back twenty years, and I found it unnerving.

'Well... maybe. But that was ages ago.' Vicky's own eyes were beady – with booze or rebellion, who knew? 'And she's never invited us to a swanky all-expenses-paid trip to the Med before, has she?'

'Give me one reason why we'd want to go anywhere near her?' Hannah was unequivocal.

'Personally, I could really use some time off from the café. Get a bit of distance, you know,' Vicky blasted on. 'And from Dave, if I'm honest.'

'What's up with Dave?' I returned to the custard and the relative safety of the hob, the air thick with tension now.

'Nothing really.' She avoided our gazes. 'Except the fact that he just sits around watching TV all day, or does his stupid free-running. It drives me mad.'

I resisted saying 'again'. They'd always been an odd match.

'Oh dear.' Spooning the gloop carefully into a jug, I added more sugar. Hannah needed feeding up; her collarbones were protruding above her scoop-necked jumper. 'Look, it might *sound* like a laugh,' I said cautiously, 'but do you really think Jodie's going to be fun? Specially when none of us have spoken to her for so long.'

'If we know one thing' – Vicky topped up her wine – 'it's that Jodie's fun. And she always threw amazing parties, give her that much.'

I felt a great throb in my chest at the memory.

'That's two things,' Hannah said flatly.

Pushing the bad past away, I allowed myself to remember the Dive, and then our Royal Mews flat. The constant revelry and never-ending shenanigans – thumping music and late nights, impromptu soirees and mini-raves, someone always crashing on the sofa. People stayed because our home was a hive of fun, where everyone wanted to be – for a while, at least. Party Central, and we were the Queen Bees. Or Jodie was.

Until...

I swallowed hard. Until it all fell apart spectacularly.

'You can't argue with the fun bit.' Vicky was bullish.

Not long after that, Jodie betrayed us, revealing our innermost secrets in print, one by one; dishing the dirt in the name of journalism, using us to climb the career ladder, leaving our reputations in tatters...

'I can.' Hannah's voice had more bite now. 'I can definitely argue. I'm keeping my promise. I won't go to Ibiza.' She pulled her bowl of pudding towards her resolutely. 'Remember that when she fucks you over again. Don't say I didn't warn you, 'cos I won't be picking up the pieces.'

There it was. The angry language that sounded so ugly in Hannah's mouth because it was so rare – and that steely edge again.

As steely as the spoon she attacked the dessert with.

But for all Hannah's hidden depths, I knew how soft she was inside. She was so loyal, and clearly devastated that we might break our promise.

EIGHT

HANNAH

I mean, a fortieth? Come on! Now that was a joke, and not a funny one at that. Jodie was no more forty than I was a catwalk model.

Far nearer fifty, I'd guess.

And amazing parties?

Not even a joke. I couldn't believe it.

Did they not remember the total carnage? The devastation Jodie had left in her wake? Locking ourselves away for months before we could pick ourselves back up. Dusting ourselves down afterwards, as if from some horrible accident, bloodied and trembling.

I wasn't allowed to go home until the Virgin Mary spoke to my mum and told her I was ready to atone – and I was still paying the price now.

Worse: did the other two not remember our vow? That we promised one another we'd never let her do it again? Never give her the chance to get too close to us.

Simone put the custard down on the table almost nervously, and I took the jug, choosing my words with care.

'And don't forget' – I poured the yellow liquid over my

pudding – 'the fun just meant Jodie ended up addicted. To everything.'

I looked at Vicky's full glass. 'So much fun, she nearly died at least once.'

'Well, she's done her time in rehab, hasn't she?' Vicky declared. She obviously had other things on her mind. 'I'm pretty sure she's clean.'

We'd all seen the big interviews Jodie gave last year about 'going sober' – we'd shared them on email with the odd emoji and little comment.

But I had an inkling what it was Vicky didn't want to remember, and why she might want to go to the party so badly.

NINE
SIMONE

'Everyone can change, hon.' Vicky fiddled with her vape, and I felt a swell of irritation at her carelessness. 'And it's not like Jodie hasn't been through the mill herself.'

'I'm sorry, but leopards and spots, Vick.' Hannah put her spoon down.

'Well, she's still sober, according to the internet.' Vicky's fashionably short hair was sticking up on end now. 'Look, let's just ring the number, see what's actually what.' She pulled her invitation out and reached across the table for Hannah's phone. 'My mobile's nearly dead – use yours?'

'No!' Hannah moved her phone back so quickly, she knocked over her wine. 'Oh God, sorry, Sim!'

'It's fine.' I fetched a cloth, glad of something to do with my hands. 'No harm done.' But the pool of liquid was the colour of old blood.

'I have to keep the line free,' Hannah apologised. 'For the carer.'

'Use the landline,' I suggested to Vicky, but she was already jabbing in the number.

The fact that we could often finish each other's sentences

always made us feel like family, but now I felt a twinge of annoyance at her tenacity.

Bolshie Vicky had come out to play tonight.

'Hello,' she said loudly into the receiver, and my stomach fluttered with nerves. Finally, the moment of truth.

Shaking her head impatiently, she put the phone on speaker.

'*Hola!*' said a tinny voice, and we all craned forward, not quite with bated breath but not far off.

'So glad you called to join us!'

It was a recorded message: female, dulcet, Americanised – and unrecognisable to me.

'Is that Jodie?' Hannah's frown deepened. 'Doesn't sound like her.'

'No,' I agreed, 'you're right, it doesn't.'

'Shush!' Vicky flapped her hand at us. 'I can't hear.'

'We're so thrilled you can make Jodie's big bash,' the message continued. 'The great news is – it's all on Jodie! The most exclusive villa is booked on the idyllic island of Ibiza, and everything's included: flights, fine wines, dining and dancing. We'll email your plane tickets and collect you when you land; just get yourself plucked and waxed, and to the airport of your choice. All you need is a bikini, shades and a party dress or three. Then just sit back and relax while we party like it's 1999.'

Jodie had always been a huge Prince fan.

'And remember – if you're not on the list, you're not coming in!'

Then the voice wished us 'Happy holidays, one and all' and the message clicked off.

'Weird. And is she gay now?' I was confused.

'Why?' Vicky frowned. 'What do you mean?'

'Well, who's that?' I gestured at the phone. 'I mean, whose voice? A girlfriend? It's definitely not Jodie.'

'Probably an assistant, knowing her.' Vicky grinned. 'Come on! It sounds ace – and when did we last have a girls' weekend?'

'But... wearing a swimsuit in front of people I don't know.' I pulled a face. 'Or any people, in fact. *Literally* my idea of hell.'

'Oh, love—' Hannah's phone pinged, and I bit my tongue as she read the message. 'Sorry. You're beautiful, Sim.' She had composed herself: the Hannah I knew and loved. 'We don't even know who else is invited.'

'True,' I agreed. 'God only knows who might be there.'

'It might just be us though.' Vicky wasn't giving up, but Hannah had.

'Thanks for a lovely dinner, Sim,' she said, looking around for her coat. 'But I've only got the carer for two hours.'

'Stay for coffee?' I didn't want her to leave with everything so messy and unsorted. 'Please, Han.'

'A nightcap, more like.' Vicky went to Hannah and cupped her face. 'It'd be really good for you,' she wheedled. 'Sunshine and sleep. Not being rude, honey, but you look ill.'

'Ill?' Hannah pulled away from her. 'I'm fine.'

'No, not ill.' I patted her arm. 'Just tired.'

'Please don't worry,' she insisted. 'It's just Dad's wandering, poor old thing. Wakes me up most nights now.'

'So maybe, angel,' I forced out, 'maybe you *could* use a break? There's time to sort some decent care out, isn't there? If Jeff can't help.'

'But why...' And Hannah's eyes filled with tears, which made my chest hurt. '*Why* would either of you think anything to do with Jodie would be relaxing?'

'I don't want to go without you, Hannah,' Vicky implored, and there was something in her tone that made me look up.

'Well, if you do go, you'll have to,' Hannah said forcefully, just as the front door banged.

Two pairs of feet in the hallway: one stomping upstairs, the other headed for the kitchen. That didn't bode well, I thought distractedly.

'Sleep on it, Han?' Vicky opened the French windows and exhaled her vape into the night, a nasty sweet concoction that made me feel sick. 'Old times and all that?'

Or maybe it was the memories making me nauseous.

'No thanks. Also, it can't be her fortieth, can it?' Hannah walked to the door. 'And you're mad if you think it'll be fun.'

'But...' Vicky trailed off. For the first time, she looked uncertain.

'Also, could we not mention this to Mike?' I said urgently as the footsteps neared. 'I haven't told him about the invitation yet.'

He hated Jodie with a real passion.

'Honestly' – Hannah turned, trying not to cry – 'after what she did, you must be desperate to even think about going! How can you completely erase the past?'

TEN

THEN

JANUARY 2002

It was a busy Friday night in the inappropriately named Bar of Life, nicknamed Dizzy's after the house speciality, the Dizzy rum cocktail, and rushed off my feet, I was seriously regretting wearing my strappy sandals.

It was even busier than usual – and that was really saying something in this place. We were the buzziest bar in the town, mostly groups of students like me getting hammered, alongside the city's young professionals coming in with cash to flash.

One of whom was standing in front of me now, ordering a huge round of overcomplicated spirits. An estate agent called Cooper – Coops to his friends – from the local branch of Ashtons – I knew that because he'd taken me out a few weeks ago on a whirlwind date, and also because he kept shouting to his mates about his massive commission this month.

You are a massive arse, you mean, I thought.

After we'd gone out that one time, I'd never heard from him again.

Part of a group who regularly met here before Saturday football games in town, tonight he'd arrived outside with a screech of rubber, The Prodigy blaring as he parked badly, ensuring his Porsche was visible through the bar's main doors.

'Fancy a spin later, Simone?' He leant close. 'I know a nice little spot.'

'Sorry.' I tried hard to sound polite rather than cross. 'I'm busy.'

'I'm sorry I didn't call, babes,' he wheedled. 'I've got keys to a gorgeous place on the Nottingham Road. Amazing four-poster.' He cocked a suggestive eyebrow. 'Know what I'm saying?'

'Thanks.' I attempted to hide my exasperation. 'But I'm working late tonight. That's £46.55 please.'

'Your loss.' He thrust a gold American Express card towards me.

'Sorry.' I met his eye for the first time. 'We don't take Amex.'

'You're joking, right?' His tone was chilling. 'Just take it, yeah?' And then I was pretty sure he muttered, '*Bitch.*'

'Please.' My heart sped up the way it always did when someone was confrontational. 'We really don't take it. Do you have another card?'

'No, babes. And I want these drinks – now. So sort it.'

The customer's always right, they taught me on training day. But what if this one wasn't?

'I'm thirsty.' He picked the tray up, and he still hadn't paid. 'Put it on my tab.'

'No tabs, sorry. You know that.' Management were strict here.

'Tough.'

What if the customer was rude, even if you'd once dated him? What if he swore at you; what if he walked away without paying?

My colleague was busy chatting up this guy's mate. Our manager, Tom, was upstairs, helping with a private party, and the bouncer was dealing with the ever-growing queue outside.

There was just me, and I had two choices.

'Stop, please!' I commanded, as forcefully as possible. 'You need to pay.'

'Yeah? And who's gonna make me? You?' Cooper smiled a nasty smile. 'You're a proper minger anyway, and you need to lose some weight.'

'Oi,' said the girl standing beside him at the bar. 'That's bang out of order.'

'Is it?' He looked her up and down. 'And who asked you?'

I felt a frisson of something. Fear, maybe?

'*I* asked me.' She grinned at him. 'I think you should apologise. And it's not true anyway. She's way out of your league.'

Or excitement, perhaps, that a stranger had just stuck up for me?

'*You* might be, sweet-cheeks.' He smirked at her.

There was an odd tension between them. Almost as if he wasn't actually that confident of what he was saying; as if she'd pricked the bubble of his enormous self-confidence. He wasn't a lot taller than her, though she wasn't super tall herself – just wearing high-heeled boots, dark hair bundled up on her head.

'I said you should apologise.' She wasn't grinning any more, just staring at him.

He shook his head and started to move away, and she grabbed his jacket. There was a small tattoo of an anchor on her wrist, I noticed absently as the sleeve of her fur-cuffed jacket slid back.

'Say sorry.'

'Don't touch me!' he spat.

'Yeah, and who's gonna stop me?'

He took a moment to contemplate her, and I held my breath, preparing to come round the bar to help; but then, as if by magic, he turned and put the laden tray down and murmured, 'Sorry.'

I watched, amazed, as he reached into a monogrammed

wallet, GC, pulled out £50 in cash and handed it to me. He didn't wait for the change.

'What a total dick!' The girl winked at me as we watched him skulk into the crowd.

'I'll say,' I agreed fervently, feeling both awed and shaky. 'God, thanks for that. You really didn't have to get involved.' I smiled at her. 'I'm glad you did though. Thank you!'

'No problem.' She stuck her hand out, the one with the anchor on the wrist. 'Jodie.'

'Hi, Jodie.' As I took her hand, 'Common People' by Pulp came on the jukebox. It was a hot little paw, adorned with many gold and silver rings of different sizes, at least one on each finger. 'Buy you a drink to say thanks?'

'Is the Pope Catholic?' She grinned. 'I'll have a double Jack and Coke, ta, babe, with one maraschino cherry.'

And just like that, we became firm friends.

Just like that, we entered each other's lives, and for the next few years or so we were almost inseparable. I'd never known anyone like her.

Best friends forever.

ELEVEN
SIMONE
MARCH

'Evening, my beauties.' Mike waltzed in; kissed Hannah's cheek, ruffled Vicky's hair. 'Not leaving 'cos of me, I hope?' He was joking: rhino-skinned, he was usually oblivious to female tension. 'If I paint my nails, can I join in?'

His joke was bad, but I saw a flash of the boy I'd fallen in love with, despite the fact we were both middle-aged and exhausted.

'Ha!' Hannah, who rarely lost her cool, had almost regained her composure. 'Nice to see you, Mike. How are you?'

'Good, thanks, sweetheart,' he said reflexively. His first lie. 'Any leftovers?' Without further ado, he began to spoon chilli straight from the pot.

'Can you give Hannah a lift please, Mikey?' I watched him absently, still feeling sick, but now because of the disgusting way he was shovelling food in. 'I've drunk too much.'

'Thanks, but I'll cycle.' Hannah belted her coat tightly, only emphasising how thin she'd become. I tried not to feel jealous. There wasn't much about her life to envy, but I hated my own curves. Another reason not to go for a weekend in the sun – baring flesh.

'No way.' My husband went in for another spoonful. 'Give me two secs.'

'Is Tiger OK?' Pointedly I handed him a bowl, keeping my voice down.

'Tiger? Yeah, just in a sulk about some boy.' He didn't keep his voice down though. 'You know what teens are like.' He rolled his eyes at the others.

But neither of them did really. It was a shame, I always thought, given how loving Hannah was, that she'd never had kids. She'd been so good with ours when they were small. And she knew what I'd been through before I had my children – how hard it had been for me to have a baby at all.

Vicky, on the other hand, didn't have a maternal bone in her body. She'd never wanted kids; had been unequivocal about that since we'd first met.

'I just don't want to be tied down,' she'd say. 'I like sleep and holidays and my own company too much.' Though I suspected her own father had put her off being a parent. 'I'll love your kids instead.'

Sometimes – just occasionally – I envied her the freedom of her unfettered life, though recently Dave, her partner, seemed to be more hindrance than help. 'My ball and chain,' I'd heard her joke a few times, in front of him usually. He'd lost his job a while back, and most of his time 'looking for work' was spent in front of daytime TV.

But in my own home, parenting my teens was turning out to be *much* harder than anticipated, leaving me feeling completely stupid for not seeing it coming. And I worried where Tiger's wild side came from.

My beautiful girl was usually moody these days. She'd flunked her exams badly last summer and was having to retake, but she just shouted if I tried to help. And I worried constantly about social media and what she did on it, but it was hard to police it much without huge arguments.

I felt I couldn't do right for doing wrong, and somehow it meant I'd found myself clinging to Mason's babyhood with unattractive desperation. I just wanted to keep them both safe, like I had when they were tiny.

After the disaster of tonight's dinner, the notion of another Tiger drama was tiring. We three old friends were all infinitely more careworn than when we'd first met, and now even the idea of Jodie's party had divided us.

An uncomfortable thought niggled: that try as we might, we didn't work the same way without Jodie. That she'd always been the gel between us, and even though she'd decimated the friendship, something else had been destroyed along with our trust.

'Vick, d'you need a lift too?' I wanted the night to finish; to just be here with my family, even if it meant teen drama.

'I'll get an Uber.' Vicky stashed her vape. 'No worries.'

'Don't be daft.' Mike relinquished his spoon reluctantly, swiping up his keys. 'Did you tell the girls about your job, Sim?'

'Simone!' Hannah managed to look enthusiastic. 'That's fantastic!'

'Ooh, you're a dark horse.' Vicky topped up her glass, to my irritation. 'What is it?'

'Not an actual job yet.' I shot my husband a look. The ad had landed in my inbox last week, but I hadn't even decided whether to go for it yet. 'It's only an idea.'

'You *are* going for the interview at least though, aren't you?' Mike returned my look, and I shifted my weight uncomfortably from foot to foot.

'Can we talk about it later, love?'

Mike had been super stressed since going it alone with his chauffeur business. Not surprising, given the hours he was working, doing most of the driving himself. We badly needed the money another job would bring.

If anyone would know how to secure the role writing for an

online magazine, it'd be my first and worst best friend. So my own motives were less than pure for considering Ibiza.

Whatever I told the others, I still missed her so much.

But I *didn't* miss the fact she'd ruined my chance at a proper career. That was still hard to forgive.

TWELVE

HANNAH

How could they honestly think any party with Jodie could be a break?

Break your heart, more like, a little voice whispered.

I waited for Mike on the front step, gazing into their cosy living room.

From out here in the spring chill, it looked so warm and inviting, and I felt a wave of yearning for a family of my own; for what I didn't have and seemed unlikely to ever manage now.

But would I really have been happy with someone like Mike? He was nice enough, but to be honest, he'd always struck me as a bit... controlled. Though maybe that was understandable, given the past.

And Vicky's partner Dave was nice enough but always struck me as deadly dull.

No point settling, is there? Better to be alone. Who had said that?

I could guess.

I would have settled though. I was very happy with the idea of settling once.

The logs in the wood burner flared suddenly and my eye was caught by... Hang on, what *was* that?

On the mantelpiece, beside a big photo of a young, just married Simone and Mike, gazing misty-eyed at each other in their wedding finery – what a lovely, memorable day, despite everything having just fallen apart finally – there was another frame.

The whole group of us outside Dizzy's. Boys in the back row flicking Vs, making bunny ears behind the girls' heads. I stood on one end, smiling broadly, wearing that old pink pinafore I'd loved so much. Vicky was in her tracksuit, like Sporty Spice, we sometimes joked; Simone smiling so much more convincingly than these days; Jodie in the middle in her fake fur as usual, jumping in the air, arms extended like a star, hair flying.

How could Simone bear to have that reminder of everything we'd lost in her front room?

For a second, I felt such a sense of loss I couldn't even bear to look at it.

Then I looked again.

It wasn't us at Dizzy's at all, I realised with a shaky laugh. It was a group of Tiger's mates in front of The Ivy in town, her sixteenth birthday.

My phone pinged yet again, and I fished it out, praying it wasn't the carer saying Mum had fallen again, or Dad had started swearing at her.

It wasn't.

Please just LEAVE ME ALONE!! I texted back quickly, then turned the phone off, slamming it into the bottom of my bag.

But I knew they wouldn't.

THIRTEEN
SIMONE
THURSDAY, 9 JUNE

Gatwick Airport

The blonde air hostess's smile is so fake, her face looks like it might crack in two. She's huffing around above my head while I murmur apologies; rearranging the overhead locker we've apparently messed up by shoving our bags in desperately, boarding so late.

But while I'm embarrassed, Vicky's oblivious. She's already engrossed in the in-flight bar menu, having just upended her bag all over the floor searching for her 'alternative' flying remedy, though I'm pretty sure she doesn't need anything else after the gins she's already downed.

I'm also thinking the second drink was *definitely* a big mistake this early in the day, because it's gone straight to my head and I should know better than to let Vicky persuade me, and I'm also convinced several people are scowling at us, when there's a commotion at the plane door.

I stare up the aisle, praying it's not trouble.

Or should I say *more* trouble.

I've been making a mental tick-list of the other passengers I've seen, conscious that there may be people we know on the flight. We're still not sure who else is on Jodie's 'exclusive' guest list – if anyone.

The hostess bangs the locker shut with a passive-aggressive, 'Please do be a little more careful, ladies. We don't want any accidents, do we?'

'No, sorry,' I say.

As I peer round her, I think I recognise the face smiling apologetically at the steward by the door. I grab Vicky's arm. 'Vick, that's not... Is that...'

Vicky looks up. 'Oh... wow!'

I've never been so surprised to see anyone – so surprised and pleased – as a flushed Hannah hurries up the aisle, apologising as she bangs elbows and toes with her little wheelie-case, a price label still attached, the air hostess glaring at us as if to say: *I might have known she'd be a friend of yours.*

'Han!' Vicky is ecstatic as she reaches us. 'I can't believe it.'

'Room for one more?' Hannah looks almost shy.

'God, yeah! But how did you make it through the gate? We were the last ones on, and they were moody enough with us.'

'I said it was a family funeral,' Hannah stage-whispers, obviously amazed at her own daring.

By now the air hostess is apoplectic, and the skinny man by the window is refusing to engage with my hopeful winning smile, so there's no way he's going to offer up his seat. My neck prickles; I have the uncomfortable sensation someone's staring at me.

'I'll order some fizz!' Vicky waves the menu. 'Soon as we're airborne!'

'Madam!' The poor woman's about to bust a gut as she directs Hannah towards the back. 'Please just take a seat quickly. We're about to taxi for take-off.'

'Sorry. I'll just...' Hannah shuffles off, mumbling apologies, and plonks herself down a few rows behind us. We smile and wave back at her, and I feel a surge of optimism that it was the right choice to come.

But then I get that sensation on the back of my neck again, as if I'm being watched, and I close my eyes for take-off.

FOURTEEN
HANNAH

I fasten my seat belt, smiling apologetically as the air hostess snatches my case from me, hurrying down the back of the plane to stow it elsewhere.

I couldn't let my friends go without me in the end. In these circumstances, we belong together.

I need to be here to make sure they're OK.

If we're going to see Jodie, we need to stick to our promise to take care of each other.

It doesn't matter that they've broken the original one already, to never see Jodie again.

It doesn't matter much, I suppose.

I am really trying not to let it matter.

I peer around my headphoned neighbour to look out of the window.

I watch the brown and green of England falling away beneath us, the toy cars on the grey roads, the neat boxes of fields as we head towards the dark blue of the coast, and I take a deep breath.

I think, *Here we go. Now we'll really see what's what.*

I hope it'll end all the speculation about Jodie's motives, and they'll remember once and for all why we've avoided her for so long.

And most importantly, I hope I can try to keep my best friends safe as we do it.

FIFTEEN
VICKY

By the time I'm seated on the plane and we're taxiing for take-off, I realise I'm *possibly* a bit more drunk than is sensible. But continuing to coat my nerves with alcohol seems like the only solution for both my nerves about flying and my growing ambivalence about the trip.

When I thought back in freezing March that all three of us would go and face Jodie together, it had seemed like such a good idea: a girls' weekend, a reunion with us all there to get each other through the difficult bits. To deal with the thing that had hung over us for so many years. And I wanted to get away from Dave, if I'm honest. He's been pretty mean recently.

But when Hannah point-blank refused to come, I felt devastated.

So now that she's turned up, obviously it's time to celebrate!

Until the drinks trolley comes down the aisle, I'd entirely forgotten my purse was so nearly lost. But fishing it out of my bag, I remember the anonymous woman who found it in the airport bar.

Or in the ladies', as she claimed to the barman.

As I think about it, I feel as if someone's watching me from the back of the plane, but when I turn and scan the visible rows for anyone I might know, I can't see a face I recognise.

I order three little bottles of rosé Prosecco and a strong coffee, and scrabble in my purse for my debit card.

There's a scrap of paper wrapped round it – a duty-free receipt probably.

But no, it's handwritten – a note, I realise, as I unfurl it:

BE VERY CAREFUL, MY DEAR ONE, OR YOU MAY BE IN DANGER.

SIXTEEN
SIMONE

Ibiza

The party started for most of the youngsters on board the flight before take-off, their clamour rolling down the plane in intense waves of excitement.

Briefly we joined their 'vibe', as Tiger would say, Hannah sneaking down to perch beside us, toasting our trip with over-priced Prosecco, until an irritated steward asked her to, 'Please move for the trolley, madam.'

But if I was honest, I didn't feel excited at all. I just felt anxious.

Vicky soon dozed off, so I dug my book out, a modern thriller about toxic motherhood, but it was really hard to concentrate.

Maybe it wasn't very good – or maybe it just reminded me of things I didn't want to think about right now.

Eventually I abandoned it to gaze out of the window, relishing the sunlit peace above the perfect white clouds, the sky cornflower blue tinged with gold. I hoped Mike would be OK with the kids; that Tiger wouldn't give him the runaround about visiting my dad. Mike had dropped me off saying he hoped I had the most brilliant time, and I felt so guilty for not being straight with him. Mason hugged me tight, but Tiger wouldn't even say goodbye.

The beautiful soft clouds were a brief respite, the last bit of peace in a long time, and then I felt those eyes boring into me again.

But when I turned, it was just the air hostess asking if I had any rubbish to get rid of.

As soon as we disembark, my semi-serene state of mind dissipates.

Vicky's sobered up now, seeming brighter than I feel, though that might just be the expensive concealer she bought in duty-free.

I'm increasingly apprehensive about what might happen this weekend, and pretty jaded from the early start, the morning drinking taking its toll. But it's the nerves about what comes next that are really getting to us all – or at least I imagine so.

Vicky's brightness fades and Hannah is very muted, though that's normal for Hannah. As we follow the signs to Passport Control, I notice that she's checking her phone constantly, a new habit of hers.

In the queue, it's hard to talk over the noise of excitable Gen Zs. I attempt a joke about being up all night being different these days, but it falls flat. Mainly because it's a bad joke, but also because joking suddenly seems pointless, while joking about partying is particularly inappropriate, given what we're headed to.

And I realise that perhaps we're all keeping an eye out for Jodie herself.

As we round the corner, the muscular customs police lounging against the wall come as a surprise, all with guns strapped to their chests, two holding big dogs on leashes. The dogs look infinitely more lively than the nearest officers, a man and a woman, who appear both bored and as if they're waiting for someone, which is a trick in itself. They lend the corridor a strange air of unease, and I'm keen to get out of the airport and into the afternoon sun.

As Hannah stops to adjust her sandal, Vicky and I linger by the exit.

'Very continental.' Vicky nods at the nearest officer. 'Do you reckon a big gun means' – she measures with her hands – 'a big dick?'

I grin.

From her recent sniping, I've gathered how deep a rut she and Dave are in, and she's also mumbled something about making a mistake that I haven't understood. The eye she casts over the two officers suggests some kind of unreadable interest.

The woman looks at Vicky briefly, but the male officer appears unaware of her; he's busy restraining his dog, keeping the leash short, studying the melee of passing passengers, who all begin to hurry as they near the final hurdle to freedom.

His gaze snaps round without warning.

'You!' Handsome and doe-eyed this policeman might be, but I feel a great wash of anxiety at his heavily accented English. The same anxiety I always feel near police these days. He points at us. 'Go on.'

'We're just waiting...' I gesture down the corridor at Hannah, who's now looking at her phone again. *Hurry up*, I urge her internally. 'Our friend—'

'No.' He is authoritative and impatient. 'Go through.'

'What?' Vicky says crossly. 'But—'

'You are in the way. Move, *now*.'

As I do what I'm told – no one's going to argue with a man with a semi-automatic strapped to his chest – I cast an eye back, willing Hannah to hurry so I won't feel we've abandoned her.

It's with an awful sense of unease that I see the Alsatian dog nearest her start to pull at its leash, whining and panting.

'Hannah Cleary?' I'm sure I hear a Spanish voice say, but too quickly we're swept up in the herd and pushed through the exit.

There's nothing we can do but wait.

Vicky goes to the loo, and I lean on my case, desperately wishing I could lie down, and text Mike to say we've landed.

'You need to go and let your hair down, baby,' he insisted the week after the dreadful dinner. 'Hannah's got a lot on her plate – don't let her put you off. Have a break from us with your mates. I can take care of all things Tiger.'

'What about Mason?' I said, but in the end, I acquiesced when he kept telling me I deserved it, though I was less than honest about Jodie's involvement. And Mason's easy still, safely through the worst of last year's drama.

But I can't stop checking faces as other passengers pass me. I'm jittery; picking people out, thinking I know them, expecting to see Jodie at every turn.

A bleached-haired girl in enormous dark shades and a short gingham jumpsuit clomps through the arrivals hall in her chunky heeled boots, smiling beatifically, long gold chains swinging. I watch her pass through the doors, pausing outside to light a cigarette with black-nailed fingers, and I envy her obvious ease, her smooth face, her peace of mind as she hails a cab and disappears.

The serenity of youth. Though there's something about her that seems kind of familiar. Maybe I'm just thinking about Tiger.

It's not just being here that makes me feel nervous; it's the past year with Tiger: the bitten nails, the late-night puking after too much vodka, the Rizlas and filters scattered round her room in amongst crumpled clothes and little plastic bags I feared had once held weed.

I'd never understood that being a mum would mean this – which was completely stupid, given my own misspent youth.

Except it feels like I was pretty tame compared to my daughter.

Ten minutes later, Hannah still hasn't emerged, and I'm debating whether to send the text to the car, as instructed in the email that came with our plane tickets, or to wait until she joins us.

Vicky's distracted, scrolling through her socials for pictures of her café. She's all about PR.

Text now or in a minute? It's no big deal, and yet it goes round my head as I feel stress mount. It's ridiculous, I tell myself crossly, trying to remember to breathe like the therapist I saw once for trauma taught me.

Get a grip, Simone, you silly thing: how can this *feel stressful?*

Once again I feel like someone's staring at me, and I look round, but everyone seems to be hurrying by.

'You had an admirer on the plane,' I tell Vicky, putting my phone away determinedly.

'Admirer?' She frowns. 'Don't be silly.'

'Yeah. Some woman kept gazing at you.'

'You're making it up.' She scrolls on. 'You always did have a vivid imagination.'

Maybe I *was* imagining it – but her comment makes me feel a bit mad.

'It's why you were so good at writing,' she murmurs.

Not good enough, neither of us says, but I notice her fingers falter on her phone. I expect she feels sorry for me. Failed at professional life at the first hurdle. Hiding behind being a mother.

Then I remember the past few years with the kids, and think, I'm not even particularly good at that.

'I'm going for a job that's just come up. A local magazine,' I say, but before Vicky can answer, my phone chirps in my bag.

'That'll be Hannah.'

But it's the car company, saying that the driver's waiting for us when we're ready.

As I'm wondering whether to go and get us all some water, a short woman in a navy-blue uniform approaches.

'Señora Dillane? Your friend is' – she checks her clipboard – 'Hannah Cleary?'

'Yes.' My chest feels tight. 'What's happened?'

'Come this way.' She gestures back towards customs.

'Is Hannah OK?' I sound as breathless as I suddenly feel, but she doesn't answer, trotting along in her sensible shoes as we drag our bags back the way we've just come, silent until we reach a muted neon-lit corridor of doors that don't bode well.

'This is where you bang up the drug cartels?' Vicky asks cheerfully, and I gaze at her in astonishment.

How can she joke?

In a horribly bright side room, a tear-stained Hannah sits alone, scrunched tissue in one hand, passport clutched in the other.

'Sorry,' she mumbles as we come in. 'I'm so sorry. I didn't mean to be a pain.'

'Why, what have you done? Don't tell me' – Vicky's trying to joke, but even she looks worried now – 'you tried to smuggle some crack cocaine in?'

I prod her hard.

'Or heroin?' It's like she can't stop. 'Or maybe meth?'

'Shut *up*, Vick,' I mutter, watching the uniformed woman's face. 'It's not helping.'

Hannah just stares at her hands, and I can see from here that they're shaking. She's trembling all over, in fact, looking utterly terrified, and it makes me more fearful.

'It's not a joke, miss,' the woman is telling Vicky, who at least looks contrite now. 'We have strict laws in Ibiza about drugs. Whatever you British may think about this "party" island.'

She makes quotes with her little hands round the word, and I think, this woman obviously hates us.

'But I don't *take* illegal drugs,' Hannah says plaintively. 'I never have.' It's obviously not the first time she's declared this in the past hour.

'That's not what our information said,' the woman retorts, but she walks to the door and throws it open.

'What information?' Vicky asks as the woman ushers us out.

'Go now,' she commands, as if we're the most stupid people she's ever met.

Frankly, right now, I feel like that might be true.

We comply as quickly as possible, Hannah scrambling to her feet as fast as she can, me willing Vicky to keep quiet.

'And you, miss' – the woman looks at Hannah as she scurries past – 'you are fortunate this time. Be sensible, *sí*?'

'*Sí, gracias.*' Hannah nods, head down.

In single file, we follow the signs back to the exit, and none of us speaks again until we're standing outside, breathing in the warm, fragrant air beneath the spiky palm trees.

The noise of jets taking off rings in our ears, along with our own shocked silence.

SEVENTEEN
HANNAH

I know there'll be a million questions from the other two, but I just want to get to wherever we're going; to be somewhere private and lock a door behind me and breathe.

To stand under clean water and let it wash the past horrible hour off me.

The very last thing I want to do is face Jodie now.

As I pass through the airport's sliding doors, the warm air hitting my skin is such a relief, I think I might cry.

But I've done enough of that already today, so I bite my inner lip hard and attempt a smile instead.

'Like, what the hell?' Vicky shakes her head at me. 'What on earth happened there, hon? You auditioning for *Ozark*?'

'Please,' I say, as Simone links arms with me, guiding me past the taxi rank. 'Can we just talk about this later?'

'But...' Vicky's frowning in a way that says no. 'I don't get it.'

'I just... I feel really odd right now,' I mutter. 'I can't... Please.'

It's obvious that she's desperate to ask more, but under Simone's clear-eyed gaze, she just about restrains herself.

'There's the car,' Simone almost yells, waving at the silver

Mercedes parked in the pick-up bays, a smart chauffeur holding a board with her name on. 'Sorry we're so late!'

He literally tips his hat, then takes our bags with a polite bow. 'It is no problem, *señora*.'

How this miraculous car has arrived, I'm only told later. Right now, I have the definite feeling I'm being treated like a child – and also right now, that's fine by me.

And as I slide into the back seat and close my eyes, for a moment letting myself savour the pleasant warmth of the late afternoon, the air smelling of pine forests and something else exotic that I can't name but that stirs a deep memory somewhere, I let myself believe things might be OK.

We drive away from the airport, away from those scary officers, past the tall palm trees and into the middle of the beautiful island.

And for once, I make sure to put my phone on silent.

Never mind home, never mind my elderly parents.

For now, I have to rely on them being in good hands if I want to hold on to my sanity and take this next step towards peace.

I turn the phone off to quieten both my own head and the terrifying texts.

EIGHTEEN
THEN
MARCH 2002

It was a quiet spring evening when the trouble at Dizzy's really started.

I'd been down south, visiting my parents. Since my mum's MS diagnosis, she had bad weeks and, loving her so much, I found them hard to witness. Already distressed, I arrived home to the news my landlord was selling up.

Seeking comfort, I fled to Jodie's place for wine. Frankly, it was a dump: one cramped room in a smelly house on the London Road, the shared bathroom Dickensian in its squalor. But Jodie didn't seem to mind, and her tolerance intrigued me.

'I've been thinking, babe.' Halfway down a bag of nuts and some cheap plonk, her face lit up. 'How about us finding a decent flat together?' She adjusted her fake specs, this month's look being 'sexy secretary'.

'That's a brilliant idea!' I almost shouted. 'Yes, let's!'

Honestly, I'd never met anyone like Jodie before. More exciting than all the nursing students on my course put together, and as fiercely loyal as a tiger – if they *were* loyal, that was. I didn't tell her that I might have to move back to Plymouth soon, to look after my poor mum. I was so distracted, my studies had gone to pot, and I thought it was only a matter of time before I returned to my dead-end life on the estate where I'd grown up.

'What do you *really* want to do?' Jodie asked when I said I might give up nursing. 'If you're not going to be the next Florence Nightingale.'

'I don't know.' I did know actually, but Jodie was just so cool and sorted, I didn't want to sound stupid.

'Go on.' She stared at me intently. 'Spill.'

'Well, in my dreams...' I flicked the pages of a glossy magazine, 'I'd work on women's magazines. I love them so much.'

'Bit different from wiping people's bums, babe.' She raised an elegant eyebrow. 'Writing for *Vogue*.' She peered critically at a fashion spread. 'Dreadful outfit. Do an evening class then, babe. I might sign up for one myself.' Her sigh was dramatic. 'If I could only find the time.'

Which made me smile.

I had no clue how Jodie survived financially. Her cashflow was ambiguous – she signed on at the Job Centre twice a month – yet her lifestyle seemed extravagant. When we eventually found the new flat, already nicknamed the Dive, she produced the whole deposit while we looked for another flatmate.

'Yeah.' I looked back at the magazine. 'Maybe I will.'

I was late for my shift that Wednesday because, to my own surprise, I'd signed up for a journalism class at the local FE college.

At least Dizzy's was quiet. It was match night, and the management – aka my boss, Tom – had so far refused to install TV screens.

'Sorry.' I dragged my Dizzy's T-shirt over my rollneck. 'I'll take over now.'

Bending down to re-tie my lace a minute later, I heard the door open and then slam shut.

'You again,' a voice slurred over the bar. A very drunk voice. 'Time to make things up to me, you sexy little slut!'

With a pounding heart, I stood to find Coops, the estate agent with the American Express card I'd dated once, wearing a tracksuit and a football scarf instead of his usual suit.

'I want a drink now. A double vodka!' He thumped the bar with a fist, clearly drunk; sweating and red in the face. 'All on the house, yeah?'

I looked at him.

'Actually' – he licked his bottom lip with a fat pink tongue – 'make it a triple and a quickie round the back.'

It was a split-second decision. 'I don't think I can serve you in this state, sir.' Politely I pointed at the notice about the right to refuse.

'Serve me *now*.' He tried to meet my eye with his bloodshot ones, and reached across the bar to grab my wrist, but I stepped back quickly, my heart racing.

'Hey!' Tom hurried across. 'What's the problem?'

'This bitch is refusing to serve me.' Cooper staggered slightly. 'Tell her to give me a drink. Right *now*.'

'You can't use that language in here, mate.' Tom, usually a pretty cool customer, was annoyed. 'Looks like you've already had one too many.'

'Who asked you?' the man sneered.

'No one.' Tom was polite. 'But as I'm the manager, it's my prerogative—'

Cooper took a swing at him, but it was so ill-judged and off-target, he lost his footing and fell clumsily against the bar.

'Mate' – Tom grimaced – 'I'm not going to say it again. Please get the fuck out of my bar.'

'Your bar, is it?' Cooper sneered, but he staggered off, grumbling, into the dusk.

'Thank you,' I said to Tom, my heart still pounding.

An hour later, there was a huge crash, and broken glass flew into Dizzy's like lethal rain.

The girls at the table nearest the door screamed as tiny fragments pattered into their hair and drinks. Someone had just put a baseball bat straight through the glass panes in the main doors and was ramming it up and down as hard as possible.

'Fuck! Someone call the police – *now*!' Tom practically leapt over the bar amongst the still-flying shards. 'Ladies, move up the other end, quickly!'

'I'm on it, mate,' a young man said, phone to his ear. 'Like a duck on a crust.' He winked at me calmly, despite the continuing carnage. 'Yeah, police, please. Quick smart, yeah?'

Cooper was visible outside, along with two thugs in football shirts. Once they'd finished with the door, they hauled their heft inside and proceeded to smash up the nearest table with their bats while Cooper leant in the doorway, smoking.

The air was full of threat and fury, and I felt beyond sick as the table turned to matchwood.

Unsure what else I could do, I fetched a broom just as – thank God – a police van screeched up outside, siren blaring, lights flashing.

As the officers bundled into the two guys by the door, Cooper met my gaze. Before I could move, he'd grabbed me by the neck of my T-shirt. As he yanked me towards him, I dropped the broom.

'It's all your fault.' His spittle hit my face. 'You should have just served me.'

'Get off!' I pushed at his hands uselessly. 'You're hurting me.'

'Not as much as I'd like to,' he leered, so close I could smell his horrible beer breath. 'You silly little girl.'

He tightened his grip, and I started to choke – then suddenly his face kind of crumpled and his knees went from under him. He let go of my collar, and as I collapsed back onto the bar, I realised that someone had just whacked him on the head with something hard.

The broom.

Whoever it was had caught him before he hit the deck. Laid him neatly on the floor, stepped over him and helped me sit down on the nearest bar stool. 'You OK?' It was the boy who'd called the police.

'Yes.' I nodded. 'No. I don't know.'

'Ambulance?'

'No.' I rubbed at my stinging neck. 'I'm fine. I think.'

'OK then.' He had very bright eyes and thick lashes, and he reminded me of someone, but my brain was too fuzzy to think who. Someone off the TV, maybe, I thought vaguely. 'If you're sure.'

'Yes,' I croaked, sounding more certain than I felt.

'Well in that case,' he said, grinning, 'I'll skedaddle.'

The police removed Cooper and his mates from the bar.

'We'll take your statements tomorrow,' the arresting officer said to us. 'They're not going anywhere in a rush.'

It turned out that the three of them were part of a football gang who liked nothing more than an organised rumble. Thwarted by the evening match's cancellation, meaning the rival team hadn't turned up, they'd come back with vile energy to burn, looking for trouble.

'Dear me.' Jodie, resplendent in emerald-green fake fur, arrived in the aftermath. In one hand she held a leather brief-case, in the other a lit cigarette. 'Looks like the cavalry beat me to it!'

'I'd put that briefcase down.' Tom passed her on the way back from showing the officers out. 'They might see it as an offensive weapon.'

'Looks like I missed the fun.' She flicked her ash straight onto the floorboards. 'What a shame. Has anyone rung here for me?'

'No.' My sore neck was throbbing now, and I was near tears. 'Where've you been?'

'Job interview.' Jodie tapped her nose mysteriously. 'Maybe my fortunes are about to change.'

'Oh yeah?' I tried to sound interested, but really I was just upset.

'Yeah.' She put the case on the bar and sat. 'Now, sorry if you're wounded and all, but can I get a Jack and Coke? It's been a long day.'

I bit my tongue and reached for a glass.

'Oh, and babe? Don't forget the cherry.'

'I thought that bloke was just one of those flash twats.' Tom poured us all a glass of brandy as he closed up early. 'Not a bloody football hooligan.'

'I never trust estate agents, specially not from Ashtons,' Jodie said loftily. 'I'm not surprised he's a thug as well.'

'What do you know about Ashtons?' I asked.

'Oh, you know. I saw them about our new flat.' She shoved her empty glass towards Tom. 'But they weren't as welcoming as I might have hoped.'

'Oh, I forgot.' Tom fumbled behind the till. 'Someone called for you earlier, Jodie.' He handed her a folded note. 'Left this.'

'Ta.' She pocketed it without even looking at it.

The alcohol went some way to dull the pain of the bruises on my neck, but I was really shaken, and I wanted to go home.

I'd been upset by Jodie joking around after I'd been attacked. But there was something else I couldn't put my finger on.

Not that night anyway.

NINETEEN
VICKY
THURSDAY, 9 JUNE

Ibiza

The sun's beginning to set now over the west of the island, and I'm nodding off in the back of the car, shattered, head on Hannah's shoulder, when the electronic peal of a phone snaps me back to reality.

On the edge of a pretty market town, our driver pulls over in front of a luxury apartment block to take the call, clicking the central locking on as he does so.

The complex looks pretty swanky, I think, yawning. It'll do me just fine, thank you very much!

As I listen to the conversation, my schoolgirl Spanish fails me, the man speaking so fast I have no chance of keeping up. The only words I think I do understand are 'too late' and 'boat'.

I'm just about to take a photo of the flaming sky to send Dave when the driver hangs up, taps something into his sat nav and pulls off again down the road.

I sigh internally. I'm tired, and one of my bad headaches is threatening. The huge row with Dave at dawn wasn't all that unexpected, it has to be said; it's been brewing for weeks, but it still upset me. He was dead set against the Ibiza trip – he thinks I'm mad, given what happened before – but I think I deserve a break. It's been really tough recently.

When the taxi arrived, we left on bad terms, me slamming the front door and then shouting at him through the letter box like a kid.

No, this morning was hardly the ideal start to any day, let alone a holiday.

I've texted him to say sorry, but judging by the terse reply, he's obviously still aggrieved. And I feel guilty that I was so nasty.

Nerves often bring out the worst in me.

But I haven't shared any of this with the others. Not about how bad things have really been at home these past few months, which meant consequently I *probably* drank a bit too much earlier, now also not helping my mood much.

Nor has that stupid note I found in my purse helped, the note I scrunched up and threw away; or all the waiting around for Hannah for what felt like hours, worrying about her.

Now all I fancy is a swim and a long, cold drink on a cool terrace, overlooking that crystal-blue sea.

What I most definitely *don't* fancy is facing Jodie for the first time in years.

About ten minutes after the call, the driver pulls up again at the top of a deserted track, beside a small vineyard.

A dusty track winds past it as far as the eye can see, through arid red earth, cactuses and wiry shrubs.

Hunched over his phone, the man's texting, and Simone and I swap glances across Hannah's sleeping form.

Suddenly, out of nowhere, I feel uneasy about being in this car. I'm tempted to try the door, just to see if it'll open.

'OK?' Simone murmurs to me. 'What's up?'

'This is it, I reckon,' I mutter back. I could really use a cigarette, but my vape's in the boot, with the rest of the luggage.

'What do you mean, *it*?' Is it my imagination or does Simone suddenly look as fearful as I feel?

'We're about to have touchdown.'

'Is that even a saying?' Simone is always so pedantic about words, and for some reason, right now it really annoys me. 'Don't you mean lift-off?'

'I mean Jodie, hon, whatever you want to call her.'

There are lots of jokes I could make, but I don't, because I'm watching the driver jab at his screen now.

Perhaps he's had instructions to do away with us.

'He's just using the sat nav,' Simone murmurs, sensing my unease. 'Probably trying to find some remote exotic location. You know what Jodie's like. Doesn't do things by halves.'

We both know what she's like – that's the problem.

Or we used to anyway.

The track through the cactuses and pink oleander trees is so bumpy, by the time we pull up outside a rustic brick-built finca at the end of it, my teeth feel like they've been shaken loose. When the driver releases the central locking, I don't think I've ever exited a vehicle so fast.

But as I stand in front of the ramshackle old villa, I think that whatever I was expecting, it definitely wasn't *this*.

'We can't be here, can we?' Hannah sounds uncertain.

'I hope not,' I say dolefully. 'Surely not!'

Flanked by stumpy palms and long grasses, the building must have once been impressive – *once* being the operative word.

Arched doors sit between browning cascades of native bougainvillea, and a chipped stone fountain gently plinks water, but while there's something almost grand about the place, it also looks like it's starting to collapse slowly into the earth.

Everything seems incredibly dusty, the ground beneath the shuttered and iron-barred windows full of potholes and loose stones.

Plus, it's deserted. There's no Jodie; in fact, there's no one around at all, by the looks of it.

Simone joins us. 'This isn't what I was expecting,' she murmurs. 'I thought it would be a bit flash. Or at least nice.'

'It probably *was* nice' – Hannah's smile is shaky – 'a hundred years ago.'

'Have a good stay, *señora*.' With a small bow, the driver hands me something and steps away.

An envelope, my name printed on the front. *Victoria Jones*.

Lord, the bill! I haven't got any euros, I realise, if we're meant to pay him. The invitation definitely said *All expenses paid*, and my credit card will take care of the rest, so I didn't bother to get cash.

I'm still worrying about what to do when the Mercedes purrs off down the track. It takes all my willpower not to shout at him to stop and take us with him.

'Perhaps the real villa's behind this one?' I say hopefully. 'Down on the beach?'

It's so humid now. Simone, wrestling to pull her hair off her face, is just asking, 'Now what?' when Hannah yelps and footsteps on the gravel behind me make me whirl around.

'*Buenas tardes*.' A plump little woman in a black dress has appeared from nowhere. She bows her head.

'Oh gosh, you scared me.' Hannah's laugh is as shaky as her smile; she's obviously still on edge. 'Sorry!'

'*Por favor*.' The woman, unflustered, ushers us towards the thick wooden front doors, holding a set of old keys that jangle louder than my nerves. Keys like a jailer's, I think, absently, on a rusty old ring.

'Has anyone else arrived?' Hannah asks, at exactly the same time as Simone says, 'Is Jodie here?'

But the woman shrugs apologetically. '*Non hablo Inglese.*' She unlocks the door, switches on a light just inside it, and hands Hannah the key ring.

'*Lo siento,*' I try, but my Spanish seems even worse than it was an hour ago. 'We're guests of Jodie Austin?' But the woman just gestures at the open door, taps her watch and melts away, much like the driver did.

'Looks like this really is it then,' Simone sighs. 'Not quite the promised luxury, is it?'

'Are you surprised?' Hannah says.

'It is a bit typical of Jodie,' I agree. Expect the unexpected. 'Might be lovely inside though...'

Together, the three of us step into a dim open-plan room that smells like funerals. It's decorated with ancient lacquered Spanish fans that look like a flamenco dancer might have dropped them fifty years ago, and old wooden shutters stand ajar onto an overgrown garden full of lush plants.

It isn't lovely at all of course. It's museum-like and smelly.

Through the undergrowth, the edge of a pool is just visible, at least, and the furious flamingo pink sunset flaming across the sky, shocking in its vivid glory.

I push open a shutter. While the ocean's definitely there somewhere at the end of the garden, little white triangles of far-off yachts gliding across the horizon, it's firmly on the far side of a tall wire fence.

'We just need a bit of livening up, girls!' I declare stoutly. 'Music and wine'll sort us out.'

'Will it?' Hannah says morosely.

'Yes, mate!' I look round for a stereo, but there's none.

The kitchen at least has a few modern appliances. I open the tall fridge: other than bottled water and cava, it's empty.

'Look.' Hannah points as I grab a bottle of fizz. The dark-wood dining table's been laid. 'That's weird, isn't it? It's only set for three...'

She's right: around a vase of lilies and a blue bowl of over-ripe mangoes and oranges – three place settings.

I snatch up the white linen napkins; they cover plates of cheese and salami, olives and a basket of bread, a small jug of oil. 'Well, this is good, isn't it?'

'I don't know.' Hannah shrugs. She looks traumatised still. 'Do you trust that food?'

'And' – Simone appears from her quick recce, slightly breathless – 'there's only two bedrooms open. All the other doors are locked, and the upstairs... well...' She points. 'The bottom stairs are actually broken. Like... It's weird – it's as if someone's taken an axe to them.'

'An axe?' I suppress a shiver. 'Are you sure?'

'Is there a bathroom at least?' Hannah asks anxiously.

'Yes, thank God, though it's circa 1970.' Simone points again. 'End of the hall.'

'I'm going to get in the shower before you throw me out.' Hannah smiles unsteadily. 'I bet I pong.'

'Don't be silly,' I say weakly, not because she does, but because everything's starting to catch up with me. The anticipation, the row with Dave, too much booze earlier.

And this place – well, it's definitely *not* what I signed up for.

'What's that?' Simone points at the envelope I'm still holding, as the bathroom door clicks softly behind Hannah.

'God, I forgot. Can you read it please, hon?' I hand it over and fall back on a leather sofa so old dust flies out. 'My specs are buried somewhere.'

'"Fantastic to see you",' Simone begins. '"We're so pleased you made it this far."'

'Fantastic,' I repeat, removing the foil from the cava deftly. 'But where are *you*?'

'And hang on.' The furrow between Simone's brows deepens. 'Doesn't that sound a bit ... weird?'

'Why?' Outside, I can just about see the pool glittering under the last of the evening sun, though it's in the midst of a jungle.

By far the best idea in my opinion is to pour ourselves a glass of this chilled cava, don our swimsuits and dive in to wash off the dust and grime. And all the cobwebs that I'm trying not to notice.

'Like... we might not have made it at all.'

'Presumably it just means she's glad we came.' Simone might well be right, but I don't want her to fixate on it.

'"So sorry you're late and missed the boat" – missed the boat literally or metaphorically?' Simone muses aloud as I pop the cork and sip at the froth, for want of a glass.

'Just carry on, Sim.' I stifle my sigh. A bluebottle is buzzing mercilessly at the edge of one of the windows, bashing itself against the cloudy glass. 'Is there any actual info?'

'"You can join us tomorrow",' she reads on, frowning.

'OK, look, don't worry about it now.' Grabbing my case, I head towards the bedrooms. 'Let's get changed and have a swim before it gets dark. We can read the rest later.'

'Hmm.' Simone's unconvinced. 'Sounds more sinister than that to me.'

Sinister?

'Stop worrying,' I push the first heavy old door open, determinedly not thinking about the note on the plane, Hannah being stopped, or the fact that we seem to be staying in a Hammer House of Horrors filmset.

Hannah's bag is sitting by one of the narrow single beds. The yellowed lacy covers look practically Victorian, and a tortured Jesus on a cross is nailed above each bed. Good Lord.

'I'll share with Han.' I pop my head back round the door,

trying hard to remain cheerful. 'You have your own room, enjoy your break from the kids.'

But in truth, I'm nowhere near as convinced as I sound, particularly when I see the expression on Jesus's agonised face.

Jeez, as Simone would say – literally.

Just the idea of seeing Jodie again is making my guts churn, and now we have to wait even longer in this horrible house.

But what silly games are being played already?

I take a slug of the cava as another fly smashes itself against the glass. How much longer is anybody's guess.

TWENTY

SIMONE

The creepy old villa is reminiscent of some kind of institution, tinged with the musty damp smell of an unloved home.

It groans with heavy dark furniture and weird moth-eaten tapestries; a wicker birdcage with two fake canaries inside gently sways high up in one corner.

At least I *think* they're fake and that they weren't once alive.

I peer closer – but it's hard to tell from down here if they're stuffed.

According to the old guest book on the pockmarked chest in the hall, the depressing house is called Finca Maria. My phone tells me that *finca* means a farm. But it's more like a prison.

In fact, it resembles a kind of old-fashioned asylum.

Not at all what I was expecting. A hundred miles from what I expected.

What *was* I expecting though?

Jodie's voice echoes in my head: *Expect the unexpected, then you're always prepared.*

I know why Jodie always expected the worst. It wasn't hard to understand once I'd begun to learn a bit about her, about the fluctuating poverty of her childhood and the way she had to learn to survive.

But right now, just being here is starting to freak me out a bit, if I'm honest. Every single reason I chose to come to Ibiza has completely fled my mind: the idea of peace, love and harmony seems remote – and seeing Jodie has become even more complicated.

It's not even a nice house. It's horrible, but at least we can take solace in knowing we will be moving on again – to somewhere much better than this, I pray.

I force myself to concentrate on the end of the note.

Do click on the iPad for further instructions, it says. *See you tomorrow.*

iPad? What iPad?

I scan the dark room, and as I spy the device, shiny and new and incongruous on the mantelpiece, propped against a tarnished brass candlestick that looks like a murder instrument from *Cluedo*, I notice something else blinking down.

A CCTV camera, also incongruous in this frowsty old setting.

Outside on the road, beyond the cypress trees that protect the *finca* from view, headlights flash on and off briefly, and suddenly the question suddenly seems to be:

Who exactly is watching us?

'A customer was asking for you,' Tom remarked one lunchtime after I'd been off sick. 'Wanted to check you were OK after our little incident.'

'Oh?' I was behind the bar, unloading the glass washer. 'Handsome dude, was he?'

Tom smirked. 'If you like 'em fat and forty.'

'Funny.' I tried to hide my disappointment, remembering the boy with bright eyes. That night was never far from my mind. 'Any idea why he wanted to know about me?'

'Who wouldn't want you, babe?' Jodie said. She was sitting at the bar, tapping away at some new-fangled thing she called a BlackBerry – like a phone mixed with a computer, but tiny. She practically lived here now, despite the fact that we'd now moved into our flat – the Dive.

I blushed at her compliment. 'Why thank you, kind lady.'

Jodie was such good company; such a cheerleader. I loved having someone permanently on my side. The oddness of the bar fight had been long forgotten; her brief lack of empathy.

Forgotten, apart from the bad dreams that disturbed me.

Sometimes I woke in the night clawing at my neck, thinking I was choking.

At least I might have something to write about now for my first college assignment, if I could face it. My tutor, Pat, was a great proponent of the fashion in feature-writing for digging deep, being honest and personal. What he called 'confessional journalism'. 'People want to read the truth,' he'd told us.

'Said he'd come to apologise for something,' Tom said.

'No idea.' I pushed the washer shut. 'Shall I change the menu?'

'What – from burger to burger?' Jodie pulled a face.

'We've got a new chef actually.' Tom sounded irritated.

'A chef? Bit posh, babe, for Dizzy's. By the way... Oh, hang on.' She held out a dramatic hand, tapping on her tiny keypad. 'Sorry. Big party soon, if you both fancy it.'

'Never turn down a party, eh?' Tom had got Jodie's number by now; understood she was *always* up for a party – though despite her best efforts, not her number in real life.

He said he was 'spoken for', making it sound like something from the Great War. His girlfriend was travelling for a year, and he never so much as wavered romantically, for all the pretty girls in Dizzy's.

But I knew Jodie wasn't used to being turned down, and I guessed that for her, Tom was Dizzy's star attraction, while he didn't mind her almost permanent residence, as long as she paid for her drinks. Which she sort of did, via an ever-growing IOU to me. She constantly assured me she had money in the pipe-line, and I tried not to worry, taking ever more bar shifts now I didn't get my nursing grant any more.

'Nick, my mate, said I can bring anyone.' Jodie ignored Tom's jibe. 'He's off to some fancy New York film school, leaving this dump well behind. Along with his poor girlfriend, Hannah.'

'New York!' The nearest I'd been to the States was a

weekend in Disneyland Paris for my mum's fortieth. 'God, lucky him.'

'Party's at a warehouse on the canal on Saturday night. Gonna be DJs and decks and all that jazz.'

'Not jazz then, by the sounds of it.' Tom emptied the float into the till.

'It'll be banging.' Jodie poked her tongue out. It was a neat pink tongue, a bit like a cat's, but her flirting made me uncomfortable, watching her persistence backfire.

And the lunchtime rush soon distracted me from wondering who the fat-and-forty man asking for me was.

'Pleased to meet you.' He thrust a meaty hand into mine. 'I'm that reprobate's boss.'

'Reprobate?' I wouldn't call this man fat; more solid. Big and tall, with slicked-back dark hair, he wore a grey suit that, though I was no expert, looked far more expensive than something from a chain store.

'Or should I say ex-boss, from Ashtons. I've just set up on my own – property development.' He produced a card with a flourish. 'Robert Perry, at your service.' A mock bow, almost a click of the heels, ruined by a wink. 'You want to avoid those nasty football hooligans in future, my dear. No manners, those rascals.'

I read the card – *Perry's Properties, Robert Perry MD*. 'Do you mean Cooper, whose mates smashed up the bar?'

''Fraid so.' He shook his head sadly. 'Might be of comfort to know that the silly sod's lost his job while he waits for his hearing. And personally I won't touch him with a bargepole now.'

'No,' I agreed. 'Well, I can see why.'

'And you're OK, are you? After the little contretemps?'

I didn't know what that meant, but I nodded anyway. 'Yes, thanks. I'm fine. People helped me.'

'I'm glad.' He smiled. 'Good to have friends you can rely on. Let me buy you a drink.'

'Ah, I'm OK, thanks. Need a clear head for work.'

'Your call.' He was polite enough, but there was something disquieting about him. His imposing size maybe, thick fingers covered in black hair, a gold-and-red signet ring biting into his flesh.

The memory of nearly choking flooded my mind, and I took an inadvertent step back.

'Good friends? My ears are burning.' Jodie waltzed into the bar, draped in emerald fur. 'If she doesn't want it, I'll have that drink, thanks, Mr' – she prised the card out of my fingers – 'Mr Perry. So, yeah, if you're offering.'

'I am, pet. And you must be...'

'Jodie Austin.' She smiled. 'The one and only. Sorry I'm late. Double Jack and Coke please. And a maraschino cherry.'

'I'd love to see your cherry.' He winked again, this time at Jodie, stroking his hair back with his pudgy hand. This time I felt actual physical distaste as he handed me a twenty-pound note. 'Keep the change, pet. I'll get us a table.'

Something was going on here I didn't understand.

'Lovely.' Jodie widened her eyes at me, and irritation flamed right through my body.

'What are you doing?' I muttered.

'Come on, babe.' She flashed me her most brilliant smile as I piled her glass with ice. She knew she'd overstepped a line. 'Have a drink with us *please*.'

'I'm working, Jods.'

The new chef, Vicky, popped her head out of the kitchen. Jodie was right: definitely more cook than chef, though she still seemed pretty posh to me. She lived in her family's big house outside town; they even had horses, I'd heard.

'Seen Tom?' She looked stressed, her hair all up on end.

'Changing a barrel. What's up?' I was glad of the diversion.

I'd never felt properly annoyed with Jodie before – apart from the night I'd nearly choked.

'Oil's run out.' Vicky pulled a face. 'I can't cook anything without it.'

'No problem.' I grabbed my jacket. 'I'll go to the shop.'

I needed fresh air; I wanted to leave Jodie and the smug property developer laughing at each other's jokes in the corner.

Slowly, since we'd become flatmates, I'd gleaned more about my friend, but she was very private about her family. All I really knew was that her dad had been in and out of her life since she was tiny, and her relationship with her mum was fraught. The one thing I'd learnt for sure was that Jodie had undoubtedly grown up with an eye for the main chance.

And I was starting to wonder how far she'd take it.

TWENTY-TWO

VICKY

Ibiza

I wake in the night with such a bad headache, it feels like I'm being forced down into the pillow by a heavy weight.

For a while, it's impossible to move, but eventually I push myself out of bed to hunt for painkillers.

But creeping across the room half dressed, having collapsed into bed after some cheese washed down with cava, I remember my handbag is in the living room. I'll never make it that far.

The en-suite bathroom cabinet reveals nothing but a cracked powder compact and an empty tube of toothpaste. But Hannah's wash bag sits beside the old marble basin; *she* might have painkillers.

Shit! It's full of pill bottles – literally chock-full, I realise, squinting at the labels in the half-light. Xanax, Ambien, OxyContin: things I'm pretty sure aren't available in the UK, even on prescription.

Wow. Who knew? Though Hannah's nothing if not a dark horse...

Without thinking too hard, I help myself to a Xanax and

some paracetamol – the most modest pills in the bag – and wash them down with tap water. I slip another Xanax into my pocket just in case.

Back in bed, I'm just starting to feel floaty when a noise gets inside my head, making all the tiny hairs on my arms stand up.

Music.

Simone must have got up. Not the world's best sleeper, perhaps she's out in the living room, watching Spanish TV.

Headache receding a bit, I force myself up again.

But when I pass Simone's room, the music swelling in volume, she *is* asleep, curled on her side.

And it's really eerie, the music – something dark and classical, something I grapple to remember. I think perhaps I recognise it, but I can't quite place it.

All I want to do is switch it off.

The living room is dark though, and the TV isn't on, and it takes me a while to locate the source. I eventually realise it's coming from an iPad leaning on the old mantelpiece.

Fumbling around in the dark, I jab at the screen until it stops, then check what it was: Mozart's Requiem.

Rattled, I think that perhaps now I'm up and wide awake, I'll just get myself a tiny drink of cava to help sleep come again.

But suddenly light floods the room, washing through the unshuttered front windows, and I hear my own loud gasp.

And then, as quickly as the light came, it all turns dark again.

My heart's beating really fast now; too fast, pounding like my head was. I inhale, trying to steady myself as I stand there wondering what I ought to do.

This house is at the bottom of a track, and there's no road nearby; we're pretty isolated, aren't we? So why would anyone be driving down here at this time of night?

I have two choices, it seems.

As I hurry down the hallway, a figure lunges out at me, and a scream rips through me.

'Oh my God!' Then I realise it's a life-size Virgin Mary statue, smiling down beatifically from an alcove.

Laughing shakily, disoriented, I find the front door behind its heavy curtain and unbolt it with shaky hands.

It takes a long minute – Hannah was very insistent we lock it properly before we went to bed – and I catch my finger on the last bolt at the bottom, blood springing immediately.

Stifling a curse, I pull the door open, taking a beat before stepping onto the porch, moths fluttering towards the room behind me.

'Hello?' My voice echoes in the dark.

As I peer into the gloom, I can make out dim lights through the trees, the small squares of lit windows. Another building, another house beyond this one, through the olive grove.

A working farm? Perhaps the owners of the vineyard we passed, or of the trees that are everywhere around us.

I don't know, and I'm not going to find out now.

My heart still beating too fast, I hurry back inside and slam the door.

Despite my brief burst of courage, helped no doubt by the Xanax, I'm very careful to lock it again; to check that each and every bolt is slid home before I stand, blood rushing to my still aching head.

As I tiptoe back towards my room, thoroughly unsettled, movement catches my eye.

In the murk, without my glasses, I see a figure on the other side of the pool.

I glance into Simone's room again, but she's gone. Nor is she in the bathroom at the end of the hall.

But then I realise that the French window from her room onto the terrace is ajar.

It must be Simone outside – talking urgently by the looks of her body language, pacing under the stubby palm trees, gesticulating furiously, the bright flash of her phone screen the only thing I can see properly all that way away in the dark.

I creep back to bed, very carefully so as not to wake Hannah, but as I pull the musty antique cover over me, I feel a sudden chill. I've remembered why I know that music, and when I last heard it.

That hideous funeral, all those years ago.

TWENTY-THREE

HANNAH

I wake early to Vicky's gentle snoring in the bed beside mine, sheet over her head, her tufty hair just visible on the pillow.

In the night, I heard her shuffling about in the bathroom, but I lay very still and kept my eyes tightly shut, like I did when I was a kid, petrified of the dark. Petrified after my mum used to tell me the Devil would get me if I didn't say my prayers exactly right.

Last night I knew that it wasn't a monster or a demon like my mum used to threaten; that it was only Vicky, my dearest old mate, wandering around, but that didn't make me feel much better.

Most of all, I absolutely didn't want to talk.

What happened at the airport keeps whizzing round and round my head.

Trapped in that airless room, all I was aware of was pure terror. The handsome blank-faced officer lounged against the wall, hand idly resting on that intimidating gun, gazing at me like I was something very strange he'd never seen before, while the woman kept barking at me that they'd had a tip-off – a *soplo*, they called it in Spanish.

'But what is there to tip off?' I begged them. 'I don't understand.'

But they just kept retorting, 'We know the truth, so tell us. Drugs.'

I could see they didn't believe me, whatever I said, and it reminded me of another time; an earlier time when I had begged to be believed and my pleas fell on deaf ears.

And so even though they let me go – with no word of an apology, of course – I just felt... violated, I guess is the best word for it.

As I was finally released from that oppressive little room; as I traipsed down the corridor with my friends, supposedly on a holiday but in reality even less ready for this reunion than ever, all I wanted to do was turn round and board the next flight home.

But I knew I couldn't.

I have to be brave, I remind myself now.

I have a job to do.

The horrible spooky old house and the music playing in the early hours didn't help my dark mood.

Unearthly and strange, when I heard it, when I realised I wasn't dreaming it, I buried my head beneath my pillow, burrowing away from the world outside as it got louder.

But now that dawn has broken and daylight has returned, there's a dash of hope in the air.

Through the slats of the old wooden shutters, I can see a beautiful blue-skied morning. As quietly as possible, I pull my cardigan over my nightie, creeping past Simone's room, where she's curled on her side in the big bed beneath a painting of a placid Virgin Mary.

In the weird old living room, I open the shuttered French windows onto the garden, lush ferns curling down the path. I breathe in the damp, warm Ibiza air, the smell of pine trees flooding through me again.

The finca is a bizarre place. It's like something from an old film, full of wicker birdcages and quirky antique chests and—

Something stops me in my tracks.

Breakfast has been laid out for the three of us, I realise with a jolt. On a crisp white cloth are plates of glistening green melon, baskets of bread beside little pats of yellow butter, two jugs of bright juice. And a big cafetière of hot coffee, the irresistible smell floating up.

'Hello?' I call nervously, peering into the kitchen. '*Hola?* Anyone here?'

I check the dim pantry behind the kitchen, but there's no sign of anyone. And the other two are still asleep, so who has done all this?

In the middle of the table, I see a handwritten card, the writing an elegant calligraphy, swirly and ink black:

GET READY TO JOIN THE REAL PARTY

Be at the jetty by 10 a.m. Please don't be late!

There's a small hand-drawn map attached to the back with a paper clip.

Thank goodness – we're not staying here for the whole weekend after all!

The map shows a path through the gardens, by the looks of it, leading to a jetty on the beach, the sea depicted by small waves like a child might draw at primary school.

But... Oh God, that must mean a boat.

Two wasps land on the melon, followed by a third, their pointed stings trembling up and down on the sweet fruit as I stare absently ahead.

I used to love boats – I spent my early years splashing about on the river near my lovely gran's house – but not now.

Now I would do anything to steer clear.

When Vicky, Tom and I left Dizzy's to go to the party that night, Jodie was missing in action.

She'd been away for reasons that, as usual, remained mysterious; something to do with a phone call she'd taken at the bar last week.

But I'd overheard another call on the flat's landline last month that had disturbed me deeply. Something about her dad and prison and money, with Jodie very upset, tearful even as she muttered into the receiver; more upset than I'd ever seen her.

Afterwards, she plastered a smile on and asked about my evening class.

'Are you OK?' I'd ventured bravely, and she lit a cigarette and said, 'Not now, Dilly, yeah?

I did, though, have a sneaking suspicion where she might be going, or rather, who she might be seeing, but as yet I had no proof.

And really, given my misgivings about that meaty, lustful man who'd turned up at the bar the other week, I didn't want any.

.   .   .

The party was already heaving as we walked along the canal path, house music banging out into the cold night, silhouetted figures dancing in the windows of the old warehouse.

You couldn't miss it if you tried: the half-derelict building lit with old-fashioned torches that flamed by the entrance; the front windows glass-less, strung with multicoloured fairy lights.

'Cool place to live,' Vicky shouted over the blaring music, and I noticed how she'd tucked her arm through Tom's. In fact, I wasn't absolutely sure they hadn't got it on a few weeks ago, despite his professed love for his globetrotting girlfriend, on the night Vicky moved into our flat. Jodie had missed it, away on one of her mysterious trips.

Tom seemed to have this effect on all the girls – all except me, I thought sometimes; maybe because he was one of the good guys, who seemed sadly rare.

'Don't Jodie's mates actually live there?' Tom pointed at a row of quaint houseboats moored on the canal, fifty yards past the warehouse we stood in front of.

'About bloody time too!' Jodie was waiting at the top of the stairs, backlit by the flaming torches, arms extended like a naughty angel in tiger-print fake fur, partygoers thronging around her. 'I've been here at least five minutes.' She had a beaker of wine in one hand and a joint in the other.

'Ha! Some of us actually work for a living.' Tom popped the cork on his fizzy cider and, watching it froth down the stairs like white lava, I had the sense of everything suddenly speeding up as the music changed to a tune I recognised in a shuddering flash.

Cooper and his stupid Porsche.

It wasn't a memory for now; I pushed it away fiercely. *Now* I was going to have fun with my mates.

'New coat?' Vicky stroked Jodie's arm as we drew level. 'Very fancy, oh charity shop queen.'

'Some of us have to be, babe.' Jodie offered me the joint. 'Dilly?'

'No thanks.' I hated being stoned.

'Ah, my little innocent.' She kissed my cheek, and I embraced the warm glow of friendship along with a blast of weed; a feeling that had died a bit since Vicky had moved in. I liked her, but she'd definitely caused a threat to my bond with Jodie.

'All for one,' she liked to cry, brandishing an imaginary sword, 'and one for all!' She used the Three Musketeers analogy a lot; the only book she'd read at boarding school apparently.

But I couldn't help feeling she also liked Jodie more than me.

'Come and meet my mate Hannah.' Jodie grabbed my hand.

'Love to,' I replied, but as her eyes narrowed, I realised she was watching something over my shoulder.

I turned to see Tom and Vicky giggling madly together.

The expression on Jodie's face was indecipherable as she pulled me towards the dance floor.

'Where've you been?' I shouted over the din. 'I was worried.'

'Well...' Eyes dark and diamond-sharp, she considered me for a second. 'I went to see that Perry geezer,' she admitted.

'What?' I knew it! 'But *why*?'

'A little business proposition.' She didn't hide her grimace this time. 'Might be good for us all.'

I sincerely doubted that. 'But, Jod—'

'Let's dance.' She chucked her joint away. 'Save the lectures for— Oh, here's Hannah!' She fell on a tall, thin girl. 'Hannah lives out there.' She pointed down at the canal. 'On a boat called *The Dandruff*.'

'*The Daffodil*! But it's only temporary.' Hannah wore a funny pinafore and round glasses that gave her a studious look. 'House-sitting.'

She didn't really look like a Jodie kind of person, though I hadn't met many of Jodie's old friends, now I came to think of it.

'Boat-sitting, you mean.' Tom and Vicky had joined us. Tom offered Hannah his bottle, and shyly she took a polite swig.

'How do you two know each other?' I asked.

'Went to school together as kids, didn't we, Han?' Jodie threw her arm around the girl's bony shoulders. 'Kept me out of bother before I moved away.'

'I'm not sure about that.' Hannah rolled her eyes affectionately. 'You always were the life and soul.'

'Well, you showed me the straight and narrow, babe.' Jodie kissed her cheek. 'Where's your other half?'

'Dunno.' Hannah pushed the specs up her nose. 'Dancing?'

Oh no, she's going to cry, I thought, feeling awkward, but she didn't.

'He's quite...' She paused, choosing her words carefully. 'Drunk.'

'Are you an artist?' Vicky, trying and failing to assemble a roll-up on her knee, pointed at Hannah's paint-stained pinafore.

'Oh.' Abashed, Hannah glanced down at herself, almost guilty. 'I do paint if I have time, but mainly I study bookkeeping at the Adult Institute.'

'It's quite a look,' Tom said, but in a nice way. 'I'd love to see your work, Hannah.' His eyes were shining. Was he drunk too? I wondered. 'Do you ever show it?'

'Ooh!' Jodie hopped around as the DJ cranked up a remix of 'Alphabet Street'. 'I love this tune. Let's dance!' She headed for a handsome boy, shirtless and sweating, on the dance floor.

'Must be so romantic,' I said wistfully. 'Living on the water.'

'If you don't get seasick.' Hannah pushed at her glasses again reflexively.

'And do you?' Tom wanted to know. 'Get seasick?'

'No.' Hannah grinned. 'Grew up on boats with my grandparents.'

When we joined Jodie, she introduced us to the sweaty Nick, Hannah's errant other half. He kissed Hannah passionately while everyone danced around them; kissed her until her glasses were skewwhiff and she giggled madly.

I remembered that laugh for a long time afterwards. It was one of true happiness.

'Have you got your door key?' I found Vicky on the rickety balcony later, chatting to a curvy girl in a tracksuit. 'Mine's at work, I just realised, and I really want to go home.'

'Oh no, hon!' Vicky's eyes were pinned and bright, and she was holding the girl's hand. 'Meet my new mate—'

'Hi,' I said. 'Sorry, but your key, Vick? I'm going to ring a cab.'

'Ah, come on, don't be boring.'

'Honestly, I'm so tired. I need my bed.' I shushed her with my finger. 'An hour ago.'

'OK.' She shrugged. 'But I put my stuff in Jodie's bag.'

'Any idea where she is?'

'Ask Hannah?' Vicky pointed to Hannah, who'd just wandered up to Tom to chat.

But neither of them had seen her for a while either.

In theory, it was quicker to find Jodie than return to Dizzy's, but even though I searched all the rooms, I couldn't find her anywhere – until she suddenly appeared on the dance floor, completely dishevelled.

'Dilly!' She grabbed me, spinning around with her arms in the air before collapsing in a crumpled heap, laughing. 'I love you, silly Dilly!'

'I love you too, but I've been looking for you for ages,' I said, trying not to snap. She was more out of it than I'd ever seen her, and it freaked me out. Normally she had the constitution of an ox, consumed whatever she wanted without it touching the sides – but this was different.

'Are you OK?' I tried to pull her up. 'Where've you been?'

'Don't be so bloody nosy.' She tapped her nose. 'Just like my bleeding mother, always going on at my poor dad.' Her face was changing faster than her words, and her voice took on an odd whine. '*Where've you been, Alf, where've you been?* On and on. Fucking nagging old cow. No wonder he did one.'

'All right!' The cold blast of her anger took me aback. 'Sorry I asked.'

'Have you seen Nick?' Hannah was at my shoulder, peering down at Jodie, sprawled on the floor.

'No.' Jodie's face was still riddled with fury, as if she'd forgotten where she was. 'I bloody haven't. Stop asking questions, all of you.'

'Has he got a mobile?' I asked.

'Yeah,' Hannah said, 'but he's not answering. It's just ringing out.'

'I saw him,' the girl Vicky had been chatting to piped up. 'Nick.'

'Where?'

'On the canal path.' She gestured towards the houseboats. 'About an hour ago. He didn't look that clever, I must say. Stumbling around.'

'Oh dear,' Hannah groaned. 'I did think he'd overdone it a bit. Probably gone to sleep it off, knowing him.'

'Yeah. I did tell him to get his head down.' The girl looked at Jodie, still on the floor. 'Did you see him?'

'What?' Jodie tried to get up. 'Who?' It was painful to watch. Her legs were like rubber, or a newborn calf's.

'Oh, for God's sake, Jod.' I offered her a hand up. 'Concentrate! Hannah's looking for Nick, and I need Vicky's door key, which you've got.'

'It's in my bag.' She gazed around uselessly, her eyes unfocused.

'Yeah, and that's *where*?'

Some kind of expression passed over Jodie's face as she finally took my arm. I hauled her off the floor, the girl gazing at her.

'I have no clue.'

'Oh God.' Hannah was staring out of the window. 'Oh my God.' She began to push her way through the crowd. "Scuse, please, just let me past...'

As one, we turned to follow where her gaze had just been.

'Oh no!' Vicky breathed. 'Is that...'

My breath caught in my throat.

'Jeez! Someone call 999!' I croaked. 'Quick!'

'I will.' Tom was fumbling for his phone. 'I am.'

'What?' The girl stepped forward to see. 'What are you all...' She breathed out. 'Oh *fuck*.'

On the dark canal, brilliant orange flames were licking up and around the deck of the last boat in the row.

The Daffodil.

And as we watched, horrified, and the music in the room died away, there was a popping noise, almost like fireworks, and then a huge bang.

Right in front of our eyes, the far end of the houseboat exploded.

TWENTY-FIVE
SIMONE
FRIDAY, 10 JUNE

Ibiza

'There's a storm warning,' I announce bleakly, ladling more sugar into my strong black coffee and peering at the little hand-drawn map. I'm struggling to function properly this morning after such a disturbed night, and my apprehension is heightening by the second. 'They must want us to get on a boat, but I think it might be pretty choppy.'

I check the weather app on my phone again: those little black WARNING! triangles still there.

Perfect: another (stormy) day in Paradise. Exactly why I came.

In fact, I'm trying hard to remind myself why on earth I *have* come, as Vicky noisily sucks the flesh off a melon rind.

'Storm? No way, hon. Just look at the sky.' She stretches luxuriously, showing off her toned stomach. She's in a much better mood than last night, now she knows we don't have to stay here. 'Whew, this melon's gorgeous.'

'I don't know, Vick.' I feel mutinous at her dismissive words, but I could also almost laugh at myself. I'm acting like my daughter, whose elfin chin juts out immediately she gets scared, whose fear makes her rude.

And that makes me think of the text message stream I've received since landing in Ibiza: every single woe right there in black and white on my phone.

So much for the all-hallowed 'me time' of the wellness industry.

'What do you think, Han?'

Hannah's curled on the old chair by the open window, in a pretty blue-and-white sundress, reading an ancient guidebook to the Balearic Islands she's found on the shelf.

'I reckon we'll be OK, Sim.' She smiles at me, and I see a glimpse of the old Hannah, the one who hasn't been around for a while. 'We're together, after all.' She looks more refreshed today, the colour back in her cheeks. 'There's some amazing plants and animals on these islands, you know.'

So what's up with me?

But I know the answer really.

Terror.

I'm scared – not of the possible storm, which is only a yellow warning anyway, not even orange or red – but of this meeting.

Of the possible – no, the *more* than likely – impending showdown.

'Who were you on the phone to last night?' Vicky asks idly as I struggle with the sticky zip on my case.

'What?'

'Need a hand?'

'Thanks, I'm fine.' Except the zip's making me sweat even more than this heat. And somehow I've forgotten how bad I am when it's really hot, especially these days. 'I'll manage.'

'I saw you.' Vicky pushes the case flat for me, despite my words.

'What?' My stomach clutches uncomfortably. 'When?

'Last night.' She says it patiently, like she's talking to a child, or a very old person. 'Outside on the phone? Talking. I just wondered who to.'

'No one.' I almost lose my balance as the zip suddenly flies round where it's meant to go. 'Phew, thank goodness for that!'

In the night, lights swooshing back and forth over my bed woke me in a sweat, and when I switched my phone on to check the time, notifications started pinging madly, ramping up my anxiety.

That infinite stream of Mother texts:

Dad won't let me do this... Why have you left me when I need you here?... Can I have some money to go into town today?... Chelsea called me a doggo... I'm freaking out, I can't breathe...

All of it at once, thick and fast.

Why does no one warn you properly about teenagers?

And of course, the guilt was pure and immediate, and Vicky's right, I *did* go outside, but—

'Come on.' Hannah appears in the doorway with her own little case. 'It's after half nine already, and I reckon it'll take a while to walk down that mad garden.'

As we close the door behind us and stick the keys under the mat, I'm not sorry to say goodbye to this weird old place that smells of musty curtains and dead mice and rotting leather.

I just wish I had a better idea of where or what we're going to next.

TWENTY-SIX
VICKY

Dragging my bag past the slimy algae-filled pool – the pool I didn't dive into last night once I'd actually seen and smelt it up close – I'm trying my best not to feel annoyed by the other two.

Or rather, by Simone, who seems to have turned into the Voice of Doom overnight. Hannah, conversely, appears to have cheered up a bit since the airport drama, which reminds me – I need to find a time to ask her discretely about all her meds.

'It's so hot already,' Simone groans, pushing her way through the jungle-like vegetation. 'I'm praying the next place has air con.'

But we're here, it's a truly beautiful island, and I'm going to make the most of it; certainly before it all goes wrong – that's my reasoning anyway.

'At least it's not rainy England,' I say firmly. 'Just enjoy it, mate, why don't— Oof!' A big feathery frond Simone has just let go of whacks me full in the face. 'Oi! Careful.'

'Sorry,' she calls, but from the rigid set of her back, I'm not sure she didn't do it on purpose.

We fight our way through the jungle in silence until we reach a little wooden gate that opens onto the beach.

It's as pretty as a painting – azure sea lapping the white sands ahead of us, a bunch of stripy parasols clustered in the distance – but there's no clue as to where to go next.

'There.' Hannah points, and she's right: a long wooden jetty is just visible on the bend of the beach, a few hundred metres along.

As we near it, it's soon clear that there's not a soul nor a vessel nearby – just blue sea, far-off yachts and a huge sky.

It's empty – which is becoming both irritating and a recurring theme.

'Now what?' Simone stops mid trudge. 'It's boiling already, and there's literally no shade out here.'

I do remember this Simone, the one who struggled with dreadful depression after Mason was born; the one who hasn't felt really sure of herself for years; the one who becomes negative rather than asking for help.

'I'm really wondering,' she sighs heavily, 'whether this was a good idea.'

'Again?' I mutter. But my initial response – to tell her to just bloody cheer up – is tempered by the fact that things are starting to seem overly complicated; too much hard work.

But all of us, I'm guessing, have our own agenda for being here, and it's that that's driving us on.

'It'll be fine.' Feeling more sympathetic, I squeeze my beloved mate. 'Honestly.' But I don't really believe my own words until Hannah points her elegant arm again.

'Think that's for us?'

A shiny black speedboat is zipping through the gentle waves towards the jetty, the name *Scylla* emblazoned in white across the side, a man in a peaked cap behind the wheel. He raises a cheery hand in greeting.

Thank God! We hurry across the sand, which is hard work, arriving sweaty and panting as the slick boat pulls up at the end of the long jetty.

'Señora Dillane?' the guy calls, throwing a rope over a metal post. 'Señorita Hannah and Vittoria?'

'Sí!' I give him a thumbs-up. 'That's us! Thank you.'

'Welcome!' He holds out a hand to help us in, and I feel infinite relief, as if someone else has finally taken charge of events.

Now it only remains to see what Jodie has to say.

Antonio, as the badge on his white polo shirt informs us our smiling captain is called, is charm personified.

He stows our luggage beneath the seats and deftly pops a bottle of real champagne, handing us each a glass. Plastic – but a glass none the less, and never more welcome, I think, trying not to knock mine back in one.

This is so much more like what I expected of the trip!

'Is Jodie there already?' asks Hannah, who has actually accepted a drink.

Antonio shakes his head, his teeth a flash of brilliant white in his sunburnt face. '*Non comprendo, lo siento, señorita.*'

'Never mind.' Hannah raises her glass to us. 'It's just nice to be on the water in this heat.'

Thank God. I wasn't sure she'd get on a boat at all. But I think of the pills in her overflowing wash bag, and the cogs of my brain creak into action.

'Cheers, girls,' she calls above the revs of the engine.

'Cheers,' we cry back.

It's so beautiful, it feels pointless to worry right now. As if to emphasise the feeling of letting go, an enormous school of fish dash alongside us, silvery fins flashing in the morning sun as they fly under and over the water, and I feel a great rush of adrenaline.

Even Simone looks happier now as she joins me at the front, Hannah at the back, trailing her hands in the water when she can, watching the jumping fish.

We're off! Where to exactly, I'm not sure, but at last we're really on our way to the reunion; to some proper R&R.

Oh, come on! chimes my sensible head. *Only time will tell what the weekend will actually bring.*

But I'm not listening. I chug my champagne back, grabbing the bottle from the ice bucket to refill; not thinking too hard about what Hannah might have taken to be this serene.

My own Xanax must have worn off now, but it did the trick, and I'm glad I stashed one away for emergencies.

Belatedly I remember the lights outside last night, and the fact that I opened the front door to face them, like some silly heroine in a horror film – no doubt made bold by medication. I can laugh about it in the sunshine.

If you've got to face your demons – and who am I to judge? – well, this surely is the way to do it.

TWENTY-SEVEN
HANNAH

When I look back at the beach, the funny old finca that reminded me too much of my parents' crumbling church is no longer visible.

I stand in the bow of the boat, enjoying the breeze flitting around my face. My two best friends sit happily in the prow, looking as relieved as I feel to be out of that place. I wave at them both, and they wave back.

But as we gather speed, a figure on the beach we've just left begins to run towards the jetty.

'Wait!' I call to Antonio. '*Señor!*' I gesture frantically at the figure, too far away to place.

But the beach is dropping away now quickly, and Antonio just grins back at me.

'Is OK, *señorita*,' he calls.

As I meet his Ray-Banned gaze, I remember Simone's earlier fears about a storm, and I wonder – is that what might be hurrying him on?

'No worry, OK?' He gives me a thumbs-up, and I have no choice but to believe him.

Because as the boat forges ahead, it's obvious he has no intention of turning back.

'Where are we going?' Simone shouts over the engine as we zip past yet another idling superyacht.

'Don't know, don't really care,' Vicky calls back, waving up at a woman sunbathing on the deck of the yacht, lithe and tanned in a tiny red bikini. 'It's kinda exciting, don't you reckon?'

The woman tips her straw hat, and Vicky blows her a kiss – and I look again at my old friend, curious. And then we're past the yacht and heading out to sea, leaving the coast of Ibiza behind us.

Holding my hair with one hand to stop it flying madly in the breeze, I keep my gaze trained on the horizon, as I was taught a long time ago. I watch the shimmering fish flash through the sea in front of us as if they're guiding us, the spray hitting my face, reminding me I'm alive.

Perhaps I *have* forgotten that recently; perhaps I do deserve to have a little fun.

'Oh no,' I hear Simone mutter as she sits beside me. 'Oh no, dammit!' She's squinting at her phone.

'Everything OK?'

'What?' She looks up, eyes wide, as if she's forgotten where she is. 'Oh yes, sorry. It's nothing.'

But it's evidently not nothing, as she starts to type furiously.

I'm guessing there's yet more drama at home. Tiger has been giving Simone a hard time over the past year or so. She may be gorgeous, my god-daughter, but she's as wilful as her mum was when she was younger.

But Simone will share when the time's right, I have faith, and I allow myself to trail my hand in the water and watch the fish fly.

· · ·

After another ten minutes or so, the boat begins to track to the left, and in the distance, a tiny island comes into view. Nearing it, I can see it's surrounded by a ferocious-looking defence: big grey rocks that lunge unexpectedly out of the calm ocean.

Antonio slows down and steers expertly between these rocks that make me think of prehistoric monsters. Occasional golden patches of sand are visible on the sea floor, but mainly the depths are scary and unseeable.

Transfixed for a moment, I drag my gaze upwards.

Is this our final destination?

The little island is very lush, covered in the pine trees that Ibiza is famous for, as well as what I think are probably olive and almond trees. And as we near, I catch a glimpse of a long white villa high above us, in the midst of what looks like an orange grove.

As fast as it appeared, the house vanishes again as we round the headland, slowly chugging through the last of the great fanged rocks into a small golden curve of beach. A brightly coloured boathouse sits to one side; inside, an upturned rowing boat is just visible, painted pastel blue, but there's no jetty like the one we just left on Ibiza.

Antonio grins and mimes. 'Jump, *señoras!*'

Wishing I'd put my swimsuit on beneath my dress, I check my phone and then stow it away carefully.

There's no signal on it at all, I realise belatedly, but that's probably just because we're down so low on the beach. It'll be fine. As soon as we climb up to the villa, normal service will resume.

Except the truth is, I'm not sure what normal service actually is any more.

The real question is whether, after meeting up with Jodie again after all these years, things will ever be normal again.

TWENTY-EIGHT
SIMONE

Isla del Diablo

Standing on the warm sand of this verdant little island, the thing that's been niggling at me all morning snaps into focus as the *Scylla* turns back towards Ibiza.

Of course – Scylla was the six-headed sea monster from *The Odyssey*; the terrible monster with a fiendish face and a voice like a dog, who used to pluck sailors from their boats as they passed, devouring them whole.

A great shiver goes through me, despite the sultry heat. As I watch Antonio manoeuvre the boat skilfully through the toothy rocks, I just about resist the urge to shout, 'Come back!'

Last year, Mason and I read a picture-book version of *The Odyssey* each night before bed, poring over the garish pictures of gods and goddesses, the magical and awful creatures those brave voyagers faced, but as the speedboat fades into the distance, the memory is less than reassuring, especially when I think of the messages that recently pinged up on my phone.

'Look!' Vicky cries, and for all her enthusiasm, I'm sure I

hear relief in her voice as she points at the wooded slope leading from the beach.

A laminated pink arrow indicates a set of stairs winding between the trees.

'C'mon.' She's off, trailing a smoke cloud, Hannah behind her. At least she's found her vape.

But I wait until the *Scylla* disappears entirely from view, feeling a strong sense of foreboding as it does.

I check my phone again for a signal – in vain – before I start to follow my friends.

At the foot of the steps, beside a hand-painted sign that reads *Isla del Diablo*, Scylla's terrifying teeth fill my mind, and I wish I was back on the boat and heading anywhere but here.

Home, preferably.

TWENTY-NINE
VICKY

It's hard work keeping upbeat when you're so unsure of an outcome; of what's round the next corner. Despite the champagne on the boat, the nerves about seeing Jodie are really biting now.

So when I reach the top of the stairs and see the villa in all its glory, I feel a wash of emotion so strong, I collapse on the edge of a sunlounger.

'Hello?' Hannah is calling, seemingly indifferent to the opulence. She walks up a small flight of marble steps, across a sundeck and onto a long, covered veranda. 'Anyone here? Jodie?'

It's the antithesis of the strange old house we stayed in last night. Truly impressive, even if Jodie always was queen of the blag.

'How the hell did she swing this?' I ask a sweating Simone, who's just appeared between the last trees, horribly out of breath as she hauls her bag behind her.

'Remind me not to wear flip-flops next time we go on a trek. Oh, gosh! Wow!' She gazes around her. 'This is gorgeous!'

It *is* gorgeous. All pure and pristine white, freshly painted by the looks of it, the villa is long and sleek, one end covered in cascades of magenta bougainvillea flowers. There are huge windows and cream canopies, hanging pod-chairs under big parasols dotted around the wooden sundeck, a smaller white building peeking out behind the veranda.

And the view! Overlooking the beautiful Mediterranean, Ibiza in the distance, a mosaic-tiled infinity pool sparkles in the sunlight, surrounded on three sides by loungers and a four-poster sunbed, white muslin curtains wafting gently in the breeze.

A brilliantly green sculpted garden slopes up behind the villa into more trees, while on this side, a stripy tepee stands on a lush lawn, a row of yoga mats laid out in front.

The whole place is like something I could only ever have dreamt of.

And yet once again, there's something discordant; something a bit off.

It's deserted.

'I've still got no signal.' Simone frowns, holding her phone this way and that, as high as she can. 'And I really need to call home.'

'There's probably a landline inside.' I can't be bothered to get up right now. 'Or use the Wi-Fi. Call through WhatsApp or FaceTime.'

'Good idea.' She looks relieved. 'I'll go and find the password.' She disappears after Hannah into the house, passing a modern metal sculpture I don't quite understand. I think perhaps it's meant to be Cupid.

I loll on the lounger, inert, feeling for a moment like a cat in the cosy patch by the fire; enjoying the sunshine warming my bones. It's the most glorious day, and we're in the most amazing setting: me and my two best mates.

The only fly in the ointment is that our host being our treacherous ex-friend Jodie. So the fact that she's apparently not here might turn out to be a good thing.

When I open my eyes again, half the garden is in shade and the cicadas are going for it – an afternoon chorus of chirrups.

My mouth tastes like I've swallowed a pint of sawdust and I'm gagging for a glass of water. Stretching my stiff neck, I wince. My shoulders are hot and tight, and I touch my skin gingerly – ouch! Lord only knows where that factor 50 is that Simone bought me at the airport. We've only been here five minutes and I've already burnt. I can't believe it was only yesterday we were drinking gin at the airport.

The creepy note in my purse flickers into my brain.

With an impending sense of dread, I look round for my bag, but it's not here.

In fact, all the luggage is gone. The girls must have taken it inside.

A strange tinkling noise nearby makes the hairs on my arms stand up. It's eerie, like something from my nightmares.

'Hello?' My voice actually sounds shaky. 'Hannah? Sim?'

No reply. A band of fear tightens round my chest. What *is* that noise?

I haul myself up. I don't know how long I've been sleeping, but the sun has moved across the sky, throwing long shadows. As I walk towards the villa, I see that the deck is covered in broken glass. A champagne flute, by the looks of the intact stem. But as I bend to pick it up, a scream erupts from inside the villa, high and clear, filling the air.

Without thinking, I start running.

Towards the noise, the scream that now stops and turns to sobbing.

THIRTY
THEN
SPRING 2002

In the ensuing chaos of the fire, in amongst the shouting and the flames and the billowing black smoke from the burning house-boat, it was hard to keep track of who was where.

It was like hell had broken its banks onto the canal: the wail of the sirens; the blue lights of fire engines flickering across the canal and mingling with the orange flames; the acrid smell of burning.

Hannah was hysterical as she tried to board the boat, held back first by friends and then, as she resisted, by a couple of burly firemen.

I felt almost overwhelmed by the noise as we tried to help and didn't know how; as her crying grew louder, and ambulances arrived to treat the injured, followed by local police.

The one thing that became quickly obvious was that Hannah's boyfriend Nick was nowhere to be found.

He had left the party a while ago, as Vicky's new friend had said – probably because he'd been so wasted. Everyone had seen him out of it earlier; it transpired he'd taken quite a lot of Ecstasy on top of drinking at least a bottle of vodka, and it looked like he had gone home to lie down.

The speculation went on until the fire was out.

A fireman came to notify the police that there was definitely a body on the boat, and the police asked if we knew who it might be.

Hannah stopped crying and just collapsed, like Jodie had earlier on the dance floor; dropped down onto the canal path and didn't move.

After the police had tried and failed to take a statement from Hannah, and the paramedics had checked her over in the ambulance, we were driven home. We took Hannah back with us to our flat, on the insistence of a weeping Jodie.

The paramedics had given Hannah a sedative when she refused to go to hospital. Jodie, on the other hand, was sobering up faster than I'd expected, and kept wittering on in the car about how great Nick was and how much he loved Hannah, until I wanted to tell her to just shut up.

It was obviously hysteria, but with Hannah sitting there in the front, it was deeply uncomfortable too.

'Hon' – Vicky was bolder than me – 'put a sock in it, yeah?'

Hannah, though, was silent: almost catatonic in her deep shock. She didn't speak at all, just stared ahead, wringing her hands over and over. She had nothing of her own, we realised, so we peeled her out of her filthy clothes and put her into an old T-shirt and shorts of Vicky's.

We made her tea full of sugar, which she didn't touch, and put her to bed in my room, sitting with her until at long last she fell into a deep sleep.

'Poor, *poor* thing,' Vicky whispered as we backed out of the room. 'I can't bear it.'

I shook Jodie, passed out on the settee, her own battery having finally run down. 'Should we call her parents?'

'What?' Jodie gazed up wide-eyed, her face a mess of kohl and mascara. 'What's happened?'

'Hannah's parents?' It was nearing dawn. 'Shall we call them?'

'I don't know,' she mumbled. 'I guess. Oh God, poor Nick.' The tears began again.

'We'll do it in the morning.' Vicky was decisive. 'I'm knackered.' And the two of us crept to bed in her room, me on the truckle bed.

'Do you think Nick...' I was tentative as we lay in the dark, dawn starting to seep round the curtains. 'I mean, do you reckon he was on his own? On the boat, before...' I couldn't quite bear to say it aloud.

'I don't know, mate.' Vicky attacked her pillow, trying to get comfortable. 'And I'm not sure I want to. It's not going to help, is it?'

Soon her breathing slowed and she too slept, but I couldn't drop off.

I stared up at the ceiling for ages, confused and angry and deeply, deeply shocked.

I didn't know Nick at all – I'd barely spoken a word to him last night – but he'd been so young, his whole life ahead of him.

All wiped out by one terrible mistake.

But whose mistake had it been?

When we got up the next day, Hannah was still asleep, and Jodie was nowhere to be seen.

Family business, she texted me when I called. *Can't talk, soz. Back soon. Take care of Hannah for me please.*

It wasn't a question – it was a typical Jodie request, i.e. a thinly veiled order. And it seemed presumptuous, given the circumstances – although it was also what I'd started to understand was typically Jodie – that we, who'd met Hannah precisely once, would take care of her.

Deep loss and tragedy were hardly a good starting point for any friendship. Or so we first thought.

Dizzy's kitchen happened to be shut that week for refurbishment, so Vicky spent the most time with Hannah, at home in the flat. And although she said she couldn't really get Hannah to talk, she did get her out walking, tramping up the local hills more than once with a flask of tea.

Jodie would call and text intermittently to check in, but to all intents and purposes, she'd vanished.

When Hannah's parents arrived to take her back to the Peaks, Vicky and I were both relieved.

'She's lovely,' Vicky said as the front door closed behind Hannah for the final time. 'But she's totally traumatised, and I'm not a professional.'

The following week, Jodie missed Nick's funeral, held up in Manchester – work apparently – so Vicky accompanied Hannah, 'for solidarity', she said.

It was a dreadful affair by all accounts; one I couldn't face attending myself and, though I felt guilty, it wasn't as if I'd known Nick.

Once that was over, I imagined we'd seen the last of Hannah, and much as I'd liked her, I was busy with my own life.

So when Jodie suggested Hannah move in, it was a surprise to me how quickly the four of us became inseparable.

For all my doubts, we worked remarkably well together as flatmates, considering we were squashed in tighter than sardines.

Soon we were socialising together: relentless drinking and

dancing and impromptu partying nearly every weekend, and sometimes on week nights too.

The Three Musketeers became Four now; the Spice Girls, we liked to joke, minus one.

Our friendship was forged in flames, we'd say ruefully, and while we obviously all wished it hadn't been so tragic a start, in the end it brought us together as the most bosom of buddies.

For as long as it lasted, at least.

THIRTY-ONE

HANNAH

Isla del Diablo

Arriving on this island and finding Jodie immediately seemed by far the best idea. The only idea, in fact: to get the 'greetings' over with, and to say what I came to say.

But it soon became clear the villa was empty.

How utterly different it was to Finca Maria. Luxurious, if you liked this sort of thing: all metal and glass and shiny surfaces; the biggest plasma screen I'd ever seen on the wall in front of huge leather and velvet settees, offset by wild oil paintings of the sea and sunsets; an expensive Sonos stereo system. In the open-plan glossy kitchen, there were Gaggia coffee machines, high-spec juicers and useless gadgets like waffle makers.

How the other half live, eh? All right for some, isn't it? Shame about us though. I heard my mother's voice as clearly as if she was in the room; saw her lips purse into that horrid thin line brought on by a lifetime of berating a God who kept letting her down. Then atoning.

All the endless atoning.

Opening the fridge with a savage rattle, I grabbed the first food I came across – a great ripe nectarine – and bit into it viciously.

Sweet juice dripping down my chin, I walked to the glass table in the main room.

There was literally no one here, but there *were* four long white envelopes laid out. One for each of the four of us, all sealed.

I picked up the one with my name on it, followed by a hand-drawn heart. They all had a symbol, in fact, now I looked more closely. A card symbol...

Hannah, our Queen of Hearts. And, oh, that took me back to the days of the penthouse flat on Royal Mews.

Opening it, I saw it was a key card with a number.

Number 2.

I was never number 1.

First the worst, second the best...

I chucked the nectarine stone away in a gleaming bin marked *Composta*, washed my hands in an explosive jet of water over the kitchen sink, then, key card in hand, padded barefoot down the long corridor to the right of the main room. I realised the numbers here went from 5 to 8, so I turned and went down the left-hand corridor.

Number 2 had my name on the door in flouncy print. It was last but one from the end, the corridor capped by a glass box of a window with the most breathtaking view over a craggy sheer rock face, straight onto the sea.

The room itself was far more tranquil than that staggering drop: fresh lilies in a vase, and a green mosaic bath in front of a picture window that looked over treetops down to the sea. A huge double bed could have homed a whole tribe, while the marble-tiled en suite was twice the size of my parents' bathroom.

I went back outside.

Simone had vanished somewhere, but Vicky was snoozing on a sunlounger. Careful not to wake her, I tiptoed around, taking all our bags inside and depositing theirs in the lounge, bypassing the champagne flutes someone had left out on the table, along with an empty ice bucket.

Back in number 2, the air conditioning made it so cool that, for all my guilt over the planet, I flopped straight onto the giant bed.

I needed to get my jumbled head straight.

Where on earth was Jodie? We were one and a half days into a four-day break with still no sign of her.

Except was that *really* surprising? Being reliable had never been Jodie's strong point.

In fact, it was the exact opposite of her life ethos. Given her family background, that wasn't so strange.

I realised it was getting very cold in here, and I grabbed the air-con remote to turn it down – but it wouldn't budge.

God, it was cold, so cold I was shivering. Icy, in fact. I went to the door, but when I turned the handle, it seemed to be stuck and I rattled it, more frantically now.

An unexpected noise sliced through the silence. A piercing scream, breaking the quiet hum of the air con, that made my skin creep all over as now I heaved at the door, but it still wouldn't open.

More than frightening.

It reminded me of a threatened animal, of a fox I once saw cornered by a huge slobbering dog straining on its leash in the local park.

But I couldn't get out of the freezing room, my sweaty hand slipping on the handle as I turned it frantically...

'It's nothing,' Simone keeps saying when I find her, smashed hand mirror in smithereens at her feet. 'I've just cut my hand a bit, but it's fine, really.'

I don't mention seven years' bad luck, but it crosses my mind nonetheless. My mother wouldn't approve of me even knowing that superstition, picked up from my lovely nan long before Mum managed to knock that kind of silliness (evil) out of me. *No new shoes on the table, no wearing green on Fridays.*

'It was so stupid of me,' Simone is muttering. But it doesn't look like nothing, and she's obviously shaken to the core. As if she's seen a ghost, in fact, as I uncurl her hand carefully, so I don't mention the fact that I thought I was trapped in my own room just now.

'Let me see, Sim...'

'What's happened?' Vicky barges into the room, holding what looks like a glass dagger. 'I heard screaming.'

'Watch out!' I point at the glass on the floor.

'More glass!' she says. 'There's broken glass everywhere on this island.'

Even if the cut isn't that deep, there's a lot of blood. A *lot*.

'I'm OK.' Simone looks rueful. 'Sorry. I just cut myself a bit, that's all.'

'A bit?' Vicky lets out a breath. 'I thought someone was dead, mate.'

'I'm sorry, I think it was just the shock. And wow, Vick.' Simone attempts a grin, but it's watery at best. 'You look pretty burnt, angel.'

'Like a beetroot, you mean?' Vicky glances in the long wall mirror, wincing at her reflection. 'Blimey, I do, don't I? I fell asleep.' She looks at us for a moment, and I think she's about to reprimand us for not waking her up. That certainly used to be her style: blaming others for her own actions. But she thinks better of it. 'So what did you do, mate?'

She peers at the bleeding hand as Simone sits heavily on the edge of the bed – her room an exact replica of mine, except for a yellow and gold colour scheme rather than greens.

'I picked up that little mirror on the dresser 'cos I had something in my eye, and... I don't know...' She gestures uselessly. 'It must have just slipped through my hand.'

It doesn't really make sense though, I don't say, because how did she cut herself like this if she'd dropped the mirror on the floor?

'Ew!' Vicky pulls a face. 'You're better with blood than me, Han. You be nurse and I'll see if I can find a dustpan and brush. I need it for the terrace too. Someone smashed a champagne flute.' She drops her glass blade into the bin.

In Simone's bathroom, I wash the blood off carefully, using tissues and cotton wool, and I'm relieved to see the cuts are mainly surface ones. 'I think it's probably OK, Sim, but I wonder if you need an X-ray?' I study the worst of the lacerations. 'Check how deep it is?'

'An X-ray?' Simone glances at her hand and shakes her head. 'No, it's fine, Han, I'm sure.'

'I don't know, it's usually good to get these things checked.' But I know I'm overcautious these days, indoctrinated by my hypochondriac parents. Sometimes I think I spend more time in A&E than the actual staff.

'And is your phone working anyway?' Simone asks. 'Because mine still isn't, and I can't find the Wi-Fi modem. So right now, I don't know how we'd contact anyone if we needed to. And actually, I do need to.' Her anxiety is palpable, building as she talks. 'I still haven't rung home.'

'No luck finding a landline then?'

'Doesn't seem to be one. Not that I can find anyway.' She opens the shiny cabinet and rummages around, pulling out a first-aid kit. 'But this is well stocked, at least!'

I feel how hard she's trying to normalise the situation, but right now none of it feels very normal. Being on a tiny island in the middle of the ocean waiting for a friend I haven't spoken to for so many years isn't normal.

A friend? More like an enemy, I hear the little voice say. *Let's be real.*

'We'll find the Wi-Fi soon, don't worry.' I tread cautiously round the broken glass in my sandals. 'Look, it's your call about the hospital. You're probably more knowledgeable than me anyway, so you decide. Now, where's Vick with that broom?'

Exactly as if she just heard me, a great shout comes from outside – a Vicky shout – and my heart begins to race again.

THIRTY-TWO
SIMONE

'I think I saw a boat headed this way,' Vicky shouts from the terrace, dustpan in hand, pointing towards Ibiza.

Sun in my eyes, I can't make out much except the vast glittering ocean.

'I reckon Jodie might be on it,' she says.

'Surely she'll arrive on the Royal Yacht,' Hannah jokes, but the humour's not heartfelt. 'Knowing her.'

But we *don't* really know Jodie any more, do we? That's the point.

Maybe it's the shock of the blood; more likely it's the shock of what I found in my bedroom, the picture left beside the bed, but without warning, I retch violently behind a planter of tumbling herbs.

'God, sorry.' I wipe my mouth on the hem of my dress. 'I'm really sorry.'

'Simone' – Hannah strokes my back calmly, as if I'm a child – 'it's OK. Just breathe slowly. That's it, in and out.'

'Hon!' Vicky's hopping up and down. 'You're all right, aren't you, Sim?' In that moment, I sense how much she wants me to be OK – or needs me to be.

Nervous energy literally vibrates out of her.

'Bit better now?' Hannah's face is solicitous as she helps me straighten up again. 'Come and sit down. You've had a shock.' Our eyes meet for a split second, and I wonder if she saw the picture too.

Then she's leading me back into the shade, and I let myself be guided into one of the bright basket chairs set round a funky table.

Leaning back, I close my eyes for a second. There's an eerie tinkling coming from somewhere, and nearer, I can hear a bee, or perhaps an angry wasp. Its buzzing intensifies as if it's preparing for attack.

'Well I never,' a familiar husky voice exclaims somewhere behind me. 'So which one of you bitches thought this was a good idea?'

THIRTY-THREE
VICKY

Only Jodie, I think, the minute I hear those words. Only Jodie would announce her arrival with that statement.

I swing round – and *of course*, there she is, finally.

Hands on hips, blank-faced and scarlet-lipped, eyes hidden behind huge zebra-print shades, she doesn't really look much different to the last time I saw her in the flesh.

Older, sure, in as much as we all inevitably look older, and a twenty-a-day habit won't have helped her skin – though knowing Jodie, she'll have been visiting every expert out there to be peeled and Botoxed or whatever else people do today to promote eternal youth.

Still boasting that big mop of hair, she's wearing a leopard-print shift over an emerald-green bikini, hoop earrings swinging, fingers still covered in glittering gold rings and topped off with a multicoloured manicure. Most of the jewellery fake, no doubt, unless she invested her fortune in precious metals.

But there's no arguing she looks good; you'd glance again if she passed you on the street. She's dramatic, Jodie; she's always been a life force: drawing the eye immediately – the colours, the glitter, the stance.

Yet the weird bit is, standing there in front of us, she seems unsure of herself. And that's not the Jodie I remember; that Jodie was *never* uncertain. For all her brave words, she's obviously surprised to see us.

More than surprised, I'd guess – shocked.

'Charming,' I snap. 'Who wouldn't think being invited on an all-expenses holiday was a good idea?'

'Sure.' She shrugs. 'I get that. I mean, *I* did.'

'But *you* invited us.' Simone's frowning now, clutching her cut hand. 'We're here for you.'

'What?'

'Yeah,' Hannah chimes in. 'For your birthday.'

'Your "fortieth".' I can't resist the elaborate quote marks.

But Jodie's still looking nonplussed, despite the massive sunglasses, and so far, this is not going at all as I'd anticipated.

'Er, no.' She shakes her head slowly. 'I definitely didn't invite you, babe. I had no idea any of you would be here.'

THIRTY-FOUR
JODIE

I can't pretend it's not a shock to see them here.

Minutes ago, I was merely ruing the fact I'd brought so much luggage as I hauled myself up the stairs from the beach, anticipating at least one more trip down again in the heat to retrieve the heavy-duty make-up box that accompanies me everywhere these days.

I was not at all prepared for *this*.

I'm gazing at Vicky's back. She's standing on the far side of the dramatic infinity pool, gazing at the sea – and yes, there's Hannah, and oh my God, last but not least, never least, Simone, sprawled in a chair, clutching her hand, which is wrapped in bloody tissues.

Hannah's much too thin, I can see straight away, but Vicky looks good, it must be said. Toned and athletic in her white vest and shorts – apart from those lobster-red shoulders. Bet they bloody hurt.

I take a deep breath.

'Well I never,' I drawl. 'So which one of you bitches thought this was a good idea?'

As one, all three turn – and it's immediately obvious I misjudged that badly. Yep, from the look on all their faces, my supposed witticism has gone down harder than the proverbial lead balloon.

'Charming,' Vicky snaps back, and, head whirring, I don't bother to defend myself; to say that in my panic, I was only channelling a famous line from that bonkbuster I used to sneak peeks of in the local library as a kid.

What was it called? *Lace* maybe?

'But you invited us.' Simone hauls herself up from the basket thing she's been sitting in. She looks solemn; paler than usual against her forest-green maxi dress; delightfully curvy and just like my darling Dilly always did, even though it's been ages.

In fact, I'm so happy to see her, weird as that might seem, given everything, I have to resist running round the pool to fling myself at her feet.

Begging forgiveness.

I push that thought as far away as possible and try to concentrate.

'For your birthday,' Hannah's saying, her voice quiet and as northern as ever.

'Your "fortieth".' Vicky sketches sarcastic quote marks in the air.

'Er no,' I ignore the dig. 'I definitely didn't invite you, babe. I had no idea any of you would be here. I meant, where's the crew?'

'We're here!' Vicky glares at me, looking like she wants a fight. She always loved all that martial-arts stuff, karate and judo and the rest. And she still looks fit and strong. I'm not sure I'd want to take her on, despite the fact that I come from good fighting stock.

I attempt a smile. 'To clarify – I meant the *camera* crew.'

They frown, exchanging looks with each other, and I can't say that doesn't rankle a bit. More than a bit.

I'm the outsider now, that's blatantly obvious. I mean, it's hardly a surprise – the one thing that isn't, in fact – but it's still tough to experience it.

I was always the centre of things when we were younger – or at least I guess I tried to be.

Yep, in retrospect, I tried very hard to be the sun around which their moons spun.

Therapy has taught me that, at least, if nothing else useful.

'Sorry. *Camera* crew?' Hannah copies my emphasis, like she's about to hyperventilate. Always was a bit oversensitive, poor lamb. 'What are you talking about?'

'For Christ's sake!' Somewhere behind me on the steps up from the beach, I can hear Mae cursing, presumably still struggling with the broken handle on her case. I can hear her, but it's not her I'm thinking of right now. (*When do you ever think of her?* my mum would say – but that's not helpful right now.)

I need to dig deep and sort this out with my old mates who have just turned up out of nowhere, because otherwise, the next few days will be awful.

Well, let's face it, they're probably going to be awful however deep I dig.

This villa, the exclusive little island itself, might be straight out of a glossy travel show, but the company... well, that's something else.

A proper shock.

I take a deep breath, push my sunglasses to the top of my head and, plastering on my best and biggest smile, march around the pool and up onto the terrace to face the girls.

Though they're not girls any more, are they?

Can't get away with that description these days; we're all women now. There's no excuse for poor behaviour; I can't behave like a teenager these days. My hangovers alone should have warned me of that at least a decade ago.

And I need this gig more than I've needed anything for a while, so...

Game face on; best behaviour at all times. I need to get them on my side, before it's too late. Before I fall into the bear pit.

THIRTY-FIVE
SIMONE

'So,' I say slowly as Jodie steps up onto the terrace in funky wedge espadrilles, stripy ribbons tied around her tanned ankles. When I look again, I see they're hennaed with elaborate designs. 'Let me get this straight...'

'Yeah?'

Truthfully, I feel like I need to sit down again, but my bum being lower than my hips will remove the last vestiges of dignity I possess – which isn't much. 'You weren't expecting us to be here?'

'No!' Jodie's smile is kind of beseeching. 'I mean, not that it's not a pleasure' – it doesn't *look* like she's finding it pleasurable – 'but I've come for work.'

'Work?' Hannah shakes her head.

She must have stopped to put those espadrilles on after getting off that blasted boat, or they'd be soaking, I find myself thinking absently.

'Yeah, no rest for the wicked. I'm filming a travel show. A segment about posh yoga retreats.' She casts her eye around the place, sizing it up. 'That's what I *thought* anyway. That I was coming to do yoga.'

'OK, hang on.' Vicky's hands are on her hips. 'So you're saying that this isn't a party?'

'A party?' Jodie looks confused. 'No. Was that what you were expecting?'

'Yeah,' Hannah says. 'We got invites. In the post.'

'Invites?' Jodie shakes her head. 'From who? The production team?'

'From you, stupid,' Vicky snaps. Anxiety always makes her grumpy.

'No, definitely not from me.' Jodie ignores the insult, poking around in the Gucci handbag slung across her chest. She finds a pack of Marlboro Lights and sparks one up as we all watch, waiting. 'So let *me* get this straight,' she says, repeating my words, 'you're all here for me?'

'Yes.'

'You've come all the way to Ibiza, or whatever this place is called' – she takes a long, pensive inhale – 'because you thought it was my party?'

'Your *birthday* party,' Hannah says – and she definitely sounds accusatory now. 'We came all this way to celebrate your birthday.'

'You didn't though, babe, did you?' Jodie begins to laugh. 'It's June, and my birthday's in November – as in "Remember, remember the fifth of November".'

'But actually, it's not the fifth, is it?' I say flatly. 'It's the fourth, your birthday. A balanced Libran, etc.' Jodie used to love a bit of astrology when it suited her to. 'A sense of justice, and all that crap.'

And, of course, she always thought it'd be far more glamorous to be born on Bonfire Night – which seems apt, now I think about it. Blowing stuff up and fireworks – Jodie's favourite pastimes.

Sometimes literally.

'If you knew it was in November' – Hannah looks at me –

'why didn't you say?'

I shrug. 'Just assumed it was a summer party. Better time for the Med.'

'Ah, Dilly darling, so you *do* remember!' Jodie looks at me with what I *think* is affection. 'I knew I could rely on you.'

And as I meet her gaze, which is the same but different – laughter lines definitely deeper, her mouth starting to show the ravages of smoking but also fuller than I remember, I'm guessing because she's had some collagen added – I have the strongest urge to either slap her or start laughing hysterically.

She frowns. 'What's wrong with your hand?'

'It's fine,' I say. At least it's stopped bleeding. And I won't give her the satisfaction of knowing her little trick worked. It must have been her trick, surely.

There's a layer of hysteria in the air so definitive I can almost taste it – like a pretty Battenberg cake, criss-crossed with sweet marzipan and icing except, in this case, I'd guess laced with something toxic too.

Arsenic, maybe. 'Anyway' – she drags on her cigarette thoughtfully – 'whatever the date, I'm really touched that you all came for me.'

'Nothing changes, I see.' Vicky holds her hand out. 'Still displaying the same monstrous ego. Give me a cigarette please.'

'Ah, Vick.' Jodie grins, handing her the pack. 'Always my biggest fan.'

A load of swearing suddenly floats up from below, and a girl – a young woman – appears pulling a Louis Vuitton case.

'My darling bub. Perhaps it's a surprise party,' Jodie says brightly.

Little Mae. I haven't seen her since she was tiny. I gaze at her pretty, cross face. It looks strangely familiar...

The girl in gingham at the airport in Ibiza, *of course*.

'Mae? Did you arrange it for Mummy? For my best friends'

– Jodie glances at us briefly, then corrects herself – 'for my *oldest* friends to be here?'

'No, Mama dear, obviously not.' Mae scowls, and though she's attractive, the irritation spoils it. 'You bribed me to come to this hole in the first place, remember?'

Wow, she looks just like—

'Hardly a hole, dear heart.' Jodie interrupts my thought, stops herself frowning just in time. Or maybe she can't frown. Maybe her face is too tight. 'It's pretty amazing, isn't it?'

'If you like this sort of thing. Give me a tent and a campfire any time over this fake shit. Sorry, guys – don't mean to be rude, but it's really not my vibe.' She stomps inside, and I try to be generous: to imagine that Tiger might have been equally irritable if faced with relative strangers. But my heart's flip-flopping all over the place, and also, I hope I've brought my kid up a *bit* better than that outburst.

'Also, the thing about surprise parties is that generally the guests are in on it too,' Vicky points out once Mae's gone. 'But no one's mentioned any surprise to us.'

'I need to talk to my producer.' Jodie grinds her cigarette out beneath her rope heel. 'Find out what's going on.' She rubs her neck as if it's sore. 'Look, it's great to see you and all that, but I really need a shower. Travelling always makes me feel filthy.' We're treated to a lascivious wink that doesn't strike true.

She begins to walk towards the villa – and then stops.

'Don't suppose one of you lovelies could do me a wee favour and grab my other bag' – she gestures at the steps – 'from down there? I've got *such* a bad back at the moment, I shouldn't really carry anything.'

We all meet her hopeful gaze blankly. What might have worked twenty years ago doesn't work now, it seems.

No, we all grew wise to her tricks a long time ago, though not in time to stop the devastation, it must be said.

'Plus, I need to call my team...' She's starting to wheedle.

The Jodie of old didn't wheedle. She was bold and forthright, and often a huge pain in the neck, but never, as far as I can remember, a wheedler.

'... so I can understand what's going on.'

'There's no phone signal,' I say dully. 'Nor Wi-Fi that I can find.' And immediately I think of what I just saw in my room, and the nausea rears up again.

'Don't be silly.' Jodie smirks. 'What kind of place doesn't have Wi-Fi?'

'If the camera crew's arriving soon, they'll be able to sort it out,' Vicky says. 'They'll be technical, surely?'

'I'll get your bag, Jodie,' Hannah murmurs, bowing her head as she crosses to the steps.

'No way!' Vicky cries. 'Get it yourself, you lazy cow.' She grimaces at Jodie.

'Ah, Vick.' Jodie grins again. 'Don't stop her if she wants to help.'

Vicky follows Hannah and grabs her arm. 'Don't. I'll go.'

And as Jodie blows them both a kiss and pulls her case inside, and Vicky stomps off down the stairs, I can't help feeling nothing has changed.

It's like being back in that hideous week when she decimated all our lives in print – all over again.

But this time, we have a choice.

This time, we're not going to take it lying down.

If it's the last thing I do, I won't let her walk all over me again.

THIRTY-SIX
HANNAH

'If *she* didn't invite us' – I plonk myself down on a sunlounger – 'well then who *did*?'

'I don't know.' Simone's looking as perturbed as I feel. 'It's all really odd.' And then her phone – the phone she's been clutching most of the day – suddenly lights up, and messages start pinging. 'Oh, thank *God*!' She's immediately distracted. 'Jodie must have switched the Wi-Fi on.'

'That's good.' I probably ought to go and check my own phone, abandoned in my room for once. I need to make sure everything's OK with my parents, left in the care of my brother and sister-in-law for once, though honestly, the temptation is not to but to just enjoy the time to myself, and the quiet, and not getting endless unwanted messages.

Simone is padding into the villa – to call home, I assume – when I think I hear a boat engine below. As I stand up to have a look, all the blood rushes from my head, and the garden begins spinning.

I grab the wall and hold on until the world rights itself.

I must have stood too fast, and I realise I'm exhausted, as

well as horribly light-headed. It strikes me we haven't eaten since breakfast, and it's late afternoon now.

Feeling slightly better, I peer over the wall, but I can't see anything from here anyway. If another boat is arriving, it must be the camera crew Jodie mentioned.

And how weird will that be?

I can't stop it, because it's already there: the panic mounting in my chest, thundering through me like a physical sensation; rushing through my muscles, grabbing at my throat until I think I'll choke, my fingers icy, my toes numb.

Breathe, Hannah, breathe. The little voice is benevolent for once. *It's OK, just keep breathing, it'll go.*

Holding on to a rough wall for dear life in an idyllic cliff garden on an unknown island, I feel like I'm not really here. I might just float up into the deep blue sky, vanishing in body like I feel I already have in spirit, and who would care? It wouldn't matter if I did...

I look up, gulping air.

The storm warning Simone mentioned at breakfast comes back to me. But the sky is clear, apart from the gulls wheeling and crying above; darker than earlier – cobalt, they call it, I think absently – as day heads into evening, but still gorgeous and cloud-free.

Finally, feeling creeps back into my fingers and toes, and I catch my breath. And as the panic recedes, it's like the fight does too.

Now that I've actually seen Jodie, it seems to have drained out of me.

If we're not here to celebrate her birthday – not that I really had any intention of celebrating it anyway – what's the point in staying? Not to watch her working, surely?

I've only come to tell her my thoughts, to say the things I've been waiting to say all this time, the things festering inside me, and now it seems too difficult. It's too late, so perhaps it's time to leave.

Perhaps it's time to go and take over my parents' care again.

I don't have the heart for revenge any more. I loved Jodie so much once, that's all I need to remember.

Jodie's text came one wet Sunday afternoon. The rest of us were slumped in front of *The Osbournes* on MTV, suffering varying degrees of hangover from a house party the previous night.

'That's literally gross, Vick!' Hannah removed a paring from her lap that Vicky had just pinged at her, busy cutting her toenails.

'Just nature, hon!' Always a joker, Vicky loved winding Hannah up in particular; she was easy prey.

My Nokia beeped and I swiped at it, hoping it was a boy I liked. 'It's just Jodie.' My shoulders slumped, though actually it was a relief to hear from her. She'd been missing in action a lot the past few months; involved in a terrible pyramid scheme she'd tried to make us all join, refusing to listen to our advice to stay well clear.

There was a definite sense of desperation about her money-making at the moment, but I couldn't get her to talk to me about it.

'And?' Vicky finished her nails.

I skimmed the message. 'She says to meet her in town asap.'

'But it's horrible out there.'

And it was cosy in here: gas fire glowing, curtains half drawn against the threatening sky and driving rain.

'I was going to do a roast.' Vicky moved on to her fingers. 'Meet her in town why?'

'Don't know. Just says "Pentagon Place, 80 Royal Mews asap. Get a cab, I'll pay. Prepare to be astounded!"'

'Where's Pentagon Place?'

'Centre of town, I think? Near the Hippodrome. The posh bit.'

'The up-and-coming bit, I think you'll find, hon. Still pretty skanky round there. But I'm not leaving here till I'm literally forced to.' Vicky chucked the clippers down and turned the TV up. 'Have fun.'

Half an hour later, she was still grumbling as the taxi pulled up outside the big black gates of Pentagon Place, a private complex on Royal Mews.

And of course, I paid the driver, Jodie being nowhere to be seen.

Her latest text had come through in the cab.

Buzz 101!

'One-oh-one?' I tried to keep my hair dry as we ran to the buzzer, the rain so intense, it drove beneath my hood. 'That's a bit Big Brother!'

'Like the TV show?' Vicky looked confused.

'No, like the book, *Nineteen Eighty-Four*?' I buzzed the number. 'George Orwell?'

'Who?' Vicky always boasted she'd barely read a book since *The Three Musketeers*, a fact she was proud of.

'The room where the bad stuff is.' I put my finger on the buzzer again and held it down. 'Hurry up, Jodie! It's pouring out here!'

'Come on up, girls.' Her disembodied voice floated out of the intercom. 'Fifth floor.'

Rain dripping off us, we literally steamed up the mirrors in the warm lift, piling out on what turned out to be the top floor.

'Where now?' Hannah whispered. It was that kind of place, plush and shiny.

'Yo!' At the end of the discreetly lit corridor, a big walnut door flew open. 'Come on!' Wearing what looked like a petticoat, her feet bare, hair in bunches like a cheerleader, Jodie beckoned us towards her.

I caught Vicky's widening eyes as we walked into the apartment.

'Ta-da!' In the middle of the big open-plan lounge with an oak floor, Jodie threw her arms up like she was about to perform a circus act. 'What d'you reckon?'

'It's OK.' A still-sulky Vicky refused to look impressed. 'If you like this sort of thing. Don't tell me – you've got a new job as an estate agent?'

'God, no.' Jodie gave a dramatic shudder. 'After what that bastard did to my Dilly?' As she wrapped her arms round me, I could smell cigarettes and that old-fashioned French perfume she always wore, which I'd associated with old ladies until I met her. 'No, this is ours.' I'd never heard her sound so triumphant. 'Ours!'

'What do you mean, *ours*?'

'I mean, you lot can move in tonight. Or tomorrow. I already have.' She threw open a door: a bedroom with plush red carpet and a breathtaking view over the rooftops. Her old leather bag – a charity-shop star buy – sat on the rumpled double bed. 'I found this place, so I get first dibs.' She padded across the room and pushed at another door. 'And look at this...' A walk-in wardrobe. 'All my dreams come true! Next stop, Hollywood.'

Hannah was frowning so hard, the crease between her eyes

deepened. 'It's very nice, Jodie, but we'll never make the rent on this place. It's properly posh.'

'That's the best bit! It's exactly the same rent as the Dive.'

'You're seriously saying' – I perched on the big beige sofa – 'this place costs the same as what we pay for March Street?'

I met her bright eyes, lashed thickly as ever with mascara and a smattering of old kohl.

'So?' she said, but her vim had dissipated. She looked really tired, I thought; her skin had a kind of papery appearance. 'What do you think?'

'That you're mad,' Vicky said flatly. 'Now let's go home for that roast.'

The four of us stood at the picture window, looking down on the rooftops in silence. Huge clouds rolled across the moody sky, threatening yet more rain as night drew in. A storm was coming.

All over the city, lights were snapping on. It was both dramatic and also nice to be warm and safely inside in this weather, watching the world unfold before us. In March Street, my tiny bedroom looked onto the wall of the next-door chippy.

Jodie put her arm round my shoulders, and I put mine round Vicky's, and Vicky scooped Hannah into the line, and we just stood there linked together: the Four Musketeers. Invincible and about to conquer the world.

Perhaps it was true, in that moment at least.

Perhaps if we had stayed together, we could have.

'It is kind of amazing,' I said grudgingly. 'This place.'

'But where've you been?' Hannah's voice was quiet.

'Yeah, we were worried, Jod.' I squeezed my best friend's hand, but she pulled away, carefully not returning our gaze.

'Just sorting stuff.' She fumbled in her fake fur. 'Anyone got a light?'

'What stuff?' Vicky chucked her some matches. 'More pyramids?'

'No.' Jodie lit a cigarette. 'I'm all done with pyramids.' She slid the balcony doors open. 'I had to see my brother.'

'I didn't know you had one,' I said stupidly. Whenever I thought I really knew this girl, I found I didn't.

'I've got several.' She shrugged, her voice carrying onto the wind. 'All by different mums. This one's the only one who's not a complete twat.'

Hannah sat on the big leather armchair. 'What's the catch, Jodie?'

'No catch, babe.' She exhaled into the rain. 'Just go back to the Dive and pack your bags.'

'But I don't get it.' Hannah was persistent. 'It's... odd.'

'It's not odd and you don't need to get it.' I saw Jodie's face literally harden. 'I got us a great deal. Just move in – or don't.' A squall of rain lashed into the room, splattering her face. 'Your choice.' She chucked the fag out and shut the balcony doors with a bang.

The rest of us looked at one another as she sauntered off to her room.

'Think of the parties we could have,' Vicky murmured.

'I do like the view,' Hannah said.

'There's so much more space,' I agreed quietly. 'A room each.'

'We can entertain.' Vicky grinned, obviously thinking of Tom, just dumped by the girlfriend now in Mumbai; Tom who she'd snogged again the other night. 'Without taking it in turns.'

'I might have room to actually do some painting.' Hannah looked excited for almost the first time since I'd met her. 'I could buy an easel!'

'All right, Picasso.' But Vicky was Hannah's number-one art fan.

'Let's say Paula Rego, shall we?' Hannah said.

None of us bothered to reply we had no clue who that was.

So we chose the apartment. It was hard not to.

And yet in the back of my mind, I knew something wasn't quite right. I knew I should probably ask more questions: but questions to Jodie rarely got answered.

Later, I looked back and wondered whether I realised that that day was the calm before the storm. But I doubt I was that intuitive.

THIRTY-EIGHT

JODIE

Isla del Diablo

Initially, I was just glad to be off that bloody boat down on the beach – or what seemed like miles from the beach, in fact, splashing in the sea up to our knees, wading to reach dry land, passing our bags in a stupid human chain. Even the fact that the boat driver – is that what they're called? – was handsome didn't help the situation.

And good God, I loathe boats with a passion. I can't remember the last time I went on one before today. Probably a booze cruise to Calais for a magazine feature – the operative word being *booze*.

But seeing them all just staring back at me... Well.

I might look like I'm just dandy as I stride into the villa, but inside I'm truly shaken and praying I don't trip over my stupid ribbons.

Inside, I start working out which Jodie I need to be right now, and my mind's going faster than the jacuzzi I spotted in the corner of this sterile, if pretty enough, Mediterranean garden.

Which Jodie... Because none of us is one set thing, right?

I'm not just Jodie the journo, or Jodie the mum, or Jodie the party girl/alcoholic. Inside I'm many things, and that doesn't make me mad; it just makes me human.

Crucially, I mustn't show them I'm more than shocked to see them. I asked for a favour as a diversion; a classic Jodie trick. Now, I have to regroup, think all this through.

I trained myself as a child to disguise emotion: I know it's always wise to hide my feelings. But just now, I failed.

Inside, I lean on the big table for a moment, out of sight of the girls.

Staring at those three familiar but unfamiliar faces – much-loved faces – all I felt was fear: rearing up as hard and fast as an uncaged animal.

As I calm down a bit, I see that there's an envelope on the table with my name on it, followed by a hand-drawn diamond. What's that supposed to mean?

I pick it up. There's a key card inside.

'Mae?' I call as I make my way through the lounge towards the bedrooms. 'Where are you, baby?'

No answer.

By now, I'm thinking that in retrospect, my opening gambit to the girls wasn't wise. I'd meant it to be funny, bold and fierce, the style I became known for in journalism, building my brand as first a saucy columnist, then a sort of truth-teller for women like me. *Sex and the City* without the saccharine, if you like.

Being bold was a way to keep everyone, and my own doubts, at bay.

But right now, who knows what price I'll pay for my first misstep—

Thwack!

There's a huge thud right by my head as something dark flies into the glass.

I duck instinctively. 'Shit!'

When I open my eyes again, very slowly, and peer out, a glossy dark bird lies on its back on the wide sill outside, looking stunned.

Or maybe, as I squint warily through the glass, *dead*?

I wrote an article once about birds that try to fly inside being seen as messengers of death by our ancestors.

And right now, looking at the spiderweb of cracked glass that the poor bird has just caused, its spiky little feet curled up to its chest, I must say this feels like a very bad omen indeed.

THIRTY-NINE
VICKY

I agreed to fetch Jodie's bag purely to give myself some time. I want to compose myself alone, my head whirling in a frenzy of emotion.

She's *exactly* the same ego-driven monster she was when I last saw her, I think, stomping down the stairs. No surprise there then.

And as usual with Jodie, absolutely no remorse, no apology!

The ground beneath my feet is stony and hot, and I wince as dry old pine needles stab my bare soles. I wish I'd put my trainers on.

But I'm not going back.

Jodie won't even think she's done anything wrong, that's the worst bit. I feel more like chucking her stupid bag in the sea than delivering it to her.

What *has* she done wrong though?

Oh, the list's as long as my arm!

Savagely I kick a pine cone out of my way, then I look at the sea and take a breath, ready to have a word with myself, as Dave would recommend.

For all his faults, he's a great emotional leveller. Which makes our disintegrating relationship all the sadder.

I love him dearly deep down, but I know he wants things from me I can't give and frankly, I just don't fancy him any more.

Plus all the money worries over the café haven't helped. It was a gamble I fought so hard to take, wanting to prove to my stupid dad that I could make it alone, without his financial help. But now I'm on the verge of losing the place because Dave can't – or won't – get another job himself. My anger starts to flare again.

It is beautiful here, completely idyllic, though – I *can* see that, even through my frustration and fury. It's like a weird sanctuary from the world; an island of the gods or something poetic like that. Not that I do poetry. Ever. I can't remember when I last picked up a book that wasn't full of recipes.

Nor am I into the mindfulness so fashionable these days, but in the midst of the pine trees, I manage to press pause, as the millennials say.

Noises creep in: small creatures rustling in the undergrowth, unusual birdsong, a nearby gecko. Eventually, feeling calmer, I continue down, taking a fork in the path through the trees and ending up further across the bay. On the beach, the warm sand trickles between my bare toes, full of tiny shells as pink as my nails, as I breathe big gulps of this pure air, thick with the scent of pine and salt.

A bird flaps out of the trees, making me jump. I grin at myself, and as the final anger ebbs away, my body begins to relax.

Before I know it, I'm stripping off my vest and shorts and running towards the sea in just my knickers.

For a second, I think I see a shadow running alongside me, through the trees, but I'm imagining it, of course, and I laugh at my own fear.

'Whoop!' I shout, for the sheer hell of it, and I think I hear a second voice lacing through my own shout, but then I realise, stupid Vicky, it's just me! My voice echoes back, bouncing off the rocks.

No, there's no one here but me.

As I wade out, spray flies against my bare skin. It doesn't matter how cold it is – and it *is* cold – it's also energising, pulsing through me like a charge, waking me as if I've been asleep for an hour, a week. Years even...

Waist-deep, I dive into the waves and swim, swim, swim, striking out for the nearest rock, which lurches out of the water like the huge grey finger of a god. Even my stinging shoulders don't bother me.

Floating like a star, face-down, in water so clear I can see tiny fish flitting past, golden sand beneath them, I raise my head to the sun and laugh out loud.

This is what it feels like to be alive, letting the stress go. Suspended safely in the salt waters of this clear blue ocean, I float—

Until something grabs my ankle hard and drags me under.

I'm choking. Gasping for breath. I can't think. I'm in survival mode, animal mode, as I battle to get free.

I break the surface, gulping frantically for air, fighting for great mouthfuls of it, kicking back against whatever's grabbed me.

I shove my foot hard onto the rock that I've bumped up against, flailing back to shore; dragging myself onto the sand, I collapse on my knees, my breath all ragged sobs.

When I'm a little calmer, I sit and check my ankle for marks. Surely there aren't sharks here... except what else could it have been?

But there's nothing to see. Just a small bruise on my shin where I hit the rock.

The ocean's surface is liquid gold in the setting sun, entirely flat, and I feel really foolish. Is it possible... did I maybe just nod off in the water for a second? Did I imagine the whole thing; was it just my own panic?

Heartbeat still galloping in my ears, I flip onto my back and try to breathe steadily and calmly, until finally my heart rate slows. I begin to relax again, hearing the gentle hiss of the sea, the suck and pull as it goes in and out, in and—

'Now *here's* a sight for sore eyes,' a voice drawls from somewhere above.

Shocked, I open my own eyes.

Groggily I realise I'm half-naked; more than half-naked, in fact, apart from my pants, still damp from my swim.

Squinting into the dying sun, I cover my chest with my hands and find myself gazing at a face my muzzy mind has finally begun to compute.

A face I know.

'You?'

I sit up, too quickly, head spinning, see the speedboat heading off in the distance now.

'What the hell are *you* doing here?'

FORTY
SIMONE

By the time I reach my bedroom, the stupid Wi-Fi seems to have cut out again. I keep trying and trying, but I can't make the connection I need to call home.

Still, I'm relieved to at least have received a message from Mike, assuring me everything is fine. Mason's sent a funny little TikTok of him and his friends playing Minecraft in our lounge, which makes me smile. How uncomplicated boys seem to be – my miracle baby – though the memory of the bullying is still vivid, and I feel my smile slip.

There's nothing from Tiger, but that's normal: it's either all or nothing with her at the moment, and she's probably sulking after bombarding me this morning and hearing nothing back – though not for want of me trying. I hope she knows I'm thinking of her.

Mike will take good care of her; I have no fears on that score at least.

What a long time ago this morning seems, I'm thinking, when movement catches my eye. Standing in my window, I see the speedboat we arrived on earlier racing towards the island. It's going a lot faster than when we were on it, and I remember the impending storm – though there's been no sign of it at all. Vicky was right – those apps can't always be trusted.

Jodie's camera crew must be arriving.

I unzip my bag and lay a few clothes on the bed, shake my best dress to get the creases out and hang it up. It's the only one that still fits well.

In the shower, the cool water feels like a balm, especially on my sore hand. I'm not religious in any way, but for a few seconds, it feels almost spiritual: like all the dirt and the bad stuff is being washed away and something more... pure is replacing it.

I grin at my own stupidity and shampoo my hair with vigour, using the expensive Aveda bottle provided.

Who has provided it though? I wonder. Did it come with the—

'Oh!' I hear my own gasp as the water turns icy. Frantically I twizzle the lever beside me, but it's still freezing.

Shivering, I glance up. To my horror, something red is beginning to run from the showerhead, the bright red liquid trickling straight onto my upturned face.

Blood.

'Oh my God!' I hear my own sob of distress as I rush out of the cubicle and I catch sight of myself in the mirror. Blood is coursing down my face like I'm Carrie in that terrifying film and I'm about to shout for help when I see my hand. I realise with a tremulous laugh that the blood must be my own, coming from where the earlier glass cut has reopened.

And when I peer into the shower, the water is running clear again from the head, the water swirling down the drain turning back to its normal translucence.

I breathe deeply, starting to feel calmer now. And the darker water, if it wasn't just my own blood discolouring it – it would be something in the pipes tingeing it red. It used to happen at home when I was little; if we hadn't run the bath tap for a while, rust or earth or something from the tank would turn the water brown and brackish.

I find a plaster for my hand, and then rinse the shampoo off as quickly as possible. But my sense of dread is strong now as I walk into the bedroom in a towel – just as a group of figures emerges from the pathway through the pines.

Dusk is here, casting its strange shadows, so the visibility's not great as I squint from the big window over the garden.

It's not a camera crew, I don't think.

No, definitely not – they have no equipment, only bags. They're a mixed group, age-wise, and—

Oh my God.

Staring across the garden, I recognise at least one... no, two of them.

I crane forward. My eyes aren't as good as they used to be, but amongst them is someone I'd never considered might be here.

When my top lip starts to tremble, I realise I'm still holding my breath. I step back and flatten myself against the wall, out of sight from the window, and try to calm myself.

Someone I'd hoped, someone I'd prayed to never see again.

FORTY-ONE
HANNAH

I'm just fetching some juice from the kitchen when I see a head bob up the steps and out of the trees, like some kind of mirage, as if I'm in a weird fairground hall of mirrors.

It's dusky now, the sky darkening as the sun finishes its slide into the sea, so it takes me a moment to realise whose body the head is attached to.

Vicky, I think, recognising her athletic gait. I raise my arm to wave.

It takes another few seconds to understand that there are other people behind her, and my arm drops heavily.

A trail of figures, in fact, three or four maybe, though it's hard to make out faces from here.

Except—

The glass slips from my hand, juice splashing up my legs, all over the fridge and the floor.

'Lucky it's plastic,' a voice says, and Simone takes the carton from my hand, her own skin warm on mine. 'I'll get a cloth.' Her hair is damp from the shower, her round, pretty face flushed. 'You OK, lovely?'

She's seen what I have. She must have.

Who I have.

The figures trail across the garden, past the loungers, one stopping to sit down, a slight figure with a great bundle of grey hair.

'I just...' I head across the kitchen towards the bedrooms. 'I need to go and rinse my...' I look at Simone and I don't know what to say. Words aren't coming out correctly. 'I'll come for the...'

I give up and hurry away.

FORTY-TWO
VICKY

'Is this some kind of joke?' I push Jodie's door open furiously. I'm so angry I'm shaking. 'You're surely taking the piss?'

'What?' She's sitting at the dressing table in a red silk kimono, massaging cream into her face. 'You OK, babe? Did you get my bag for me? You are a—'

'Sure.' I fling her case across the room, so hard it hits the opposite wall. 'So do tell me, *mate*' – and the derision dripping from the word is deliberate – 'what the fuck's going on?'

'Easy, tiger!' Jodie holds her nerve efficiently. Well, she always *was* good at that.

But as our eyes meet for the first time since she arrived, it's obvious she's not as collected as she's hoping to appear.

I know her too well, it seems, even after all this time.

'So' – she quickly rubs the excess cream onto her bare skin – 'what's happened?'

'Ah, come *on*, Jodie!' I shake my head at her in the mirror. 'Quit the act.'

'What?' Innocence personified. 'Really, I don't know—'

'Your *guests* have arrived.' I spit the word out.

'The camera crew?' She looks pleased. 'About time.'

'No, not the sodding crew. Your *other* guests,' I hiss. 'Put some clothes on and get out here now. You've got some explaining to do.'

'I told you, Vick' – she stands and slips a black dress from a hanger as if she's got all the time in the world – 'I don't know anything about all of this.'

'Jodie.' Simone's in the doorway now, holding a tea towel for some reason. 'Is this some kind of sick joke?'

Jodie drops the kimono on the floor and stands there in her lacy underwear, almost daring us to admire her. Her body's still good, strong and sturdy, but I'm not in the market for compliments.

'Kick-boxing.' She meets my eye again before slithering the dress over her head. 'So what's the problem?'

'Well, where d'you wanna start?'

'Let's cut to the chase, shall we.' Her sigh riles me even more. 'Who exactly has just rocked up?'

'Well, let's see.' Simone folds her arms and leans against the wall. 'Dear old Sue, for one. Be great to catch up.'

'My *mum*?' Jodie's eyes widen. 'You're winding me up.'

'I'm really not.'

'Oh shit!' Jodie's relationship with her mother was never less than volatile. 'That's a bummer.'

'Yeah, thought you'd like that.' Simone glares at her.

'But Sue's not the half of it,' I say.

'Really?'

'Really.' Simone's voice is quieter now, and I wonder what's going through her mind. 'Your ex is here.'

'Which one?' Jodie smooths the dress over her hips. She's taken her rings off, to apply the cream, I guess, and her hands look much smaller than normal.

'For God's sake.' Simone leaves the room, shutting the door hard behind her.

Jodie looks up at me, preparing to say something – but I don't want to hear it.

'Just get out here now, would you?' I slam back out of the room before I lose it entirely.

I'm so angry, I'm not sure which way to go first.

As I stand there, my heart pounding, shoulders stinging from the sunburn, a noise filters through a door.

Somewhere, someone is crying.

I'm not sure, but...

Maybe Hannah, I think, reading the name on the door nearest me.

But when I knock and enter, Hannah is curled into a tiny ball on the bed, dry-eyed and staring at the wall. Not crying.

'Han.' I sit on the edge, carefully put my hand on her shoulder. 'You OK?'

'I need to get off the island now please,' she says, her voice very small. 'Can you call the boat back?'

'Um, I can try.' It's almost fully dark now though, and I don't fancy her chances of leaving tonight. 'But I really don't want you to go, Hannah. Not like this.'

'Thanks.' She attempts and then gives up on a smile. 'But I have to.'

There's a knock at the door and Simone sticks her head round. 'Can I come in?'

'I need to go,' Hannah says. 'I really, *really* need to get off the island now.' The pitch of her voice climbs, the desperation audible as her breathing quickens.

'Let us help.' Simone is gentle, standing beside us. 'What can we do?'

'I just...' Hannah begins to shake. I can literally feel it under my hand. 'I'm worried about my parents, and because my phone won't work, it's making me super anxious.' She's gulping for breath.

'Yeah, I know. It's really annoying.' I'm scared she's going to hyperventilate. 'But I'm sure your brother's got things under control.'

'And maybe if you stay, just maybe it's a chance to sort some stuff out,' Simone says. 'Here, I mean.'

I'm surprised. 'Chance'd be a fine thing, Sim,' I say, and then regret it when I see the wounded look on her face. 'Sorry, I just mean...'

What *do* I mean? I think of the beach.

'... it's all pretty weird, isn't it?'

'You can say that again. But maybe this is kind of what we all need.'

Hannah makes a noise I don't quite understand, halfway between a sob and a laugh.

'Let's go out together and have a chat,' Simone suggests. 'Even if it's hideous. Then we might feel a bit better.'

'No way.' Hannah clutches and unclutches her hands frantically. 'Just let me go please, let me get away from this place...' She's tipping into hysteria.

'Try to keep calm, mate.' I remember the pill-laden wash bag from last night, and I hurry into Hannah's en suite. 'How about something to kind of chill you out?' I call.

But when I open her bag, there are no pills in it at all. It's just full of normal things, like toothpaste and face cream and hairclips. Weird.

I hear Simone saying, 'I'm going to get something from my room for you, OK, Han? Just keep breathing slowly. Vick,' she calls, 'I'll be quick. Get her to breathe in and out – in for six and out for seven.'

'OK.' I'm opening cupboards and slamming doors, searching for Hannah's stash, but there's nothing apart from a first-aid kit. 'Keep counting, Han.'

A door opens and closes again. Simone returning, I assume.

But when I go back into the bedroom, empty-handed, Hannah has gone.

FORTY-THREE
SIMONE

Rushing back with a paper bag for Hannah to breathe into – a useful tip learnt long ago for approaching panic attacks – I see a shadowy figure scurrying away from the house.

Some of the new arrivals are out on the terrace, but the figure's heading away from them, past the tepee and across the side of the garden, towards a path I've not clocked before.

Not visible, I don't think, from the terrace.

'Simone!' A panicked-looking Vicky darts into the hallway. 'Hannah's gone!'

'I think she's out there.' I point, but when I look again, the garden's empty.

'I'll go after her.' Vicky is desperately looking for something. 'Where are my shoes?'

'Don't panic, Vick.'

'But I *am* panicking,' she growls. 'I need to find her.'

'Give her a bit of space.' I lean against the wall, truly exhausted. 'Maybe she'll get her head together on her own.'

'But she's *really* stressed. I found all her pills.'

'She's tougher than you think. And I feel pretty stressed too.' I shrug. 'So stay with me instead.'

'Ah, Sim.' Vicky gives a strange half-smile. 'Don't do that, mate.'

'What?'

'Lay a massive guilt trip on me.'

'I don't mean to.' I'm not even sure if that's the truth or not. 'I'm just saying we're all a bit freaked out. Not surprisingly.'

'So' – Vicky picks her words carefully – 'did you see who's out there?'

'Unfortunately.'

'OK. So look' – she puts her hand on my arm – 'I'm here for you.'

'Thanks.' I lay mine over her strong, square-fingered hand. Dependable, like her. 'I guess maybe... maybe *this* is why I came,' I say slowly, as if realising it for the first time myself.

'Why?' She looks incredulous. 'To see the shit hit the fan?'

But who is the shit, and who's the fan?

'It mightn't come to that.'

'I'm not so sure.' She shakes her head. 'And personally, I one hundred per cent didn't come for drama. I came for a break.'

'Did you though, Vick?' I square my shoulders and begin to walk towards the terrace. 'How could that be possible in this company?'

'But we didn't know who'd be here.'

Didn't we though?

Couldn't we have guessed?

FORTY-FOUR
HANNAH

There's only one oar in the boathouse.

Beneath the single naked bulb that flickers its weak light over the rough concrete floor and the little wooden boat, that's all I can see. One oar.

But it doesn't matter, I tell myself, as I drag the boat down the beach: it'll come back to me. I'll remember what I knew when I was small, and I'll manage out there on the dark ocean. It can't be that hard, and there's a big moon tonight at least, lighting a path across the water.

What did you know when you were small though? the little voice says. *You knew how to make your confession, and to invent things that hadn't happened, to pacify the priest: things that seemed better than the things that really had occurred. You knew how to say your Hail Marys and count your rosary beads.*

But you didn't really know how to live.

You still don't.

'Be quiet,' I mutter, dragging the boat further towards the sea. It's surprisingly heavy, and I'm sweating, despite the cooler temperature now.

You only live via your parents, don't you? Pathetic. For them.

You're a forty-something woman with no real life of your own and no chance at one any more.

Except...

'What?' My fingernails are short, but they're snagging and breaking as I grapple with this vessel of hope.

When you did have the chance, you blew it, you fool.

'Shut up,' I mutter. 'Just shut up.'

The waves are rushing round my ankles now. I turn and push the boat off the sand as hard as I can, then scrabble alongside it, splashing through the water until I think it's safe to haul myself up and in, but it's harder than I anticipated and I'm clinging on for dear life as the waves take it.

It's definitely rougher than this afternoon, and the boat lurches up and down.

I land so hard that I bang my nose on the wooden seat. I feel a warm trickle of blood on my lip, but I don't care. I grab at the single oar I laid carefully inside the boat and start to row.

I don't stop to think; I just begin thrashing at the water.

Heave. I remember my nan and grandad and how we'd play pirates in their little boat on the river at the end of their garden, and I pull on the oar until the beach begins to fall away.

Heave.

'Stop!'

I peer back over my shoulder into the dark night. Someone is standing there, gesturing frantically, and I remember the figure this morning running down the beach as the *Scylla* sped off from the jetty.

'Wait! Where are you going? It's not safe!'

But I'm not stopping for anything or anyone.

Heave.

I feel alive now in a way I didn't earlier, blood pumping through me as the oar hits the water again and again. I'm getting out of here – now.

There's a terrible lurch and the boat rocks violently; so

violently it nearly tips me right out. I grab onto the side, but to my horror, the oar topples into the sea.

I've hit something. The boat has hit something.

Jaws floods my mind, the film I was most scared of as a kid; I saw it once when Jeff smuggled a VHS into the house, borrowed from a school friend, after my nan and grandad were both gone.

I didn't sleep for weeks afterwards.

But it's not a shark, I think, as something looms up out of the dark.

There is a tearing crunch, and I push myself away from the thing with my hands.

It's the huge, fanged rocks – the Devil's teeth.

The bottom of the boat must have hit rock.

Water is already coming in, and I realise suddenly how cold I am in my thin sundress. It's not warm out here any more now the sun's gone down for the day, and my feet are covered by the sea that's seeping ... no, *pouring* in through the jagged ripped wood.

Don't think of *Jaws*. There aren't any Great Whites in the Med.

Are there?

Don't be daft. The voice is helpful for once. *It's Europe, not the USA or Australia.*

But there *are* plenty of ways to drown in the dark, all alone.

'Try to row back,' the voice is yelling. 'Row back, Han, row back.'

And I recognise the voice; I'm sure I do.

I knew who it was when I saw him on the beach – and maybe that's why I had to leave.

'I can't!' I cry, but the oar's still visible, floating in the moon-light, and I reach out... If I can just reach it...

The boat rocks again as the breeze picks up, the waves bigger as all the different currents eddy past and around me.

'Row back!' he's shouting, and I realise from all the splashing behind me that he's wading in himself. 'Row back as far as you can. I'm coming to get you.'

I stretch my fingertips towards the oar, stretching until I'm fully extended; nearly touching it, so very near—

And then there's a massive whooshing noise as the boat flips over and I hit the water harder than I thought possible.

But I can't think any more, because I can't breathe. I kick again, in desperation, until I break the surface, my own gasps echoing madly in my ears.

But there's no moonlight, no sky, only darkness all around me.

It takes me a second to realise, to my horror, I'm beneath the over-turned boat.

Just before my last class of term, my journalism notebook vanished into thin air, along with the printout of my final article, about football hooligans. I'd worked so hard, researching leads and interviewing people for weeks – plus there were rumours that a national newspaper editor was coming in this evening.

I *couldn't* miss class, but I needed my book.

Perhaps it was in with the laundry I'd swept up yesterday to dump in Jodie's room? I was nothing if not the Royal Mews hausfrau; I'd learnt well from my mum, finding mess hard to bear.

Nervously I pushed her door open. Her tip of a room alarmed me; it was as if she just upended things onto any surface possible, similar to the way her messy mind worked too.

Quickly I rifled through her underwear drawer, a spectacular array of design and size – and thank God! Between a tiger-print thong and a pink plunge bra lay my trusty notebook.

As I hauled it out, a piece of paper came along with the book.

A dark pink A4 slip, bearing the heading: *FIRE INCI-DENT REPORT 8.06.2002: THE DAFFODIL BOAT, AVON CANAL.*

The houseboat fire.

Frowning, I skimmed it. It was dry and technical: details of the fire brigade's actions that night; a theory about how the fire had started – a gas canister, a dropped cigarette, the bedspread catching fire, the fire spreading.

Report of one deceased.

Attached was a set of blurry photographic images: not the body, thank God, but of the cabin, some items around the bed.

My heart thumping, I peered closer. What was that?

A bag I thought I recognised, badly burnt but unquestion-ably hers: like Mary Poppins' magic carpet bag, I'd always thought.

Jodie's bag: the bag I'd been searching for that night, that had contained the door keys I needed.

And I thought about it and realised – I hadn't seen that bag since. She'd replaced it with the vintage leather one.

As I stared at the photo, the intercom buzzed. I slid the paper quickly back under her socks and tights as if it was hot itself, grabbed my notebook and hurried out to pick up the intercom phone.

'I'm here for Jodie Austin.' An unknown male voice.

'She's not here, sorry.'

'When will she be back?' Anger tinged his accented voice.

'Later today maybe?' I felt uneasy. 'I can take a message?'

Silence. He must have gone.

Hurrying now, I pushed open the door to Hannah's bedroom. The boots I'd lent her yesterday were sitting neatly under her radiator. Perched on her bed, I pulled one on and texted Jodie.

Man called for you. I gazed unseeingly at an old baseball

jacket on the back of the door. Not very Hannah. *Not friendly; is it about pyramid thingy?*

No response. I called her.

'Sorry, babe, terrible reception,' she answered in a typical drawl, but the line was so clear, the spark of her cigarette lighter was audible.

'Is it to do with the money you owe?' I said urgently. 'He didn't sound... nice.'

'Just business.' I practically heard her shrug. 'It's fine, babe. I'll see you later. I'll have dinner on the table.' And we both laughed, because the most she'd ever mustered was a chicken-and-mushroom Pot Noodle.

But fetching my coat, I felt a piercing shaft of anxiety. What if this man, whoever he was, was waiting outside?

Still, the fact that we had a coded gate meant he couldn't get through.

The class was cancelled when I got to college; postponed, as my tutor was ill. Walking home, I couldn't shake the idea that Jodie was into something too deep; something she couldn't deal with. And then there was the fire report too. A feeling of dread burgeoned in my gut.

Back in the flat, her coat was there, the contents of her bag strewn across the table – purse, make-up, keys.

I smelt cigarette smoke. She must be out on the balcony.

'I don't know what to do any more,' I heard her say. Was the hostile man from earlier out there too?

My heart in my mouth, I crept towards the door, listening carefully.

'I'm running out of time,' she said. She was on the phone, I realised, and her tone of voice was new to me: kind of lacerat-ing; like hearing your dad say he couldn't pay the rent this month.

'I can't!' she exclaimed. 'It's on me, 'cos I promised him.'

A click and an inhale. Chain-smoking.

'It's fine...' But her voice broke, and she began to cry. 'I know it will be, 'cos it has to be...'

Apart from the night Nick died, I realised I'd never witnessed her cry before, and even then, it was a brief storm that blew itself out. But this was like seeing someone unmasked, or catching sight of an adult I'd always respected naked.

'And the thing is...' she was croaking now, trying to stifle a sob; finding it hard to get her words out, 'if I don't sort it, well – we both know what'll happen.' And she began to sob properly.

I was torn. She would hate me to see her like this. Plus, the conversation was obviously deeply private. And yet my best friend sounded so desperate, so alone, that I couldn't bear to leave her.

'Dilly?' She banged on the glass, making me jump.

'J-Just going to get some chips,' I stammered. I was like a guilty kid, meeting her gaze. For all the smudged make-up round her eyes, it was fierce. 'Want some?'

'Sure.' Fag in one hand, bottle of Jack Daniel's in the other, she smiled, but we both knew that she knew I'd heard her.

In the corridor, the lift doors opened almost immediately, and Hannah and Tom fell out, laughing; her doubled up as if he'd just said the funniest thing ever.

'Oh, Simone!' Her eyes were suddenly wide as she saw me, darting like a meerkat's. 'Thought you had your evening class?'

'Cancelled.' I tried not to look taken aback. 'Going for chips.'

'Great!' Tom's eyes shone as he held the lift doors for me, and he looked less than abashed. 'We're going to cook some fresh pasta pesto.' He held up a basil plant as if it was the rarest orchid in the world.

'We'll save you some,' Hannah said, as if trying to placate me, and I looked back at him and realised: of course, the base-ball jacket hanging on the back of her door. It was Tom's.

FORTY-SIX

JODIE

Isla del Diablo

Most of them seem to have disappeared to their rooms, pleading exhaustion, and that includes my mother, thank God.

I'm glad; I'm not up to any more confrontations right now, on this strange, never-ending day of devastating connections.

Except of course this major one.

He's still here, of course, even though everyone else has gone to bed. Well, he always was persistent.

And we always both hated backing down; both of us relished a challenge.

'So who's the lovely *young* bird with you?' I'm careful to emphasise the word. 'Always did like them on the youthful side, eh, babe?'

Gary sits opposite me, sprawled in one of the weird egg chairs on the terrace, legs splayed wide in the way a certain type of man presumes is acceptable, and all I can think is that, if nothing else, I've got to style this out.

'Well' – he keeps grinning in that familiar way that sends shivers down my spine – 'you'd know.' The ice bucket on the table behind his shaved head glints; a bottle of fizz sweats beside a group of exquisite champagne flutes that someone's kindly laid out.

'Not really.' I get up and pour myself fresh water from the jug, and if my hands feel shaky, well, I'm damned if he's going to see that.

He yawns widely, showing all his gold fillings. 'That's me done. Long day, and Daisy's waiting for me.' He hauls himself up from the chair. 'Lot of catching up to do though, eh?' He walks too near me. 'I look forward to it, *babes*.'

Malice exudes from the mocking word.

Or perhaps it's lust. I hope it isn't.

I hold my glass very tight to stop myself from lumping it round his smug head – and then my mum saves me. A rare occurrence indeed. She plods onto the terrace, surprisingly flat-footed for such a scrawny old bag, and Gary turns and disappears off to his room, on the far side of the main villa. Thank God.

'Is Mae OK?' she asks.

Just the sight of my mum's face riles me.

'Of course.' I try not to snap at her. 'Never better.'

'Where is she? I want to make sure she's checked her blood sugar.'

My fingernails curl into my fists. Always someone else to check on, eh, Ma?

'She's in her room, Mum. Where all young people live. And she knows perfectly well how to check her levels actually.'

'She's not *actually*.' My mum's frown deepens. 'In her room, I mean. Honestly, Jodie, you really ought to keep more of an eye on her.'

'She's eighteen, Mum, not five!' Good God, that fizz looks ever more tempting. 'She's perfectly capable of taking care of herself.'

'And what's that man doing here?'

Good question. 'Mum' – I put my head in my hands – 'I'm exhausted. Can you just leave it please?'

I'm actually relieved when Vicky appears. From bitching about me with the other two, I expect.

'OK, babe?' I try not to mind.

'Have you seen Hannah?' She looks around frenetically, as if Hannah might be hiding in a corner somewhere.

'No.' I pick up my Gucci bag; a very good fake from Bangkok, bought when I travelled a lot with work. 'What's up?'

'She's...' Vicky's stuttering, 'she's not...'

'Spit it out, babe.' My hand closes round my cigarettes in relief.

'She's a bit panicked.' Simone appears behind Vicky. 'She wasn't expecting' – she gestures – 'all this.'

My heart turns over.

'None of us were.' Simone gazes at me.

Oh God – of course. How stupid of me. How bloody, bloody stupid.

FORTY-SEVEN
VICKY

Hannah's room is still empty when I storm away from bloody Jodie, who as usual displays all the sensitivity of a rampaging politician.

But I do know what Hannah's like when she's angry or upset. She tends to disappear, to lick her wounds alone.

'Let's just go to bed, lovely.' Simone hugs me. 'We all just need some sleep right now. Tomorrow's a new day, and Hannah can't come to any harm here, can she?'

In her familiar embrace, I relax a bit.

Still, when I get into bed, I wish I was anywhere but here right now, and I know I'll never get to sleep.

Tossing and turning, a hazy memory floats into my head: the other Xanax I nicked out of Hannah's wash bag last night.

I get up again and find it in the pocket I stashed it in, feeling like I just hit a triple on the fruit machine.

I take half of the pill, and it must kick straight in, because the next thing I know, I awake with a start at 4 a.m., hearing voices. How strange, I think: one sounds like a child.

But I must have been dreaming.

In the bathroom, I guzzle water straight from the tap, then stumble back to bed.

I didn't shut the blinds earlier, and the moon is immense and almost full, lighting up the sea dramatically; the sea that definitely looks a little more turbulent than earlier today.

There's something floating in the water past the rocks, floating in the moon's great path of light, I realise.

Straining to see, I get back out of bed again and pad over to the window.

It's amazing: a huge fish by the looks of things – maybe a dolphin or even a whale, painted white by the moon – and I go to grab my phone to photograph it.

But by the time I've found my specs and my phone and returned to the window, my vision clearer, it's gone.

The sea has calmed again, and I collapse back into bed to dream of nothing.

FORTY-EIGHT

SIMONE

Isla del Diablo

In the early hours, I wake with a gasp.

My children are laughing outside my room.

'Tiger?' I lurch upright. 'Mason?'

The voices get louder, giggling, bouncing eerily off the walls, but as I leap from the bed, they start to fade, little feet pattering away.

I'm both icy and sweating, despite the air con, as a last giggle echoes in the corridor. Obviously I was dreaming, I tell myself – but I tiptoe to the door and open it anyway.

An empty corridor, one light flickering slightly at the end.

I get back into bed, unnerved and missing them desperately; they sounded much younger than they are now. Opening the bedside drawer, I pick up what disturbed me so badly when we arrived and slide it under my pillow.

Somehow, I manage to drift off again.

.   .   .

Despite all yesterday's drama and my broken night, I wake up starving.

In the kitchen, as I pour myself steaming coffee from a big pot on the side, I think that the only thing we can be sure of today is more tension.

Needing fortification before I venture out, I nab a slice of toast that's just popped out of the flashy Dualit, drizzle it with honey and gulp it down.

I wipe my hands, take a deep breath and step outside.

'Morning, Dilly.' Jodie waves from the terrace. She's eating yoghurt straight from the pot, wearing a sapphire-coloured kaftan over a halter-neck swimsuit, and ridiculous oversized shades.

If I didn't know better, I'd think she was nursing a hangover.

Beside her sits her mum, eating cereal that looks like bird seed.

'Sue.' I bend to kiss her cheek. I never was sure how someone so ethereal bore a child as robust as Jodie.

'Been a long time, Simone.' She smells of talcum powder. 'How are you, love? Kids well?'

'Oh, not too bad.' I smile, but I'm suddenly reminded of my children's laughter last night. 'How are you doing?'

'Jodie, my phone's still not working.' She ignores me to prod Jodie querulously. 'And I really need to ring home. Malc's op is tomorrow, poor lamb, and I should be there. I need to at least call.'

I notice Jodie clasp her spoon tighter. 'Well I didn't ask you to come,' she says pointedly. 'So don't blame me.'

'I've got no service either,' I say quickly. 'It's driving me bonkers.'

'That makes me three.' Jodie finishes her yoghurt. 'I still haven't got hold of my bloody producer, 'cos the phone cuts out each time I try him. So weird. And I can't find a router or a modem anywhere.'

Out of habit, I check my phone for the hundredth time since we arrived, but it's still showing nothing new. How odd, I think – we're all so attached to these stupid hunks of metal and plastic that we're lost the moment they don't work.

The sound of chanting floats from nearby, and my eye is drawn to the lithe young woman on a yoga mat on the little lawn. She was performing a perfect downward dog pose as I sat down, but now she's cross-legged, head bowed, sing-song voice chanting. There's certainly lots of *oms* involved.

She must be part of the yoga feature Jodie's meant to be filming, I think, watching her spring up as Jodie's ex appears in the doorway, munching toast too.

I stir a little bit of sugar into my coffee. Then I think, sod it, and spoon more in lavishly. You only live once after all.

'Daisy!' Wiggling his fingers at the young woman on the mat, his eyes light on me. 'Oh-ho! The gorgeous Simone, no less.' He heads towards the table. 'How long's it been, babes?'

'I'm not sure.' I do my best to meet his gaze. 'How are you?'

'Never better thanks. Have you met my gorgeous angel?' Did he actually just mime a love heart to the young woman?

'No.' I try to hide my surprise. 'Not yet.'

'My fiancée!' he says proudly as she steps onto the terrace in barely there Lycra and a thin sheen of sweat, pushing her hair back under a Yankees baseball cap.

'Fiancée, eh?' Blimey. What the hell's she doing with *him*?

Although, of course, sadly, I can guess. She's at least half his age, I imagine, feeling depressed.

'Good session?' He puts a possessive arm round her waist. His fingers are fat now, I see, splaying out like podgy sausages on her toned midriff. They didn't used to be fat like that, I don't think.

'Oh yeah. Done my sun salutations, daddio.' She drops a fond kiss on his shiny head. 'Now I'm going for my run.'

Daddio? My mouth drops open.

'You put us all to shame, Daisy.' Jodie grins. 'If I had any left.'

I choose an orange from the fruit bowl, wondering where I recognise Daisy from. Probably an article of Jodie's. A celebrity mate perhaps, or maybe something to do with Mae, who's started to attract attention as a singer recently.

'Sim.' Vicky interrupts my train of thought, hair slicked back from the shower, trainers in hand. 'Hannah out here?'

'Haven't seen her yet this morning.' I shake my head.

'That's because she never came back,' Vicky groans. 'I just checked, and her bed's not been slept in.'

'Just like old times, eh?' Jodie jokes. 'She'll be OK, babe.'

'And I'd believe you because?' Vicky snaps. 'I knew we should have gone to find her last night.'

'Sorry, Vick.' Jodie's read Vicky's troubled expression. 'Are you actually worried? I didn't think—'

'Did you ever though? Yes, I am,' Vicky snaps. 'Really worried.'

'Ah, come on, babe.' Jodie tries to reassure her. 'You know what she's like.'

'Yes, *I* know what she's like, but you – I doubt it.'

'Don't you think' – something's just crossed my mind, given who turned up last night – 'that... you know...'

'Hannah's always been like a cat,' Jodie carries on. 'Wandering in when it suits her.'

'Lord, that's rich coming from you, Jodie.' Vicky pulls away from my attempts to comfort her.

'Let's go and look for her,' I suggest.

'I'll go on my own.' She's obviously annoyed with me, slipping on her trainers, and I feel guilty for not understanding how worried she was.

A sudden shriek comes from the villa.

'How fucking *dare* you?'

Mae stands in the open kitchen doors, hands on hips,

bleached hair on end, eyes blazing, steam practically emanating from her nostrils.

'How *could* you?' she's screeching at Jodie, clutching something in both hands that she waves at her mother.

'What? What's wrong?' Jodie looks worried. 'Mae? What's happened?'

'Oh, don't pretend you don't know, Mum!' Mae is stomping down to the terrace now, launching herself at the table, silver bangles clicking as she throws down something that flies in the breeze like giant white confetti. Printed sheets of A4...

I pick one up.

It's a newspaper article, dated yesterday: a photograph of Mae, another blurry photo of Jodie and a young man, maybe taken in a club or from a CCTV camera. Their heads are very close.

CELEBRITY JOURNO POACHES DAUGHTER'S TOY-BOYFRIEND!

'Oh dear, love, that's bad,' her dad says comfortably, not sounding like he thinks it's bad at all.

'And you can piss off too.' Tears are coursing down Mae's face. 'Like you care, you absolute *arse*hole.'

'Ah, come on, babes.' But it's clear he's not amused. 'That's a bit strong, eh?'

'Mae!' The colour drains from Jodie's face. 'It's not what it looks like.'

'And what's that? That my mum's a slag?'

'Mae!' Sue reproves her granddaughter, but it's not very convincing either. I'd lay money on whose side she's on, and it's not Jodie's.

'Where did this come from?' Vicky frowns at the article.

'I dunno,' Mae snivels. '*The Sun*?'

'No – I mean, how did it come to be here?'

'That's not the point, is it?' Mae cries. 'The point is, my mum shagged Slug!'

'Slug?' Gary explodes into false laughter. 'With a name like that, I'm surprised anyone wants to shag him.'

'Shut *up*, Gary, you total twat. We all know you love a nickname. And I didn't shag him.' Jodie's standing now, arms extended to her daughter, imploring her. 'I swear, baby.'

'Really?' Mae looks at her with nothing short of hatred. 'And you think I believe that for one second?'

'Sorry, but... is your phone working?' the girl called Daisy interrupts. 'Mine just won't.'

'Who cares right now?' snaps Vicky, so rudely I double-take.

'OK, but— God, what's that?' Daisy runs to the edge, pointing down towards the beach. Something is floating in the water, just past the last of the big rocks.

'A dolphin!' Jodie claps her hands joyfully. 'Or a whale?'

'Don't be stupid,' Vicky scoffs. 'That's not an animal.'

She must have her contact lenses in if she can see that far.

'It's not a dolphin,' says Daisy loudly, staring down. 'It's definitely not a living creature at all.'

I step closer to the edge and realise she's right. It's nothing so romantic.

It's not romantic at all.

It's the little rowing boat, upside down, floating out to sea.

We'd spent so little time together in Royal Mews that towards the end of November, someone – probably Jodie – suggested a house party. The halcyon days of our flat share were sliding towards the past; the shine had worn off faster than I'd ever anticipated.

The tensions were obvious. Jodie was extra skittish recently. Always out, exhausted when she was home, either sleeping or tapping away on her infernal BlackBerry. She said she was done with pyramid schemes, but we thought she was still hawking them around, looking for prey.

Vicky was fed up with Hannah because of how much Hannah hung out with Tom, while Tom had stopped showing any sort of romantic interest in Vicky at all. At least Jodie didn't seem to care about him any more, distracted by whatever her work was.

I coped with Jodie's mess, tidying up after her constantly, but Hannah obviously hated the way Jodie was half naked most of the time, and the way she and Vicky both borrowed our clothes without asking. Vicky just acted a bit entitled some-times, but Hannah, it struck me, came from a very ordered home and struggled with the chaos often swirling around Jodie. Keeping the peace was tiring.

My issue with Jodie was that she was so seldom home. All work or play with her, and pathetic as it might sound, being an afterthought hurt.

Since the houseboat fire, I'd avoided big parties, but I hoped this would bring us back together.

The night before the party, I trudged home after my Dizzy's shift thinking about the lead I'd found for my final college article. He'd promised to tell me about the organised fights still happening between rival football fans.

In the flat, in the dark, it took me a second to understand that it was someone else's breathing I could hear and not mine.

Someone was there, I realised shakily, my eyes adjusting to the gloom.

He had Jodie pinned up against the fridge, one hand round her throat, one up her skirt, leering down at her.

'It's time to pay up, girlie.' His voice was full of a dark and lewd desire that turned my stomach.

'Is that right?' Jodie's voice was raspy as she laughed up into his face – but not in a way that suggested a joke. No, it was in a way that said *I dare you*; animalistic, her teeth almost bared. 'Is this how you like it then?'

'You know it is,' he growled.

I stood transfixed with horror until she sensed me there, her eyes swivelling to meet mine over the man's shoulder.

As soon as they did, she pushed him in the chest, and he glanced at me then let her go, smoothing his hair back, adjusting his tie.

'You're such a hoot, pet,' he said to Jodie, but it was me he winked at as he turned. 'Loves it, you naughty girl, eh?'

'That's me.' She smiled, a strange, knowing smile. 'A real naughty hoot. Don't you reckon, Dilly?'

What weird game was this between them?

'I finished early,' I said stupidly, putting my bag on the table, next to things that didn't belong there. His open briefcase, a chequebook.

'Dilly's an aspiring journo.' Jodie shook her skirt down. 'Gonna be the next Lee Miller, aren't you?'

'Who?' The man shut his briefcase.

'War correspondent,' Jodie replied knowingly, as if I hadn't told her that recently.

'Oh. Well, I enjoyed your article,' he said.

'What?' My stomach plunged.

'I said' – he pulled a fat cigar out of his jacket – 'I'll enjoy seeing that – the next big thing. Your fame and fortune.'

'I'll see you out, big man,' Jodie purred, leading him towards the door by his lapel.

And I realised then who he was.

'What the hell are you doing with *him*?' I asked her when she came back.

'What do you mean?' She washed her face and hands at the sink, fag in mouth, eyes narrowed against the smoke.

'That's Robert Perry, isn't it?'

'What if is it?'

'Er – he's twice your age, for a start.'

'So?' She turned the tap off and dried her face on a tea towel, wiping off the scarlet lipstick that had bled round her mouth. I stared harder. *Was* it lipstick?

'And he's...' How could I describe the horrible feelings he elicited in me? 'He's...' Words failed me. 'He's not nice.'

'Needs must, babe.' Jodie pulled a bottle of Jack Daniel's from a bag. 'He's minted.'

'Oh my God!' How unbelievably stupid I'd been. 'Is this his place?'

'What?' She broke the seal on the bottle.

'Don't play dumb! His.' I gestured wildly at the door. 'Robert Perry's.'

'What if it is?'

'So *why* would he let us live here so cheap?'

Jodie drank long and hard from the bottle. Then she met my eye with a blaze of the defiance that was always just out of sight; that she struggled to damp down.

'What you don't know' – she wiped her mouth – 'won't hurt you, babe.'

Bottle in hand, she walked to her bedroom and shut the door.

I followed, flinging it open. 'And why's he read my article?'

Something like remorse flickered across her face. 'I read it,' she had the good grace to admit. 'The one you've been working on forever.'

'Oh yeah?' It was in my room, and it wasn't ready. 'Why?'

'I reckon I can help you.' Peering into the mirror, she drew a big flick with her kohl eyeliner.

'How?' I felt a knot in my belly. This was all going too fast for me.

'Get you someone to talk to.' She smudged the kohl a bit.

'Someone involved in football hooliganism, you mean? I think I found a lead.'

'*Football hooliganism!*' she mimicked, slicking on more bright red lipstick, retying her side ponytail. 'You're such a granny.' She stepped into the walk-in wardrobe, which looked like a small hurricane had just occurred. 'Platforms or stilettos?'

'Jodie – what's going on?' I was more insistent this time.

'Mind your own business, babe,' she said, but now her voice was dull.

Still it was like an actual slap. And when she left, I didn't see which shoes she'd chosen, because I was too angry and upset to care.

Nor did I hear her come home that night; I was so tired, I crashed out quickly.

But I really wished I had talked to her about Robert Perry again.

FIFTY

VICKY

Isla del Diablo

The histrionics between Jodie and her daughter are crazy, but I can't say I'm surprised. Jodie's always lived her life like she just plugged her hand into a socket.

Not surprised, maybe – but I *am* concerned about Hannah, and why everyone else isn't more worried. Especially after seeing the little boat floating out to sea...

Daisy keeps staring down at the water and saying, 'Was that the only boat?' with a kind of sick look on her face, but who cares about the *boat* right now, when Hannah's life could be in danger. *Must* be in danger.

And Simone's concentration is just off generally. God knows where her head's at; she's even irritating me. 'Simone,' I'm trying to say, but I'm drowned out by the shrieking Mae.

Meanwhile, Jodie's more concerned with her daughter and the fact that – by the looks of it – she's gone and shagged the poor girl's new boyfriend.

But why would anyone be shocked by *that*? I'm thinking – just as Hannah wanders out of the trees.

I start towards her, but I'm pulled up short when I realise she's not alone.

Him.

Before yesterday, I thought I wouldn't ever have to see him again.

Heartbreak from Royal Mews crashes in my head like the waves breaking on the beach below, and I have to turn away to catch my breath.

'Hannah!' Simone cries, oblivious. 'Are you all right?'

'I'm fine,' Hannah croaks, but she's shuffling like she's been hobbled in a chain gang, Tom catching her up to walk close by her shoulder.

And seeing my mate appear like that when I really thought she might be dead brings such an overwhelming rush of emotion, relief tempered by anger, that I turn to jelly inside and out.

I sit down quickly, while Simone murmurs something like, 'See, I told you she'd be fine.'

She doesn't look very fine though, poor Hannah. She looks like she's been dragged through many hedges backwards; her hair straggly and tangled, her dress salt-stained beneath a checked shirt I don't recognise.

'I could use a shower,' she's saying, and I notice that her hands and knees are grazed. I want to offer my help, but Simone, the semi-trained nurse, is already at hand, fussing gently in that unique caring way and leading Hannah to sit.

'She nearly drowned,' I hear Tom mutter.

And I have to say, he doesn't look much better, his face all scratched, his hair, longer than when we were young, on end, his eyes reddened, from lack of sleep maybe.

'We got lost. Ended up crashing out in the hammocks in the wood,' he says. 'The stars were amazing at least – that was a plus.'

Oh, how terribly romantic, I think, staring at him, and it's so stupid, but tears rush to my own eyes.

Behind us, the squabble on the terrace is reaching a climax of dramatic Austin family sentiment, before Mae runs off, sobbing piteously.

If I disappear now myself, no one will notice I'm gone.

'Oh Jesus.' Jodie jumps up to follow her daughter. 'Just when you think things can't get any worse.'

Which, some might say, is an ethos Jodie's lived by for most of her life.

'Well, what did you expect?' Gary says, as serenely if he's a Buddhist monk – which actually he does resemble a bit. A fat old Buddha with his shaved head and those terrible sandals. He's 'rediscovered' himself, it would seem, in old age, which, given what he got up to in his youth, wouldn't be before time. And boy, does he look old. A lifetime of making money and being an arsehole has caught up with him, it seems.

'If you can't say anything useful, don't say anything at all,' Jodie hisses at him. 'God, I don't believe this is happening. Poor Mae.' She's shoving her feet into bright pink sliders to follow the girl.

'Leave her, love,' Jodie's old scarecrow of a mum is saying. 'I'll go.'

'But I don't want *you* to go, Mum!' Jodie's trying not to shout, that's obvious, and failing to restrain herself. '*I* want to go.'

'You'll just make things worse though.' Sue shakes her head.

'Ain't that the truth,' Gary agrees.

'Is it?' Jodie rounds on him. 'I mean, what the fuck are you even doing here, Gary?'

'The same as everyone else. I've come to your *fortieth*.' He imbues the number with the same weighty sarcasm I did yesterday, and for a second I actually feel sorry for Jodie. 'I was invited.'

Only briefly sorry though.

'Oh, sod off, babe,' she snaps. 'We all know by now that we're not here for my fortieth – and anyway, I can't think of anyone I'd rather spend it with less.'

'So why *are* we here then?' he asks, kind of fair enough, but we're all distracted by Sue, who's pointing down at the beach.

'Am I seeing things? Is it art?'

One by one, we gather at the edge of the garden, by the wall.

There are big looping words, I notice now, scrawled on the sand down there.

'What the hell does that mean?' Gary scowls, much less Buddha-like suddenly. Also, he smells like he's sprayed way too much cheap Lynx on.

'Tom and Hannah probably wrote it for a joke,' I suggest, but then the thought of those two doing anything together pierces my heart and I move away.

'Wrote what?' Simone peers over my shoulder, and I try not to snap at her to back off; *she*'s done nothing wrong, I remind myself.

'I didn't write anything,' Tom yawns, rubbing his eyes. 'I'm pretty sure Hannah didn't either.'

How do you know? I want to demand, but I don't.

'That's really creepy.' Jodie stares down. 'Jesus.'

The words say: *THIS IS JUST THE START*.

And next to them, someone has sketched a crude drawing.

Crude, maybe, but recognisable nonetheless as a skull.

FIFTY-ONE
SIMONE

The words on the beach are freaky, it's true, but my main concern is that Hannah's all right.

I guide her to a seat on the corner of the sundeck, under a big parasol.

'I'm OK,' she tries to assure me, 'honestly.'

Just shaken and tired after having some kind of accident on that little boat apparently.

'I know it was daft, but...' She glugs the water I've brought her like she's been in the desert for a month. 'Sorry. I just couldn't bear being in the villa last night. I...' She swallows hard. 'I lost it a bit.'

'It's Vicky who's annoyed, I think.' I don't want to admit that I was reasonably relaxed about her disappearance. 'Because of... Well. You know.'

'No?' She looks pretty vacant still, I think.

I gesture at Tom, who is perched on the swing seat now, eyes shut.

'Tom? Still? Oh gosh,' Hannah sighs. 'I thought that was all in the past. It was so long ago...'

'Well, it's good if you're not bothered now. Maybe Vicky's

upset 'cos things are so bad at home with Dave,' I suggest. 'I don't know.' I have a sudden flash of the way she looked at the lithe woman on the superyacht. 'Hannah. You don't think...' I stop. It's not my business to speculate.

'Gosh, I'm tired.' She yawns. 'I didn't really sleep in that hammock, but I couldn't bear to come up to the villa.'

'So... you took the row boat out?'

'I panicked. I wanted to leave, mainly because it feels like that choice has been taken away from us.' She pushes her hair off her face. 'I know it sounds daft now, but I was a bit... delirious, I think.'

'It's not that daft given that we're stuck here. But Hannah... Vicky mentioned something. Some pills?'

'Pills?' She gazes at me absently. 'No. Look, I'm sorry if I scared you, but I'm fine now.'

I don't want to press her more, and she says she's going to lie down for a bit. Vicky's stomped off somewhere in a mood, so I walk down through the garden to enjoy the beautiful morning.

There was brief talk earlier of taking a picnic lunch to the beach – thank God at least the fridge and cupboards are well stocked – while we wait to find out what's going on here.

Right now though, no one else is around. Tom's gone for a shower, Hannah's in bed presumably, and that girl Daisy's jogged off on her run. I suspect that Jodie and her mum have disappeared to have a 'chat' about Mae, while Gary announced he was going to try and sort the 'effing Wi-Fi' – though I'm not holding out much hope; it hasn't come on again since the brief interlude yesterday.

The setting might be beautiful, but the company is toxic. Fear is mounting fast, anxiety squeezing my guts. It's all really odd. Which one of my fellow guests is nasty enough to do something like drawing a skull on the beach? And until someone explains what the hell's going on, or Antonio turns up again to take us back to Ibiza, I realise it's going to continue to be worrying.

As I head down the terraced part of the garden, through the orange trees to the viewpoint in the far corner, my head buzzing with the events of this morning, I see a figure sitting on the love seat, looking out to sea. For a second, I think it's Tiger, and it takes my breath away.

Then I realise that it's Mae, and my heart contracts. From here, she reminds me so much of my daughter, I feel the most incredible wave of homesickness and longing for my family.

What the hell am I doing here, trying to right old wrongs that should probably be left in the past? And I can't even leave. I clench my hands against my racing thoughts.

'Hey,' I say to Mae. 'Penny for them?'

'What?' She wipes her eyes frantically, but they're red and puffy, and it's clear that she's been crying hard.

'Penny for your thoughts – it's an old saying. Can I...' I indicate the seat beside her. 'No worries if you'd rather be alone though.'

'It's fine.' She moves up a bit.

'Thanks. I don't suppose you remember me.' I sit, trying not to crowd her. 'But I remember you from when you were tiny. You were such a sweet little thing.'

'Whereas now I'm a monster,' she sniffs.

'Don't be silly, not at all.' I nudge her gently. 'I'm sure you're still very sweet – and absolutely gorgeous, of course.'

She manages a grudging smile. 'Bet you say that to all the girls.'

'Only the gorgeous ones.' I meet her smile. 'So – are you OK?'

'What do you think?' She stops smiling and glowers again. She's got a lot of earrings in the ear nearest me; almost every bit of it is pierced, and I can see a tattoo of what looks like a snake edging onto her collar bone. 'I really liked this one.' She sees I'm confused. 'Slug.'

I try to suppress my grin, but she catches it.

'I know it's silly, but he's cute. And a brilliant musician. He plays guitar in a band I sing with.'

'And your mum?'

Mae shrugs. 'Obviously thought so too.'

'Has that happened before?' I'm genuinely curious. Jodie might be a wild thing, but I'd have thought this was a step too far even for her.

'What – her shagging my boyfriends? Not as far as I know.'

And for a second, I'm blasted back in time, to the party at Royal Mews. The beginning of the end, though we didn't know it at the time.

I gather myself. 'I guess you might have dodged a bullet, as they say.'

'With Mum?'

'No – with this Lettuce guy.'

'Slug, you mean.'

'Yeah, him. And whatever happens, you're stuck with your mum.'

'More's the pity,' she says.

'She's good at heart, I think,' I say. 'I mean, I *know*, really. Just a bit... misguided sometimes. You should probably have a chat with her.'

I remember all the chats I was too cowardly to have with Jodie myself. I always backed off when I should have gone forward.

We sit quietly for a while, gazing out at the beautiful turquoise-and-silver sea and the huge blue sky, the breeze lightly ruffling the nearby orange trees, the smell of pine in the air, until we hear Jodie calling.

'Picnic party leaving in ten, you groovy people!'

'What's his real name?' I scrape my hair back and tie it up – it's definitely getting hotter as the day heads towards noon.

'Slug's?'

'Yeah.'

There's a tiny pause.

'It's Mark,' she says, 'Mark Brown.'

We look at each other, and then we both start to laugh, and we laugh until I think I might cry.

But as we stop, growing quiet again, I see the clouds gathering in the distance, and I think – they are bound for here, sooner or later.

The storm is on its way, just as the weather app predicted.

And we're stuck here, and I don't really know what that means. I feel a swell of panic in my chest – just as the shouting begins.

'Hey, everyone!' It's Jodie, louder now. 'Come back please!'

We hurry back across the grass to the villa.

'Can everyone gather round,' she's saying, and she looks properly stressed now.

'Is your phone working?' It looks like Daisy's just arrived back from her run, out of breath, a towel round her neck, her long face red, sweating profusely. 'Is anyone's?'

'Nope.' Vicky's so terse, it feels rude, and Daisy turns away abruptly, cheeks flaming.

'Still not, unfortunately.' I check mine for the umpteenth time. 'Why?'

'Bad news, people.' Daisy grimaces, hands on hips like Wonder Woman. 'I think I can tell you why the phones don't work.'

'Oh, drum roll!' Vicky's dealing with her own stress very badly. 'Spit it out then.'

Daisy seems both scared and excited to be the one to tell us. 'Well, it looks like the mobile mast's been sabotaged.'

'What?'

'I saw it on my run. Up on the hill.' She points. 'It's like someone took a chainsaw to it.'

'A *chainsaw?*'

'Surely they'd have killed themselves if so?' I'm no electrician, but that sounds dangerous.

'Locals.' Gary is sage on his sunlounger. 'Obviously.'

'What bloody locals?' Jodie snaps. She's not doing a good job of hiding her distaste for him. 'We're on a deserted island.'

Something about that idea makes me cringe.

'They hate the Brits out here.' Gary sounds so smug and mansplainy, I'd quite like to kick him myself. 'They're trying to get rid of us.'

'And that's OK, is it, Gary?' Vicky glowers.

'Well, it's not great, but honestly' – he gazes around – 'look where we are. And who' – he grabs at Daisy – 'we're with!'

'Gary!' She giggles as he pulls her towards him.

Jodie ignores him, obviously worried. 'So look, I'm sorry, but unfortunately I think we're stuck for the time being.'

'Someone's got us here under false pretences if there's no actual party.'

'Not that I know of,' Jodie says flatly. 'And I just want to know when the bloody crew's turning up.'

'I'd like to leave actually.' Vicky kicks the step with her trainer toe, like a child. 'I've had enough now. There's no Wi-Fi, there's no party, and I'm having weird dreams.'

'Me too,' I say.

'Yeah, last night it was kids running in corridors.'

'I heard them too,' I say slowly. 'Little kids. But I thought it was my imagination.'

'I tried to leave last night.' Hannah has appeared from the

kitchen, wearing a clean dress, hair tied back neatly. 'But I didn't get very far.'

'And you ballsed up the boat doing so.' Gary lumbers to his feet. 'The *only* boat.'

'Hey,' Vicky snaps at him, stepping nearer Hannah, 'leave it out!'

And I look at my old friend and another penny begins to roll...

'How do you know it's the only boat anyway?' she demands.

'Well have *you* seen another one?' He's belligerent now; the man I remember, unfortunately, only too well.

'I bet you've not got off that sunlounger since you arrived, have you? So why don't you shut up?'

'Stop arguing,' Hannah says softly. 'It's what they want.'

'Who?'

'Whoever's got us here.'

And we're all pulled up short. We look around at one another, and a sense of unease crawls down my spine.

Who *did* bring us here, and are they in this group I'm looking at right now?

And if so, what *exactly* do they want?

I'm lying on the beach, listening to the sea and trying to enjoy the feeling of heat on my skin, when all I really want to do is scream.

I watch that Daisy bird playing bat and ball with Mae. She isn't all that pretty – she has a long, sort of horsey face – but her body looks strong. I bet she's into all that weightlifting young women now seem to think is cool; I heard her saying she and Gary love going to the gym.

The mind boggles, honestly.

But what I'm mainly concentrating on is the fact that my daughter has stopped crying. Thank God. The fact that she's come to join us, my little Mae, though it's clear she's not going to talk to me yet. It's a start, at least.

I do feel sick about that stupid guitarist. Thank God I didn't sleep with him – wasn't even tempted to – although she clearly doesn't believe that. There was a reason I was in that photo, but I need her to calm down a bit more before we talk.

But more to the point, how the hell did that article get *here*?

Who brought it with them to the island?

Who wants to hurt me – or Mae – so badly, they'd share that bit of tabloid tat?

Simone appears, plodding through the trees with an ice bucket and a cool box, Tom bearing a wicker hamper they must have found in the villa's well-stocked utility room.

Tom looks a little bit fresher than earlier but still exhausted by whatever the hell went on last night.

Hannah and her suicidal tendencies? Such a sensitive soul.

Vicky has appeared from somewhere along the beach, still scowling. She goes to help Simone but studiously avoids Tom, and I remember how hurt she was that he preferred Hannah when we lived in Royal Mews.

A lifetime ago.

We all fancied Tom, which seems ridiculous now, though he's still handsome enough, I suppose.

Unlike my useless, rancid ex.

He lies inert on a rattan beach mat, a cushion beneath his head that only emphasises his double chins. Gazing at him, I wonder: does he hate me enough to try to sabotage things with Mae? Oh, I bet he does.

'So where did you two meet?' I glance at Daisy as she fetches a drink from the cool box Simone's just plonked down.

'Online.' She smiles politely at me.

'Sugar Daddies Are Us?' I can't help myself.

'No.' Fair play to her, Daisy doesn't bat an eyelash. 'Match.com.'

'And you like old men?'

'Older. I really appreciate maturity.' Her smile fades a bit now, but she meets my gaze bravely. 'I like the fact they have life experience,' she drones. I don't believe she means it. 'Young guys just want to game all the time, or get high.'

'How quaint.' I take a sip of icy water as if it's nectar from the gods and not the world's most boring drink. 'And now the truth?'

'It *is* the truth.' Her smile returns. 'Gary,' she calls, 'shall I cream your back?'

Vicky, digging grapes out of the hamper, meets my eye and almost grins.

Then, thinking better of it, she moves off to sit with Mae.

Does Mae like her potential new stepmum? I wonder. She hasn't mentioned this one before, but she loathed the last one. One of the reasons I've never married again – the happily blended family is a full-on myth.

Just look at my parents. Or rather, don't.

When I wake, the beach is deserted. They've damped down the barbecue Tom cooked some chicken on. I'm on my own.

Swatting away the sandflies, at first I'm just relieved that the sun's moved around, leaving me in the shade of the cliff, thank God, so I haven't ended up like a bacon Frazzle.

Imagine what my dermatologist would say.

But where *is* everyone?

Why did no one wake me?

It must be five o'clock at least, I think, shaking my wrist where I've lain on it, but I left my watch in my room and when I check, my phone's died.

And that doesn't seem to matter any more, given that none of them work. Which would be a relief if this wasn't all so bloody stressful.

How the hell we're going to get off this island does cross my mind now that Hannah's broken the boat, but I'll worry about that later.

Stretching my foot out for my sliders, I hear rustling nearby.

There's a terrible stink, I realise, along with the flies buzzing and hopping by my head.

Something from the barbecue maybe. Or some kind of wild animal nearby, I imagine, swatting at them again. Burying dead meat, maybe, like the foxes do with carcasses in the city. Though what this would be, I'm not sure.

I mean, what kind of creatures *do* live here? Not wolves and bears, surely – I laugh at myself – but maybe a big cat?

The idea's suddenly unnerving, and I scrabble to my feet, almost falling in my haste, and start to gather my things.

There's a rattling noise nearby now, like shale, and little bits of grit trickle down the slope behind me, around me, like something's slipping, or about to fall.

Worried, I look up.

The sun, high above me, floods my vision, blurring everything so I can't be sure, but is that a figure leaning over the walled garden?

I raise my arm and wave.

The four of us met at the local café on the day of the party to discuss outfits. Vicky had suggested we make the theme 'Dress as Your Favourite Celebrity', mainly because she wanted to wear a new catsuit.

'Everyone from Dizzy's is coming.' I salted my eggs thoroughly. 'Who've you all invited?'

'No one.' Jodie fished out a cigarette; she was hung-over apparently, drinking coffee in fake Ray-Bans and a long Afghan coat. 'I've been busy.'

'I've asked the whole studio.' Hannah scooped chips between thick slices of bread and squidged them together. 'Hope no one minds.'

'I mind *that*.' Vicky wrinkled her nose. 'It's literally gross.'

'What, a chip butty? Don't be daft.' Hannah bit into her sandwich lustily, brown sauce squirting out the sides. She was in a really good mood at the moment, which after last year's tragedy was refreshing. 'One of life's finer things.'

'You're just too posh,' Jodie ribbed Vicky.

'I've invited my tutor.' I changed the subject before Vicky

could rise to Jodie's barb. 'I'm hoping he brings his editor mate from the *Courier*.'

'Older man, eh?' Hannah teased.

'God, no.' Inadvertently I caught Jodie's eye. 'I'm not into older men.'

'Oh, why not?' Jodie drawled.

'I just prefer guys my own age.' Was she daring me to spill the beans? I'd not mentioned Perry to anyone, such was my loyalty to her. Or to her, such was my cowardice. 'Plus he's gay, so I'm hardly his cup of tea.'

She was right though: Vicky *was* posh in comparison to the rest of us, and she was in a foul mood a lot recently, the reason for which was obvious. Tom.

'You like boys, you mean, rather than men.' Jodie nodded at the young waiter. 'Though *he's* not bad if you like that sort of thing.'

'What's that?'

'Grungy. As in too dirty to shag. Like, literally dirty.'

'You'd have jumped on him happily six months ago, grungy or not,' Vicky said flatly. 'What you mean is, you want money. Men with cash.'

'What's wrong with money?' Jodie narrowed her eyes. 'Don't judge me just because you don't have to worry about it, babe.'

Vicky's dad had just announced that he'd help her buy a flat. Personally, I thought it was just a fob-off; Vicky barely saw him since he'd left her mum.

'At least I've got a job.' Vicky stabbed a tomato with her fork.

'Being a "chef"?' Jodie did elaborate quote marks. 'If you can call it that, frying burgers for minimum wage.'

'Shall we talk about how *you* make your money then?'

All eyes swivelled to Jodie.

'Are you asking me?' Jodie's voice was low.

'Not really, hon.' Vicky shrugged. 'It's up to you what you do, but don't judge me 'cos my dad's rich. He's a major tosser anyway, so it's not like I'm fortunate with my parents.'

'Ah, poor little rich girl.'

I winced. It could go any which way now.

'And weren't you judging me?'

'For what?' Perplexed, Hannah had stopped mid chew.

'For making my money on my back.' Jodie took her coffee from the waiter, whose eyes were on stalks. 'Ta. That's what you think, isn't it, babe?'

'I didn't say that.' Vicky toyed with her eggs.

'On your *back*?' Hannah pushed her glasses up her nose as she always did when she was uncertain.

'Christ's sake, Hannah, do we have to spell it out?'

'Um, well...'

Bless Hannah. Truly one of life's innocents.

'Well, are you?' Vicky stared at Jodie. 'Prostituting yourself?'

'Don't, Vicky!' I hated conflict; was a proper wuss around it, in fact, but I needed to step up. 'Let's just leave this now.'

'Just when it was getting good,' Vicky said tonelessly.

'You're being awful to each other,' I replied. '*And* it's our party tonight.'

'The party to end all bloody parties,' Jodie said. 'I might be busy.' Her eyes sparkled brilliantly, and not with happiness; that was clear. 'Working.'

'Don't be daft.' Hannah touched her arm. 'It's your party too.'

'All I'm saying' – Jodie ladled sugar furiously into her coffee – 'is none of you have a Scooby *why* I might need to make money quickly.'

'So tell us then.' I realised she was trying not to cry. 'Is it your dad?'

'I'm not discussing it, not after this.' She inclined her head at Vicky, now pretending to be engrossed in a game of Snake. 'But your eye's on the prize, Dilly.' She managed a smile my way. 'I've taught you well.'

'What prize?' Hannah asked. 'A column in the paper?'

'In my dreams.' I pushed my plate away. 'Though it would be fantastic.'

'We need dreams,' Jodie said. 'Some of us don't have Daddy's purse strings to rely on.'

'For fuck's sake!' Vicky slammed her phone down savagely.

'Don't row!' Hannah hated people arguing even more than I did.

'With respect, Hannah, butt out please.' Vicky glared at Jodie.

'Don't have a go at poor Hannah!'

'Don't pretend you care about Hannah!' Vicky hissed.

'What's that meant to mean?' Jodie was bristling now.

'Please,' I tried, but this had been lurking under a murky surface for ages.

'*I* don't know what it's meant to mean actually.' Hannah's frown had deepened.

'You've been foul to Hannah since she started seeing Tom,' Jodie fired at Vicky. 'You're so bloody jealous.'

'I'm not seeing Tom,' Hannah protested. 'We're just friends.'

'Pull the other one,' Jodie said. 'Have you seen how he looks at you?'

'No.' But Hannah's face flooded with colour.

'I'm not jealous, and you're deflecting,' Vicky shot back. 'We all know what *you* did to Han.'

My hands were clammy. I'd been waiting for this since seeing that fire incident report; wondering if it was on me to bring it up.

'I'll be looking for a flat next month anyway.' Vicky's chair squealed painfully across the tiles. 'So you won't have to put up with me for much longer.'

And she was gone; Hannah following soon after, failing to hide her pleasure about Tom, mumbling apologies to everyone.

I looked at Jodie.

'Don't!' She extended a dramatic hand, like a movie star warding off the paparazzi. 'Yes, it's to do with my dad, and no, I don't want to talk.'

'Your dad—' I started, but she stood up in a swirl of hippy coat and Chanel perfume, and I knew from experience I'd get no further.

'Let's get some more vodka for the party.' Adjusting the Ray-Bans, she produced a gold Amex card, flicking it with a tiger-skin fingernail until it vibrated. ''Cos the thing is, babe' – she hauled me to my feet – 'I don't think we've got nearly enough.'

Something was bothering me as we walked to the off-licence, something deep down and distant.

But I still couldn't think what it was.

FIFTY-FOUR

HANNAH

Isla del Diablo

When Tom half carried, half dragged me onto the shore, I was shivering so much my teeth were actually chattering, and I was confused about where I was; disoriented in the dark, despite a white disc of a moon above like a communion wafer.

More than that, I was confused about why *he* was here.

I hadn't seen him for so long, and this was all so peculiar. I got hysterical for a bit and lashed out, scratching his face badly, but eventually I calmed down.

He left me shivering on the dry sand higher up the beach and then waded back out to try to pull the boat to shore. When he failed to get it back onto the beach, we sat there for a while, side by side on the sand, not talking, watching it float out to sea.

I didn't know what I wanted to do now, but I knew it wasn't to go back up to that villa.

At first, I was freezing, but the night was warm; the stars and moon were bright, and the sea had calmed again. Tom poked around the little boathouse and came back with a couple of holey old blankets. He tried to drape one round me, but I took it from him and did it myself. He took his shirt off and spread it out to dry, leaving his T-shirt on, to my relief.

Words seemed difficult to form, but eventually I managed.

'How come you're here?' I asked quietly.

'Here with you?'

'No.' I tried not to growl at him. 'I mean here on this island.'

'Couldn't resist a free invite to a fortieth in Ibiza.' He was trying to be light-hearted obviously, but I could sense the frown in him.

'Oh yes, the great fortieth,' I replied, as if I was super-relaxed, though I didn't feel it in any way. I felt like I wasn't here at all, in fact; completely detached from my body. It ached now, probably from the desperate treading of water when I thought I was going to drown, but it was like it wasn't really part of me.

And also... It was so strange to sit here next to Tom, after all these years.

'I really think we ought to get you back up to the house,' he was saying now, but his voice seemed to go in and out, my ears full of water, my head full of pain.

Not actual pain. Metaphorical pain.

Get away from him, the little voice said. *He's not safe.*

'I'm not going to go,' I told him. 'I'm not going back up there.'

'C'mon on, Han.' He touched my arm, and it felt like someone had just stuck a thousand volts in my vein.

'No.' I stood up. *Hurry up*, the voice said.

'Well at least let me see if we can find somewhere to lie down,' he began.

Lie down with him? Never. And so I ran away.

When I woke up, there were so many unfamiliar sounds around me; like camping in the Peaks when I was a kid. Maybe there are animals in the woods, I thought, and I wasn't sure if that was comforting or not. I remembered the time my parents left me in my little tent and got up, packed up their own tent and drove off to the nearest café.

I thought they'd abandoned me forever.

A green lizard scuttled across the sandy ground, and I watched it. How free it was.

Then I spotted Tom sitting under another tree, maybe a hundred yards away, and before the warning voice could start, I told it no.

This was the Tom I once knew so well – who would never crowd me or hurt me, or want me to be scared...

And the fact that he was here made everything both better and also infinitely worse.

I turned my face away as I started to cry, silently, sound-lessly, the tears sliding into my hair and mouth.

Around 7 p.m., as Tom and his mates arrived with the sound system, our landline rang, and someone asked for Hannah.

'Try her mobile?' Vicky shouted over the chaos. 'She's at the shop.'

'Put the speakers there?' I suggested to Tom, indicating the far end of the living room. 'Then they're away from the balcony.'

'And your point is?' Jodie, tortoiseshell cigarette holder in hand, was directing cocktail-creating operations at the kitchen island.

'That the downstairs neighbours already hate us.'

'Guys.' A teary Hannah rushed in, bringing the cold with her. 'My mum's had a fall – they're taking X-rays now.'

'Oh no.' Jodie flung her arms round her. 'I'm so sorry, babe.'

'I need to pack.' Hannah clutched her brick of a phone. 'My dad can't cope on his own.'

'Not now, surely?' Vicky appeared from her room in a tight glittery catsuit that emphasised every plane of her athletic figure. A tribute to Destiny's Child apparently. 'Go tomorrow, and I'll come with you.'

'Let her go, babe,' Jodie drawled, 'if that's what she wants.'

Vicky stared at Jodie, her eyes kind of strange-looking and spinny. The two of them had struck an uneasy truce after lunch as they decorated the balcony with fairy lights and candles in glass jars. I didn't want them to start arguing again – especially not with Hannah looking so terrified.

'Vick,' I said gently, as Hannah gathered her things, 'there'll be other parties.'

'OK.' Vicky linked Hannah's arm. 'I'll come down to the cab with you.'

People began to arrive unfashionably early after Hannah left. Friends were DJing, while Tom's mate Dave from university manned the bar.

By eleven, the room was heaving.

Vicky and Jodie reconciled dramatically, involving much hugging and *I love you*s from Vicky, which made more sense after she admitted she had taken some Ecstasy: eyes even wilder, dancing ever more riotous.

Jodie, on the other hand, seemed calm so far, channelling *Thelma and Louise* in skin-tight jeans, a knotted vest top and white Stetson, along with her incongruous cigarette holder. 'For my best hot mess, Holly Golightly,' she explained to anyone who asked, flicking her ash into the ice bucket.

My own costume – low-slung combat trousers and, having lost a bit of weight recently, a crop top that *almost* skimmed my midriff – was in tribute to my favourite band, All Saints.

'You look nice,' Tom's friend Dave said. Sadly, he was sporting double denim – a fashion faux pas I couldn't forgive – and also, weirdly and to my delight, the boy with bright eyes had just walked in, wearing a leather biker jacket, a paperback book stuck in his back pocket. My heart sped up as he saluted Jodie.

'Who's that?' I asked her, trying hard not to blush.

'That, babe, is my little brother Mikey.' She passed me another mojito. 'The only decent one of my many siblings. Why?'

'Your brother?' Oh God, *of course*! Those amazing eyes. How stupid I'd been. Their colouring was completely different – he was much darker – and he was lean and angular where she was robust and strong, but still it was obvious, now I knew.

'Why?'

'He's the guy who helped me in Dizzy's that night.'

'Oh!' Jodie squinted her heavily painted eyes. 'Oh, I *seeee*...'

'See what?' I took a long swig of my mojito. Jeez, it was strong. 'I was just asking.'

'Don't lie!' She hauled me over to where he was sitting. 'Mikey, someone wants to meet you.'

'Jodie!' I was mortified, but it was too late.

'Mikey, Simone; Simone, Mikey,' she said, pulling her phone out of her cleavage. 'Do your worst. Though' – she blinked false lashes at us – 'you know what I say about mixing friends and family.'

'I owe you a thank you, don't I?' I said to him, my face rigid for some reason. 'That night in Dizzy's...'

'Oh, that was *you*, was it?' He stood, revealing his height, T-shirt riding up to show a lean midriff above faded Levis the same colour as his piercing eyes. 'Anyone'd have done the same.'

'They didn't though,' I said bashfully. 'Only *you* helped me.'

'Ah, you'll have me blushing.' He grinned. 'Forget about it, duck.'

Jodie's phone was buzzing, and she frowned at the screen as a kerfuffle started by the front door.

'Who?' I asked automatically.

'No one.' She put the phone away. 'Just an old mate.'

'I'm going to get a drink,' Mikey said. 'Fancy one?'

'Don't mind if I do, thanks.' I hoped I sounded a bit cool.

Dancing with Vicky, who kept performing outlandish slut-drops in front of Dave, so his eyes nearly sprang out of his head, I saw my college tutor Pat arrive. He'd brought a very grown-up bottle of claret but, disappointingly, not his editor friend.

'Who's this?' Jodie's radar had picked him out immediately.

'My journalism guru.' I felt a bit distracted, wondering why Mikey hadn't come back with my drink. 'Pat knows everything worth knowing.'

'Hardly.' Pretending embarrassment, Pat bonded immediately with Jodie, swapping tales of big nights in the gay clubs of Soho. When he went to grab a drink, or possibly flirt with Tom – very handsome in a checked lumberjack shirt – I danced with Jodie.

'Tell me about your dad now.' I was drunk enough to push it, and also even more intrigued now I'd met Mikey properly. I knew they shared the same father.

'That bastard?' She grimaced. 'He's not worth the breath, babe. He'll be the death of us.'

'Which *us* do you mean?' I asked cautiously.

'His poor abused family. He's accumulated so much gambling debt' – her sigh was long and quiet – 'he's gone and done one.'

'Like – disappeared?' I frowned. 'Where?'

'Spain probably. Maybe Morocco. Likes a smoke. And he's had lots of women but occasionally likes to mix it up, you know.' I wasn't sure I did know, suddenly feeling very wet behind the ears. 'But the minute he sets foot back in Blighty' – Jodie mimed a knife across her throat – 'probably curtains.'

'Jeez!' I stared at her. 'Is he really worth prison for, Jod?'

'Not me, babe! Don't be daft, even I draw the line at murder. No, the loan sharks, the bailiffs, his ex-wives, another of his *many* kids. I bet there's a price on his head, if not two.'

'Good riddance then, yeah?' I said hopefully. 'If he's gone...'

'It's not that easy, babe. He's left a lot of people in the absolute shit.' She looked woeful, and I put my arm round her. 'Properly up the creek.'

'I'm sorry, lovely,' I muttered as Tom headed towards us, followed by Mikey with my drink. 'It sounds crappy.'

'The worst thing is' – a single tear glittered in the corner of Jodie's eye – 'I really love the old bastard.'

'Sorry to interrupt.' Tom did a little bow. 'Two coppers just turned up and said turn the music down or else.'

'That'll be those effing neighbours.' Jodie rolled her eyes. A girl had intercepted Mikey, ostensibly to ask him for a light.

'And, er, either of you heard from Hannah yet?' Tom failed to look nonchalant.

'Her mum's broken her collarbone,' I told him. 'But she's OK.'

'That's good.' But Tom was obviously dejected.

'Tommy!' Vicky jumped on his back and flung her arms round his neck. 'Come and look at this thing this girl's got.'

'What thing?'

'You have to see...'

They galloped off to look at whatever the thing was, and I headed for the bathroom, trying not to feel too disheartened that Mikey was still chatting to the same girl, who was laughing up at him in her halo and wings.

'I'm off.' Pat stopped me. 'Pop into my office after the holidays. I might have a suggestion for you.'

When I returned from the loo, Jodie and Tom were dancing enthusiastically to 'I Feel Love'. Vicky, wrapped in a pink feather boa, was snogging Dave of the double denim. I hoped it would at least cheer her up a bit. The kissing, not the denim.

'What was the thing they went to look at?' I asked Jodie over the music.

'Oh' – she tipped her Stetson – 'magic mushrooms. Want some?'

'No thanks.' Something else was niggling at me; something

I'd been meaning to ask Jodie since lunchtime. But when I looked up, Mikey had vanished, though the halo girl was still there at least.

I went to look for him, but he was nowhere. Perhaps – my last hope – out on the balcony?

I slipped out. It was drizzling lightly, so I slid the door shut behind me. But there was no Mikey. Leaning on the railing to look across the city, I knew I had to accept he wasn't interested in me.

The rain didn't bother me. The crescent moon was covered by cloud, and I felt like my heart would look the same if I was dissected. Everyone had someone. Even my mum and dad had each other, and I was the permanent third wheel; always on my own.

'All right there, pet?' A voice made me jump. 'You look sad. Come and join me.'

In the shadows in the far corner, a small orange disc blazed – a tall man, smoking a cigar, wearing a black cape and a Zorro mask.

'I was just saying goodnight to my wee girl.' He put away the phone he was holding and pushed his mask up. 'I do it every night, wherever I am.'

'Oh, right,' I said. 'That's nice.'

Not any man, I realised with a jolt; *that* man, the big, solid one who'd been with Jodie the other night.

Robert Perry. Cooper's old boss.

'Come here,' he said – or perhaps it was a command.

'I'm OK, thanks.' I tried to smile and slide past him, but he'd moved in between me and the doors now.

'Are you enjoying living here?'

'Um, yes, thanks.' It was pitch-black out here; our cheap fairy lights must have shorted in the rain, and all the candles had fizzled out.

'Why don't you demonstrate your gratitude then, eh, girlie?'

'G-Gratitude?' I stammered. 'What do you mean?'

The thing that had niggled me dropped into place; the thing I'd both seen and not seen. The gold credit card Jodie had had at lunch. The name on it was *Perry's Properties*.

And I realised that although I could see the others inside, we were probably hidden in the shadows.

'Yes, pet, gratitude.' Perry put his horrible warm hand on my bare flesh and, without warning, slid it quickly under my top, his big fingers feeling the underwire of my bra, making me gasp.

Maybe he mistook it for lust – *maybe* – but it was the very opposite.

'Don't, please.' I tried to wriggle away, but I was firmly in his sights.

'Don't worry, pet.' I could see all the tiny black hairs up his nostrils. 'Jodie told me you needed some help.'

'What?' I didn't understand. 'Please' – I tried to shuffle back from him – 'let me go!'

'Ah, just my wee joke.' He splayed his hand over my ribs, pulling me forward so I fell hard against him.

My struggling made no difference at all.

'Get off!' Valiantly I tried to push him away, but he was almost double my size, and so solid he didn't even flinch. Enraged, I butted his chest with my head, but he just grasped me harder – and too late, I understood he was enjoying it. My struggle was exciting him, I realised with disgust.

'Ow, you're really hurting me!' I choked out. 'Let me *go*!'

'C'mon,' he breathed heavily, 'you like it really, girlie, I can tell. You're all the same. Don't bother putting up a fight.' He yanked at the popper on my trousers, which opened all too easily, exposing my knickers.

I tried to pull them shut again, but now he'd pushed me to the corner, against the wall, past the windows, so I was boxed in.

And even if it hadn't been so dark, no one could see me any more. I was masked by his bulk.

Now he pulled my hand away, big fingers biting into my flesh, ramming his knee between my legs to open them.

'Please.' I went rigid with fear. 'Please get off, please! People can see...'

But they couldn't, that was half the trouble; they were all facing the DJ, jumping up and down in a great pack, and my yells were behind double-glazing, drowned out by the music.

'That's half the fun, isn't it?' I could smell his stinking cigar breath, underlaid with something else, something like onion or curry sauce. 'Being watched. I bet you like being watched, girlie, don't you?'

'Get the fuck off me!' I hissed, but the more I struggled, the more I felt his disgusting excitement, onion breath wet and pungent as he yanked my knickers aside, and it was too late, it was too late, I couldn't stop him, and I could hear myself sobbing, the tears coursing down my face, moaning, 'Please stop, *please stop!*' as he grunted like a horrible fat pig – worse, not even a pig; a monster – his face red and gurning as his eyes rolled into the back of his head.

'Stop!' I screeched like a banshee, but he wasn't going to stop.

He didn't stop.

FIFTY-SIX

VICKY

Isla del Diablo

I'm making a salad dressing for dinner when Jodie appears off the beach, visibly upset, and rushes straight to her room without speaking.

Tonight's meal was always going to be tense after the events of the past twenty-four hours. Seeking my happy place, I've taken charge: plated up some cheese and salami, whipped up a Spanish omelette for everyone to share, and assembled salads, while focusing on the realisation that I *have* to pull myself together before I give myself away.

At least the cooking has helped to calm my buzzing head. Sort of.

Tom offered to help, but I'm not sure I can bear being round him right now, so I suggest he takes charge of the drinks.

'No problem. How's Hannah?' he asks, and I try to bite my tongue.

I mean, how hard can it be? I've been biting my tongue for so many years now.

'She's OK, mate, I think,' I say. 'I reckon we'd all be better, though, if we could work out what the hell was going on here.'

'It's pretty weird,' he agrees, finding some earthenware jugs in a cupboard. 'Do you reckon the tap water's OK to drink?'

'Well, hasn't killed me yet,' I say, meeting his very blue gaze. He's still as handsome as he was as a boy; more so maybe. He's kind of grown into his face, which is rugged and interesting now where it's lined. 'More's the pity, eh, Tom?'

He frowns. 'What's that meant to mean?'

'What's what meant to mean?' Gary lumbers into the kitchen. He, on the other hand, has not aged well, his bulging face pockmarked from old acne scars, his bald head shiny. He's no longer the roguish gunslinger he liked to see himself as when we were younger.

'Remind me.' I slice a tomato with a very sharp knife, careful of my fingers round the blade. 'What was that film you were nicknamed after, back in the day?'

'*High Noon?*' Gary smirks, his salmon-pink Ralph Lauren polo shirt already damp with sweat. He looks a bit like a big pink salmon actually.

'Oh yeah.' Tom puts one jug down and fills the next. 'I remember now.'

'Yeah, but' – Gary pulls a face – 'I don't like that name now. That was kids' stuff. Got no gravitas.'

Gravitas? Good Lord! I try to keep a straight face as Daisy comes in, wearing a tangerine body-con dress and perfume I recognise immediately. My mum wore it in the noughties; very retro.

'What name?' Daisy slides her hand up Gary's sweaty back.

'Gary used to be called after a film star you're too young to know.' I can't bear to watch her touch him. I turn away to fan the tomatoes out on the plate.

'Try me.'

'Gary Cooper?' Tom plonks the other jug down as I turn back. 'Wasn't it?'

'That's me.' Attempting a terrible American accent, Gary mimes blowing powder off a pistol. 'Sheriff's in town!'

'Oh, the inimitable Gary Cooper,' Daisy says knowledge-ably. 'Him with the swagger. Well, that fits, hon.' She kisses his cheek affectionately. 'You certainly got swag.'

And I meet her eye over his shoulder and think, how can she?

She looks very directly at me, and then at Tom, running her tongue over her top lip as if it's dry.

I pick up the salad and march it to the big table. 'Dinner's ready,' I call, but I'm clutching the bowl so hard, it bites into my flesh.

'Right, you absolute tossers!' Jodie appears in a lot of eye make-up and a spaghetti-strapped leopard-print jumpsuit. She claps her hands loudly, and her big amber jewellery clatters. 'Please gather round.'

People start to assemble in the living room, and while their backs are turned, I pour myself a straight vodka and down it quickly.

A huge black spider scuttles across the kitchen, so big it looks almost like an animal, and disappears under the fridge.

'Um...' I start, but Jodie's already launched into her speech.

'So, do tell me' – arms raised, she looks as if she's about to enlist God's help – 'which one of you arseholes tried to end me on the beach earlier by chucking a fucking enormous rock near my head?'

'What?' Tom looks shocked. 'When?'

Jodie scans the room, and suddenly it's as if we're all naughty schoolchildren in front of the headmistress – except this headmistress wears a malevolent grin, eyes sharp and enquiring beneath her sparkling eyeliner.

''Cos know this, whoever you are – and maybe it's the same person who so kindly brought that horrible newspaper article this morning' – she points a finger round the room, taking us in, one by one – 'I ain't going down without a fight.'

'Hey!'

I was vaguely aware of the balcony door sliding open as my head smacked back hard onto the concrete wall behind me. I was too desperate to even feel relief.

'Simone?' It was Jodie's voice, rising in pitch as she rushed towards us. 'What the fuck? Robert?' She pulled frantically at his arm – the same arm that had me pinioned against the wall. 'What the *actual* fuck are you doing?'

'Come and join us, darling.' He was panting from his exertions, scarlet in the face, his oily hair no longer slicked back but falling in his nasty piggy eyes, the other meaty hand still clamped over my mouth.

'Get off her,' she begged, and now I managed to bite him as hard as I could. He let go of me suddenly, and I fell forward, free of him at least, straight onto my knees. It hurt so much, all the air went out of me.

'You little bitch!' he spat, and I cowered away from him, pain shooting through my knees.

But he was more worried about his hand.

'You've drawn blood!' He wiped it on his trousers, which he was fumbling with now. 'You stupid bitch!'

'Get up, Dilly!' Jodie grabbed at my wrist and managed to drag me past him as he rearranged himself quickly.

But as I pulled my own trousers shut, trying to get my breath, only half aware now of what was happening around me, Perry bent down and grabbed my hair hard, yanking my head back again.

I was vaguely aware of someone else standing behind Jodie, someone I couldn't quite see, as she charged at Perry like a bull, slamming her head into him, and then I scrabbled to my feet, rage flooding through me, and joined her.

I don't know how it happened, I never would know exactly, but before any of us could do or say anything, the big man lost his balance.

He stood there for a second, his arms held out to the sky – and then he literally just toppled backwards over the edge, emitting a solitary grunt.

Then he was gone.

'Jesus!' the other man breathed, staring at the sky where Perry had been – and I looked at him and realised with horror that it was Coops, the obnoxious estate agent I'd dated once; the man who'd started the bar brawl and tried to strangle me in the process. Dressed up as a cowboy with a sheriff's badge.

I couldn't even begin to compute this one.

'Shut the door,' Jodie hissed at him. 'Shut the fucking door – now!'

Muttering, Cooper did as he was told.

'We need to call the police.' I was breathless, my head exploding with tension. 'Don't we? Or an ambulance?'

'Don't be fucking stupid, babe. There's nothing you can do for him now. We've got about two minutes at best, I reckon,' Jodie said. 'And we need to get our stories straight right now.'

'Not me, mate—' Coops started, but she looked at him and said:

'Yes, you too, *mate*. You're in this too.'

'No!' He held up his hands as if he'd just been arrested. 'Nothing to do with me.'

'Shut up,' Jodie ordered. 'I'm thinking.' She reached into her cleavage and produced a lighter; pulled a cigarette from behind her ear.

Then she put the cigarette back and came to me. She straightened my trousers and wiped my face quickly with my top, running her thumbs under my damp eyes. Then she put her hands on my shoulders.

'OK.' Her smile was more like a death mask than any indication of joy or humour. 'Slide the door back open and go inside as if we're having a right laugh. As if *absolutely* nothing has happened.'

I slid the door open, forcing a smile myself now. Jodie put her arm through Cooper's and followed me.

'Shut the door again, subtle as you like, babe,' she muttered, still grinning like a manic Cheshire cat, and I did so, clicking it carefully into place.

Cooper looked like he was about to have a heart attack.

'Cheer up,' she said, and she kissed him very deliberately and slowly. He looked dazed when she stopped, but no one else so much as blinked; too high on life, or whatever else they'd consumed.

'So.' Jodie fitted her cigarette carefully into the holder as someone put 'In da Club' on the decks. 'We are going to sort this.' She gestured at Tom, manically refilling ice trays to put in the freezer. 'And this is what we're going to do. Tom, we need you too...'

FIFTY-EIGHT

SIMONE
SATURDAY, 11 JUNE

Isla del Diablo

'You're being ever so melodramatic, love,' Sue sighs, drowning in a bizarre lace kaftan that leaves nothing to the imagination. 'I'm sure it was just an accident.' She adds ice to her drink.

'And how's that possible?' Jodie's concocting a non-alcoholic cocktail. 'A massive rock just launched itself off the side of the hill and nearly fell on my head?'

'But it didn't, did it? You're alive and well, love,' her mother says comfortably. 'Now, where's Mae's special plate? I'll take it to the table.'

'God, Mother.' Jodie grabs her drink so hard, half of it spills. 'Could you just leave Mae alone for a bit? Let her sort herself out.'

'Like you did, you mean?' Gary takes a seat at the head of the long table on the terrace.

'And who asked you?' Jodie snaps.

'I'm her dad.' He shakes his head sadly. 'I'm allowed an opinion.'

'Perhaps if you'd done a bit more childcare yourself' – Jodie fixes him with a stare – 'you would be.'

A little brown lizard flicks up the wall and away into the shadows.

'I was away working.' He unfolds the napkin Vicky's laid at his place setting. 'Earning.'

'I was working too.' I see Jodie's fist close where it lies on the table. 'I was looking after her, and also always, *always* working.'

'That's what your dad used to say,' Sue murmurs.

I move the breadknife surreptitiously away from Jodie and place it on my other side.

Jodie chooses to ignore her mother's barbed remark as Vicky puts the cheeseboard in the middle of the table.

'So, folks.' She smiles at everyone. Always the hostess with the mostest, Vicky likes to be. 'We've got a mix of salads, Spanish omelette, smoked fish, prawns and charcuterie, and cheese and grapes to finish.'

'Amazing,' Hannah says. 'Thank you, Vick.'

'Charcute what?' Daisy wrinkles her nose. 'What's that?'

'Meat.' Jodie almost grits her teeth. 'It's meat, babe. If you're a veggie, eat the cheese and salad.'

'And if you're vegan?' Mae arrives in a *Peaky Blinders* cap and tiny kilt, her vest top displaying arms tattooed with funny little symbols, including a fork on one wrist, and a spoon and dish on the other.

'Eat the bread, my darling.' Jodie smiles at her. 'And the lettuce and carrots. I don't *think* they cry when they're pulled from the ground, but who knows?'

'Hilarious.' Mae sits next to me. 'You're really hilarious, Mum.'

'I try my best.'

'Really?' Mae looks at her. 'Like you did with Slug, you mean?'

'I explained about Slug,' Jodie starts as Tom arrives at the table bearing cold bottles of Chablis.

The thermostatically controlled wine cellar is well stocked at least; I know, because I checked earlier.

'I wanted to see if you could trust him. It was a test.'

'And I don't buy that excuse, Mummy dear.'

'Who'd like a glass?' Tom begins to circulate with a bottle.

'Me please!' Mae holds her glass out immediately.

Like mother, like daughter, I think, and that makes me think about Tiger. I really, really hope she's OK; it's been over forty-eight hours since I've spoken to her, which is the longest time in…

Since she was born? I feel a clutch of panic and my palms go clammy.

Breathe into it, Simone, I tell myself.

'Not me, Tom.' Jodie puts a hand over the glass I laid for her on autopilot. 'I'm all good, ta.'

'Thanks.' I extend my own glass swiftly. I'll definitely need some help to get me through tonight.

'Me please, love.' Sue pushes her glass forward. 'I'll have Jodie's.'

'So supportive, Mother,' Jodie murmurs. 'As ever.'

'Half a glass,' Vicky mutters. 'Thanks.'

I notice she doesn't look at Tom as he pours her wine.

'So, look, could we talk about how we're going to get off this island?' I suggest quietly as Tom carries on round, exactly like the professional he is. 'Because I'm starting to feel more than anxious about it.'

'And me,' Hannah agrees. She's wearing a shapeless dark shift dress, and although she looks better than earlier, the smudgy shadows beneath her eyes are even more pronounced than when we arrived.

'I'm sure Antonio said he was coming back to get us on

Monday,' Vicky says. 'My Spanish is very rusty, but that's what I *thought* he said.'

'But as we still don't know which fucker invited us' – Jodie forks slices of Parma ham onto her plate as if they've personally offended her – 'how can we find out if that's true?'

'We have to wait it out,' Mae says. 'Which is fine by me, because I know how to live in the moment. Unlike you lot.'

'Ah, Gen Z, you are my idols.' Jodie toasts her daughter with her glass of water.

'We can't find out, since the mobiles aren't ever going to work,' Daisy says. ''Cos of the mast being buggered,' she adds helpfully.

I exchange glances with Vicky.

'But surely if your TV crew are coming,' Vicky says to Jodie, 'they can help.'

'I'm not sure they are though,' Jodie says flatly.

'Are you saying,' Tom asks slowly, 'this is all a set-up?'

'It's so weird about the phone mast.' Hannah's voice is low. She's refusing to look at Tom. 'Who would do that?'

I think about the red water in my shower yesterday – and then tell myself again it was just rust. Or the Ibizan red earth. Or my own blood from my cut hand. Wasn't it?

'This is typical of you, Jod.' Sue spikes a bit of tomato and nibbles round it. No wonder she's almost emaciated. 'Everything always a bit topsy-turvy, even as a little kid. Always getting everything wrong.' She's got a dark firefly type thing tattooed on her wrist, I notice.

'Gee, thanks, Mother.'

'Do you remember when I sent you for my paper and you brought back suncream?' Sue's smile is gappy; she's missing an upper canine.

'I got my suns muddled up, Mum. Exhausted by running to buy your fags.' Jodie lays her fork down. 'Child labour was banned in the nineteenth century for good reason.'

Sue ignores the jibe. 'You always were disorganised.'

'And your point is?'

'Well' – Sue gazes into the middle distance – 'I mean, it only got worse when you had Mae.'

'I was trying to earn a living, Mum.'

'And I was trying to take care of your daughter.' Sue turns her watery gaze on Jodie.

I can't help it, I'm fascinated. What *is* it Sue's actually saying? Is she deeply angry or just commenting? It's hard to tell.

'Whereas you were such a fantastic parent, yeah? Provided such stability' – Jodie's eyes grow ever fiercer – 'always there for me.'

'I was—'

'Was not? You were *not* always there, is that what you're trying to say?'

'I looked after Mae every day when you went into rehab.' Once again Sue seems unflustered. She's like a robot, I think. Some kind of automaton.

'Er, I think I was involved too,' interrupts Gary, dabbing at his T-shirt where he's spilled something; olive oil, maybe, his lips horribly red and slick with it.

And I swallow really hard, because I find I can barely stand to look at him. He reminds me of everything I never wanted to be reminded of ever again.

'I think I looked after myself, thanks, Gary,' Mae sniffs. 'It was only last year.' She doesn't call him Dad, I realise for the first time; I don't think she has at all since we've been here. How history has a habit of repeating itself, whatever they say.

'Anyone for a top-up?' asks Tom, and then obviously realises what he's just said. 'I mean, actually, I might have a coffee.'

'The first time, I meant.' Sue prongs a prawn. 'The rehab. Into the Priory for all that drinking and whatnot.'

'Whatnot?' Mae stares at Jodie. 'How many times *were* there?'

'*She tried to go to rehab, but Mummy said no, no, no,*' Vicky sings off-key.

'Vick!' I reprove. 'Don't be a cow.' But her eyes are doing that spinning thing that suggest she might have drunk quite a lot.

'You can talk,' she mutters, and I don't even know what that's supposed to mean. It's all so tense again in here, it's hard to tell where the next attack will come from.

'Oh, for God's sake!' Jodie stands up. 'Well done, you absolute heroes.' She starts clapping again. 'You've made your points about me, thank you very much.' *Clack-clack* go her heavy bracelets. 'Very helpful from people who I might just say... Well. Glass houses and all that.'

'Which means?' Vicky squints at her; she's definitely half cut.

'Let's not argue, people.' Daisy's eyes shine with distress. 'We need to stick together.'

'Mae, baby.' Jodie walks round to her daughter and kisses the top of her head before Mae can demur. 'You're the only one I care about, and I'm more than happy to discuss this with you.'

I can hear something, I think, but there's so much noise at the table it's hard to make out.

Jodie reaches to grab the full bottle of Rioja standing beside the cheese.

'You, Mae, but not Sue.' She gestures at her mother. ''Cos you were crap. And you know it.'

Sue shrugs and keeps peeling her prawn, its pink body obscene suddenly in its nakedness.

'And you' – Jodie points at Gary – 'how the fuck can you have an opinion when you didn't even turn up again till Mae was about ten?'

He scowls. 'You know why that was.'

'Do I?' Jodie has been prising the cork out of the bottle. Now it comes out with a satisfying pop.

Mae rolls her eyes. 'Fallen off the wagon already, Mum?'

'What's that?' Daisy looks round, obviously on edge. 'That noise?'

'I can hear it too,' I say. 'Shush, everyone, for a sec...'

'It's one night, baby,' Jodie's saying to Mae as she raises the bottle to her lips.

'Oh God!' I stand up suddenly, my calm shattered.

Children's voices echo in the room, bouncing off the walls: *my* children, a girl and a boy, eerie laughter, running footsteps. I sit again and bury my head in my hands.

'It's OK, Sim.' Hannah puts an arm round me. 'Don't get upset.'

'It's coming through the stereo system, I think.' Tom stands up. 'I'll see if I can find it.'

I just want the unearthly voices to go away. 'Please,' I croak. 'Make it stop!'

Hannah pats my back as Tom goes to the Sonos in the living room.

'Don't be upset,' Daisy repeats helpfully.

'Needs must even more.' Jodie swigs the wine.

The voices stop suddenly and it's quiet for a moment. Thank God.

'Sorted.' Tom comes back to the table.

Vicky frowns. 'But why was that playing?'

'Who knows why about anything here?' Jodie shrugs. 'It's all fucked. I'm going to bed.'

'Oh my God!' Mae screeches, pointing past Jodie.

A massive black spider trundles out of the kitchen, advancing rapidly towards the table, its body as heavy as a snooker ball.

'Ah, my friend.' Jodie toasts it with her bottle. 'Come join the party!'

'Gary!' Daisy squeals in a girlish way.

'Disgusting!' Gary grabs the floor lamp next to him, obvi-

ously about to try to squash the creature, but Hannah's too fast
for him.

'Don't!' She flies across the room and crouches, extending
her hands gently towards the spider. 'C'mon, little fella.'

She scoops it up and walks out into the garden, and I feel a
massive shudder go through me. I bundle myself onto my chair,
scooping my feet off the floor.

'What if it's a tarantula?' Mae's still visibly scared.

'Not in Spain, babes,' Gary assures her. 'They live in
Africa.'

'The Americas actually,' Tom says. 'Tarantulas. And I'm
sure it's not poisonous, Mae,' he tries to soothe her. 'Or Hannah
wouldn't have picked it up.'

But the sight of the heavy, hairy body has set off great waves
of disgust rolling through my chest.

'Like I said, I'm off to bed, and in case anyone has any ideas'
– Jodie's still clutching the wine – 'I'll be locking my door
tonight.'

One by one, people peel off to bed, and Vicky says she'll
turn off the lights and lock up. I offer to help in the kitchen, but
she hugs me and says, 'Go on, Sim, get a good night's sleep. We
might need our wits about us tomorrow if help doesn't turn up.'

I'm not sure what she means.

Later, I lie there sleepless, remembering the things I've tried so
hard to leave in the past.

Then I think of how vehement Hannah was about not
hurting that horrible creature. She was always so soft-hearted.

Tossing and turning, I wish I'd brought a drink of water to
bed. When I eventually open my door to fetch one, I see two
shadowed figures huddled together at the end of the hallway,
near the living room.

As soon as they hear me, they melt away.

But I don't want to go out there now.

I shut my door and drink from the tap, and a bad feeling gnaws in the pit of my stomach.

Before I fall asleep, I get back up and lock my door too, but all night the noise of the glassy wind chimes in the garden haunts me.

FIFTY-NINE

HANNAH

SUNDAY, 12 JUNE

Isla del Diablo

'That was brave,' Vicky says. 'Last night.'

'What?' I concentrate on pouring boiling water onto the coffee grounds. It's the most beautiful day again, absolutely perfect, a few wispy clouds in the sky, which is the bluest I think I've ever seen. A true blue – ultramarine, maybe, in the paint spectrum.

Tom has just passed through the kitchen whistling cheerily, saying he's going to see if the boat washed up along the shore.

This is meant to be our last full day here before we leave tomorrow to fly home.

The sky is like the blue of the Virgin Mary's dress. Of the porcelain statue in my mother's bedroom, but I try not to think about that.

About the bedroom I should be back in by tomorrow night.

'That disgusting spider.' Vicky pats my shoulder. 'I was really impressed. Honestly, Han.'

'What?' I look at her.

'You!' Her face floods with a happiness I haven't seen in a

long while. 'You're a woman of many hidden talents, hon. And it's so great just hanging out with you for a bit, even if it is all pretty stressful here.'

The two of us are putting breakfast together: fruit, yoghurt, cereal; the last loaf, the last few pastries in the cupboard.

Stocks are running out, that's obvious from the depleted fridge.

'Thanks,' I say. 'By the way, we're low on milk. Is there anything in the freezer?'

'Not much. It's like the Big Brother house when they blow their budget and exist on beans,' Vicky jokes, but I never watched reality TV at home. My parents didn't approve, Nick was an anarchist, and by the time of Royal Mews, it'd passed me by.

But it does seem likely someone's watching us now, just like the original Big Brother did, and I shiver as though a spirit just breathed down my neck. Those unearthly voices last night were so freaky.

'Perhaps you can do a Bear Grylls, hon,' Vicky says, grinning, 'and go and kill some wild animals for us before we starve.'

'Not my thing, Vick.' I feel almost apologetic. 'Not very Buddhist to kill something that's harmless.'

'Fair enough, mate.' She slices an apple neatly in her hand. 'But I thought you were Catholic?'

'No, that's my mum,' I say as a yawning, barefoot Daisy appears in a frilly white nightie.

'Anyone seen Gary?'

'No, thank God,' Vicky mutters.

Daisy frowns. 'What was that, Vicky?'

''Fraid not,' I say quickly. 'There's tea and coffee on the table– I made a pot of both.'

'Thanks. He must have crept out when I was asleep.' Daisy takes the mug I pass her. With her hair in plaits, she looks a bit *Little House on the Prairie*.

'I did see him actually,' Vicky corrects herself. 'Outside, about six thirty, when I came to get a tea.'

'Probably went to watch the sunrise. It *was* amazing.' I pass Daisy the milk jug. 'Go easy on the milk – it's running low.'

'He said last night he was going to climb up to try and get a phone signal.' Daisy ignores my warning and pours a lavish amount into her cup. 'See if he could check the boat for tomorrow.'

'Have you seen that big knife I had yesterday?' Vicky's searching the drawers. 'I need it to slice the pineapple.'

'Check the dishwasher?' I suggest as Daisy takes her milky tea and wanders into the early-morning sun. She's pretty gorm-less, I have to say.

'I already did. No joy.'

'So listen, what do you think *we* should do about no phone signal?' I'm saying when a wild-eyed Mae appears in a huge holey Snoopy T-shirt. She's clutching a crumpled envelope and looks like she's been crying.

Jodie follows her daughter, rubbing her eyes. 'I need coffee – urgently.' She clearly hasn't slept a wink.

'For fuck's sake, Mum!' Mae rounds on her furiously.

'Mae?' Jodie's panda eyes make her look vulnerable. 'What's up, baby?'

'This!' The girl waves the envelope in her mum's face. 'Why do you have to be such a fucking mess?'

'What did I do this time?' Jodie implores as Mae runs out of the kitchen with a sob. 'Oh dear. Was it my embarrassing tumble off the wagon last night?'

'Tumble?' scoffs Vicky. 'More of a face-plant, I think.'

'I don't know,' I say gently. 'But I'll get you a coffee.'

As Jodie's eyes follow Mae across the garden, I actually feel sorry for her. I think about how I ran away myself the other night when I saw Tom for the first time in years.

'We've only just sorted out the fact that I did not sleep with that stupid guitarist,' Jodie sighs.

'Sure about that, mate?' Vicky snipes.

'Yes, quite sure, thanks, babe,' Jodie retorts and hurries after Mae.

It's late morning, and I'm lying in the sun by the infinity pool.

It's so odd: I'm actually *trying* to feel stressed about the fact that I don't know how my parents are, or the fact that we're all on an island not knowing who invited us or if we're going to get off it – but in fact, I'm feeling better than I did yesterday.

Maybe it's the fact that I slept so deeply last night, after I returned from depositing the spider far from harm.

'Hey!' Daisy jogs through the trees. 'Gary's down on the beach if anyone wants to join him, he says, and he's planning a hike this afternoon.' She's wearing shorts, thick socks and hiking boots, despite the heat.

'I thought he'd probably just fallen asleep somewhere in the sun.' Vicky looks up from her Angela Hartnett cookbook, bought at the airport. 'It's hard not to.'

'I'm going for a power walk now if anyone fancies it,' Daisy says, but no one responds.

'Anyone seen Jodie?' Sue wanders out of the villa in that weird lacy kaftan again, clutching an old *Daily Mail* crossword. 'I need her specs. Can't find mine anywhere.'

'Not since breakfast,' I say. 'Sorry.'

'Ask Mae?' Vicky points to the viewpoint, where Mae's sunbathing topless in a pair of boy shorts, giant headphones on.

Judging by her relaxed state, presumably she's recovered from whatever upset her earlier.

But an hour later, when Daisy returns, having apparently hiked right up the hill and back, Jodie still hasn't turned up.

'Shall we wander down to the beach and take a look?' Simone suggests. Fidgeting beside me for the past half-hour, pretending to read a novel, she also looks like she slept badly, her hair wild, her face grave.

I know that beyond everything else, she misses her kids badly.

'Jodie wasn't with Gary,' Daisy says. 'Earlier.'

'They might be together now though.' Vicky raises a suggestive eyebrow.

'Oh please.' Simone looks irritated. 'Don't be stupid, Vick.'

'What do you mean?' Daisy stares at Vicky. 'You don't mean—'

'No, she doesn't,' I interject quickly. 'She's just joking.'

'Oh.' But Daisy looks unconvinced.

'I'm sure Jodie's fine,' I say, but the anxiety's contagious. 'But yeah, let's go along the beach, just in case she's twisted an ankle or something.'

'I'm not going anywhere.' Vicky puts her book down and shuts her eyes resolutely. 'It's sweltering, and everyone will be OK.'

Looking for my sandals, I wonder how she can be so certain.

'I need a shower first,' Daisy says. 'I'm pouring with sweat now.'

'Come on then, Sim.' I drag my dress over my swimsuit. 'Let's go.'

Down on the empty beach, it's roasting hot, and there seem to be a disgusting number of flies swarming over the sand, very near where I sat the other night with Tom.

There's no sign of Gary, though there's a freshly damp beer bottle on the side by the makeshift barbecue, built out of brick and a wire rack.

Maybe it's the barbecue that's attracting all the flies buzzing so angrily around it.

'Ew!' Simone flaps at them. 'I thought I'd buried all the chicken bones, but we must have left something here.'

'I didn't come down yesterday,' I remind her. I slept most of the afternoon. 'After, you know...' I trail off.

'Indeed.' She slides a sideways glance at me. 'So, you and Tom...'

'Me and Tom what?'

'Yeah, me and Tom what?' Tom appears through the trees where we found the hammocks that night. 'My ears are burning.'

I catch my breath – or maybe my breath catches me.

Shirtless, in just shorts and sliders, his T-shirt tucked into his back pocket, he's already caught the sun.

'Tom!' Simone straightens up. 'Where've you been this morning?'

'I was looking to see if there's another boat anywhere. Honestly, ladies' – he grins at us both, looking fit and vibrant – 'I didn't take either of you for a gossip!'

'Oh no.' I'm mortified. 'We weren't really...'

Seemingly oblivious, Simone's poking round the back of the barbecue.

'Relax, Han,' Tom murmurs, coming nearer. 'I was only joking.'

'Is it me or is there an awful stink?' Simone wrinkles her nose.

'God, no, it *is* bad.' Tom grimaces. 'Old meat, maybe?'

Simone pokes around a bit more, leaning right over to move something, and I'm about to suggest there might be foxes here when she recoils violently.

'Jeez!' She looks like she's about to pass out.

'What?' I clutch her arm. 'What is it? Are you OK?'

'There's a massive dead rat!' She shakes herself free to look closer. 'Oh my God!'

'What?' Fixed to the spot, I feel a stab of something in my gut.

'I'm not being funny, but...' She leans forward again and reaches out a tentative hand. 'Ugh, that is really gross!' She gags.

She always did have a sensitive stomach.

'What?' I repeat, almost unable to look, but I follow her to peer down. 'Oh no. That's really... weird!'

Tom has a look too, then hurries down the beach. He comes back with a bit of old driftwood and scoops the dead rat onto it.

'Something's had a really good go at this.' He screws up his nose against the terrible stench. 'But I mean... Well, just look!'

We can all see. Why, I have no clue, but someone has stuck a pair of shattered reading glasses over the poor dead animal's mutilated face.

Tom removes the specs with his penknife, wrapping them gingerly in a tissue from his pocket before burying the rat in the first row of trees, shoving it down as deep as he can manage with the driftwood.

'I'm not sure what might dig it up again,' he mutters, and we all glance round.

Who knows what creatures lurk in the trees? I shiver, and something visceral, very much like pure fear, travels through me.

'I mean...' Simone starts, 'it would *almost* be comical, except...'

'Except it's really horrible?'

She nods. 'Exactly.'

The three of us exchange glances.

'What the hell's going on here?' Tom rubs his head as if it's hurting him.

'I wish I knew.' Simone speaks as if her jaw has set. 'I really do.'

'Me too.' He turns towards the steps. 'I have to say, this is not turning out to be the fun weekend I was imagining.'

And I really want to ask him why he decided to come, but I can't bear any more bad news today.

Together, the three of us hurry back up to the villa.

'It must just have been a weird thing that happened,' Simone keeps saying. 'The glasses being on its face.'

'Very bloody weird though. Like, they just fell there?' Tom shakes his head, striding ahead, and I feel dazed just watching the speed he takes the stairs in the heat.

By the pool, we find Sue alone, dozing under a parasol, her mouth open like a corpse.

Is she dead? I suddenly wonder, fear crawling up my spine. She looks so still.

Simone peers down as my heart flips over. 'Sue?'

'Who's there?' The older woman wakes with a start, wiping drool off her crepey chin, just as a voice calls urgently.

'Hey!' Mae is waving as she hurries across the grass. 'You guys!'

Then she sees Tom and pulls up short.

He takes a step back. 'Oh no!' He claps a hand to his head. 'I think I left my Swiss army knife down on the...' He dashes back towards the steps. 'Won't be a tick.'

'I found this.' Mae thrusts something towards us. 'It's my mum's. I gave it to her for Christmas last year.'

A bright yellow G-Shock watch.

'I just saw it out of the corner of my eye, on the slope under the viewpoint. She was wearing it this morning.'

Oh my God, Jodie, I think, for the first time.

Perhaps something actually *has* happened to her.

SIXTY
VICKY

When the others go to the beach, I put my cookery book down and try to enjoy the sun, but it's hard to relax now.

I said I wasn't worried about Jodie's whereabouts, but the truth is, perhaps I am. I'm definitely a little unnerved by everything.

Still, I'm just nodding off when a shadow falls across me and my eyes flick open again immediately. I sit up quickly and grab my sarong.

'Hello, stranger,' a voice says.

This time, I'm ready to talk. 'Fancy a stroll up to the orange grove?'

'Sure.' She turns and strides off.

I follow her, passing skinny old Sue, who's snoring gently. I tuck my sarong around me carefully, thinking about what I'm going to say. What's *best* to say. I don't come up with much.

'I don't understand why you're with him,' is my opening gambit as we exit the small gate into the grove. It's planted in neat rows up the incline. 'What in the world possessed you? I mean, he's not really your type, is he?'

'How do you know what my type is?' She stares at me.

'Well, I could guess. I mean' – I try to make a joke of it – 'he's the wrong sex, for a start.'

'You hypocrite,' she mumbles, and my heart lurches.

'Daisy, flower, please. It's just... I don't get why you came out here with him.'

'Why do you care?' Daisy ducks under the branches of the first orange tree. 'It's nothing to do with you.'

I consider her question as I follow. Why *do* I care?

'You lost any right to care when you sacked me.'

'I totally didn't sack you, flower,' I protest. 'You know I didn't.'

'Well' – she shrugs defiantly – 'you said it was best I went.'

'I just thought, all things considered, it was probably easier not to work together, given what we'd been...' I search for the words. 'You know.'

'You mean the fact we'd been sleeping together.'

'Yes.' I try not to look around nervously, worrying who might hear. It's no one's business obviously, apart from ours.

'But on top of actually liking you, it was my job,' she says boldly. 'It was how I paid my bills.'

'I liked you too,' I say, which is true, or was back then. But I'm finding it all hard to contend with, and before I can think of a more suitable response, Daisy turns and stops stock-still.

'Look.' Her face is pink, her eyes are wet – it's clear she's struggling not to cry. 'I realise this was a bad idea. I should never have come.'

'To the island? You and me both. I can't wait to go home.'

'I meant on this walk actually, but yeah, that too. It was a mistake.' She dashes the tears from her eyes. 'It's all been a mistake. I just want to go home with Gary and get away from you and his poisonous ex. At least he really loves me.'

'Don't be like that.' I attempt a pacifying smile. 'I'm really sorry.' But she's striding up the hill away from me. 'Daisy!'

'Please,' she throws over her shoulder. 'Just leave me alone.'

'Daisy,' I call again, taking a few steps after her, but my heart's not really in it. I know deep down why she came; I knew she wasn't over the whole thing – and I deserve it really. She's right to be upset with me.

I tramp back down to the villa and take up position again on the lounger, but my heart's not in sunbathing anymore either. I can see Daisy high up on the hillside, still marching upwards, a little matchstick figure now, and I feel a throb of guilt.

A cold beer would go down an absolute treat, I think, and I get back up and wander into the kitchen.

The walk-in wine fridge is ajar. Not good in this heat, but at least I can access it easily. I slip in to take a bottle off the shelf.

The door slams behind me.

Jodie pulled Tom onto the dance floor and writhed up and down his body to that infamous Pussycat Dolls tune, a sight no one in their right minds would forget in a hurry. I clapped along, trying to look like I was having the time of my life and not like I felt it might all be ending.

And after we'd made sure everyone saw us there, having fun, I spent the rest of the night locked in my bedroom with Cooper, as agreed with Jodie.

She made very sure people saw us; busy creating our alibis.

After I shut the bedroom door, my hands still trembling, Cooper sat on the bed, but I said bluntly, 'Please. Don't.' I stared at him. 'Why are you here anyway?'

'She said you wanted to interview me.' He shrugged. 'Some article?' Grumbling, he sat on my beanbag in the corner. 'You lot are fucking trouble.'

'So are you. You owe us, mate.' I sounded far braver than I felt. 'You definitely owe *me*, and you know it.'

Eventually he dozed, snoring on and off, his cowboy hat over his face.

But I lay wide awake on the bed, freezing, clutching my

blanket in both hands. Waiting for the inevitable knock on the front door.

At one point Cooper woke up and started to say something, and I said, 'Just shut up,' and thankfully he did.

I lay there thinking, am I a murderer?

It seemed the lesser of the two horrific thoughts churning round my head. I hadn't even washed myself properly after the horrible... after the...

After Robert Perry assaulted me.

I kept thinking we should have called an ambulance; I should have insisted we just go to the police, but it was too late now.

A life locked behind bars was beckoning.

By 4 a.m., it sounded like everyone had left.

Still wide awake, I crept out to use the bathroom, desperate to get clean.

Vicky was curled up with skinny Dave of the double denim, asleep together on the settee, and I felt so jealous of her for a minute: for the oblivion; for not being party to any of the horror I'd just endured.

As I went back to my room, Jodie's door opened a crack, and I glimpsed her in the doorway, wearing the slinky black petti-coat she used as a nightdress. She was decidedly dishevelled, looking behind her to say something.

Tom was lying on her bed, shirt off, jeans on, and I felt a weird shift in my belly.

I thought of Hannah, poor Hannah tending to her demanding mother, and what she would make of all of this, and before Jodie could see me there, I hurried back to my own room, praying for sleep; for temporary oblivion.

. . .

Around 7 a.m., an insistent buzzing woke me from a dream about a courtroom, three bewigged judges sitting in a row, banging their gavels hard and calling my name.

'Simone...'

The door handle rattled, setting my heart racing, but the door was still locked, and Cooper was still there, I saw as I pulled myself up to sit; flat out on the floor now, snoring like a drill.

Someone knocked – hard.

'You in there, Sim?' It was Vicky. 'Why's the door locked?'

I mumbled something unintelligible. I felt horrendous; more than horrendous. Bruised, sore, terrified, sick. Guilty.

'You'll never guess what I've just seen,' Vicky was hissing through the door.

'What?'

'Only bloody Jodie and Tom in bed together.'

'Oh really?' I said flatly. Unconvincingly probably. I tried harder. 'Oh no!'

'And someone keeps buzzing the front door. Can you get up please? I feel like I'm about to throw up again.'

'Give me a minute,' I said. 'I'll get dressed.'

I didn't know who was at the door for sure, but I could guess.

The police.

SIXTY-TWO

SIMONE

Isla del Diablo

'Thank God you came back when you did,' Vicky is saying to Tom, as I try to calm Mae down in the living room. 'It was colder than the Arctic in there.'

'Sim...' Hannah appears from the hallway. 'Come here a minute.' She beckons me urgently. 'You'll never believe this amazing moth I just saw.'

'But if my mum doesn't turn up... Oh God! I really need to talk to her about this.' Mae produces an envelope from her bum bag, looking like she's going to cry again.

'Simone!' Hannah's voice is pressing. 'Vicky.'

'She will turn up, angel,' I soothe.

'Mae, be a mate and put the kettle on for me,' Vicky says. 'We'll have a cuppa in a minute, yeah? I need to warm up.'

Confused, I follow Hannah down the hall, Vicky not far behind me, and into Jodie's bedroom. 'A *moth*?'

'No,' Hannah whispers, pointing through into the en suite.

Vicky slips in first.

'Blimey. Just get a load of *that*, would you.'

I stand in the doorway and stare at the mirror over the marble basin.

YOU'LL BE NEXT BITCH!

It's written in big shaky letters, with Jodie's best scarlet lipstick by the looks of the destroyed gold tube in the basin.

'I'd say it was melodramatic, but I'm getting a very bad feeling about all of this now.' Vicky flops on her back onto Jodie's unmade bed. 'I didn't believe her about that rock fall – my bad – but this is properly creepy. Someone just shut me in the fridge—'

'God! And what does it mean, *next*?' Hannah says slowly.

'Oh mate, don't be so pedantic,' Vicky says.

'Hannah's right,' I agree. 'Who's first?'

'Ever the wordsmith, eh?' Vicky sits up again. 'The point is – where the bloody hell *is* she?'

'Do you think...' I say what I've wondered since earlier. 'What if she *is* off cavorting with Gary? Like, for old times' sake?'

'Unless she's had a total brainstorm, I highly doubt it.' Vicky pulls a face. 'He's looking absolutely rank. I mean, why the fuck she ever went there, I don't know.'

'Well then – *has* something happened to her?'

'What are you doing?' Mae is at the bedroom door.

'Nothing.' I hurry out to prevent her seeing the stupid words. 'Sorry, just gossiping.' I take her arm. 'Shall we go and make that tea?'

'Only if it's peppermint,' she says, and I think, oh these teenagers. In our day it was all caffeine, fags and weed; now they vape blueberry mess and prefer camomile tea and mindfulness.

Then I think of Tiger and think: maybe not.

'Simone?' Mae looks morose, sitting at the table. 'Where do you reckon my mum is?'

'Ah, you know what Jodie's like.' I hunt through the assorted herbal tea bags. 'She'll turn up soon.'

But I think of the words on her mirror and wish I felt more convinced.

'I don't know if I do really,' Mae says. 'We've not really... We've been pretty distant these past few years.'

'You and me both, angel.' I turn the kettle on.

'Why?' Mae says, and I rue my careless words. Stupid.

'Oh, you know. Just busy really. Life gets in the way.' I choose the nicest mug I can find for her, one with little hearts on. 'And we don't live in the same town any more, so...'

'What was she like when you were young?'

'Jeez,' I sigh. 'Well, how long have you got?'

'Not sure.' Mae puts her big shades on and gazes out at the sea. 'All day apparently. Or the rest of my life, if we can't get off this bloody island.'

I want to reassure her. But all I can think of are Tiger and Mason's faces, and those eerie little voices last night – and I feel a wave of horror so strong I almost can't breathe.

How *would* I describe Jodie?

Once, I would have put 'loyal' at the very top of my list, but everything changed after what we learnt to call 'the incident'.

What we agreed to never talk about.

What we were too scared to talk about.

'Fierce, passionate, funny. Changeable as the weather,' I tell Mae now, pulling myself together. 'The original party animal.'

I pour water onto the tea bag. It smells of toothpaste.

And if something *has* happened to Jodie here in this supposed Paradise? How would I feel?

'Bright, outrageous, an absolute nightmare...' I hear the croak in my own voice.

I'd be devastated, that's the truth.

I may not want to hang out with her these days, although there's a part of me that's actually quite enjoyed it this past forty-eight hours, but...

'Let's just say she changed my life forever when I met her,' I say. 'And I think, largely, that was a good thing.'

'How terribly kind,' drawls a voice, and my worst best friend walks in. 'You sound like you're writing my obituary, Dilly.' She looks completely the worse for wear. 'Now don't forget to add sexy, gorgeous and the most fantastic disco dancer to the list.'

'Mum!' Mae gets up and flies to her, and to my great surprise, they hug for a long moment.

'Unreliable,' I mutter. 'And utterly selfish.'

But gazing at mother and daughter, Jodie still panda-eyed as she rests her chin on Mae's head, I feel that terrible yearning for Tiger again.

If I don't get off this island soon, I might commit murder myself.

'I'm going to make myself a cuppa, and then I'm going to have a shower,' Jodie says with a wan smile. 'And then I'd really like to talk to the Three Musketeers alone for a minute.'

I can't believe she's just used that expression.

She actually looks nervous, and it feels like we've entered a parallel universe, where everything I've worked at being for the past ten years is dissolving into the ether, into the once-cornflower-blue Mediterranean sky – now darkening rapidly, the moon slowly appearing, on its way out to cause havoc.

Mae's taken her peppermint tea outside to sit with her grandma, who's found a magnifying glass and is flicking through an old copy of OK! from the magazine pile in the lounge.

Whose glasses were on that poor dead rat? I wonder, feeling nauseous again. Were they Jodie's? Vicky's brought her contacts. Hannah hasn't worn her glasses since we got here.

Vicky's in the pool now, ploughing up and down doing showy lengths, competing with Daisy, I think, who has the most impressive butterfly stroke I've ever seen.

It's so hot still. Maybe I just need a cold dip myself, wash all this rubbish off. Just as I think this, something shoots into my head like a thunderbolt.

'Jodie!'

I hurry into the house, down the corridor, knocking quickly.

Her room's empty.

Should I wipe out the lipstick words? Maybe I should photograph them first as evidence – but my phone's on my bedside table.

I hurry back down the corridor and into my own room, where I see through my window Jodie talking to Tom under an orange tree on the far side of the garden, which is only visible from this side of the villa.

There's no way I can make sense of what they're discussing from here, but Tom looks angry... or is it upset? The light's fading and it's hard to tell exactly, but it's obviously not an easy conversation, judging by Jodie's body language.

I grab my phone and hurry back to her room.

As I walk back into the en suite, I feel something soft and yet kind of muscular under my bare foot, and I glance down.

My scream comes out of nowhere.

With a whimper, I launch myself onto the tousled bed.

Within seconds, Jodie appears. 'What is it?' She looks worried. 'What are you—'

'Stay there!' I whisper hoarsely. 'Don't move!'

'Simone?'

Mute with fear, I point to the corner of the bathroom, where the long brown snake has now coiled itself into a deadly pile behind the clothes bin.

And I realise there's the most terrible stink coming from the bathroom too – a stink I recognise from earlier today.

'Oh my God!'

Daisy, dripping wet and wrapped in a towel, follows Tom into the room. 'What's going on? Christ, what's that disgusting smell?' She holds her nose. 'Yuck!'

'Fragrance à la dead rat, I'm guessing. Oh, and Jodie' – Tom produces the smashed glasses from his shorts pocket – 'long story but I think these might be yours.'

Jodie nods slowly. 'You see!' Her eyes look enormous as she stares round at us. 'Someone's one hundred per cent trying to kill me.'

The three of us sit round the outside table, candles lit, waiting for Hannah, who's fetching a cardigan for some bizarre reason, given the heat. Because she's too thin probably.

Tom is dealing with the snake – which so far has just meant finding an empty crate in the utility room and trying to place it over the hissing creature while he works out what to do. He's assured us he's fine, sending us outside to talk to Jodie as she requested.

The smell came from the laundry bin, in which Tom found another dead rat. Vicky suggests the snake brought it in, and everyone else tells her not to be stupid.

I know nothing about snakes, and we can't even look it up to see if it's poisonous. 'Pretty sure snakes are indigenous to Ibiza,' Hannah says.

'Big words, Han!' Jodie retorts.

But sitting round the table drinking in the last of the amazing sunset, for a minute I can almost forget our woes. I can *almost* fool myself we're back in Royal Mews, or even the Dive in March Street.

We were happier in the Dive, I think. We had better parties; we had a laugh all the time, or it seems like we did now.

We definitely had parties that didn't end in death.

'Sorry if I scared you all. I had to go off and reckon with myself for a bit.' Jodie fiddles with a cigarette, but for once she doesn't light it. She's tied her hair up off her face and scrubbed all the make-up off.

In this light, she looks almost as young as when we first met.

'Reckon with yourself?' I'm curious. 'What do you mean?'

Now the truth will finally out – maybe.

'Because I've done something bad.' Now she fiddles with her lighter.

'Everyone falls off the wagon sometimes.' Vicky is actually being nice and soothing for once, which makes a change since we got here. 'Don't beat yourself up. And it's not surprising really, what with Gary and your mum both being here.'

'Ha,' Jodie says. 'Well, thanks for the sympathy.'

'Has Gary turned up yet?'

'I don't know. His sense of direction was always crap, and so was his timekeeping.'

'We thought you'd gone off for a shag,' Vicky says.

I see a shadow pass over Jodie's face, and then I realise it's actually a bat, flitting in and out of the trees behind her.

'Don't be stupid, babe,' she fires back. 'I'd rather eat my own arm.'

'You know, it's kind of like that TV show.' Vicky seems almost excited.

'What show?' I wonder if she's drunk. It seems quite likely, given how much she's been putting away since we met up on Thursday.

'Where they drop them on an island and they have to survive.'

'*Survivor*? Except *they* can just radio through for help,' I point out. Mason loves that programme. 'And they have medics and boats on hand.'

'Anyway, look.' Jodie seems tearful – so unlike her, I'm

shocked. 'I mean, it's a bit crap, but I have to admit something to you all.'

'Don't tell me.' Hannah has appeared out of nowhere, without her cardigan, the candlelight sending strange shadows across her face. 'You did it again.'

'What?'

'Sit down, Han.' I push a chair out for her.

'You know what I mean, Jodie.' Hannah sits down very slowly. 'And I guess you're going to say that you just couldn't help yourself.'

'What's that?' Vicky points past me.

We all look round.

Smoke is trickling up into the sky.

There's a fire on the hillside, and it takes me back to the time around the terrible accident on *The Daffodil*.

SIXTY-THREE

THEN

'I've been at the insurance company.' Hannah's pretty grey eyes were magnified by new milk-bottle glasses as she sat at the kitchen table. 'They said they had more questions.'

'Are you OK?' Tom looked concerned. He was round at the Dive for a curry that Vicky and I were cooking, Jodie having just returned from a trip.

'The loss adjuster won't pay out, they said. The electrics were probably faulty. It wasn't my boat anyway; it was Nick's friend Jon's, so he's the one who's losing out, but I do keep thinking.' Hannah wiped her eyes quickly with her hand. 'I know Nick was wasted, of course, but *why* did he go to the boat?' Her expression was hard to read. Almost pleading maybe. 'Why didn't he just come and find me?'

Wrapped in a long black coat with a baggy old beanie hat on her head, she looked like a child from a Victorian workhouse.

'Just went to crash out, don't you think?' I was wary of saying something stupid. I still found her pain unimaginable. 'To sleep?'

'Who knows why anyone does anything?' Vicky sounded

sage, but her words were kind of meaningless, if you actually considered them.

'Maybe. But if I'd known...' Hannah's eyes filled again. 'I could have stopped him.'

'Or you might have been with him and died too,' Tom said bluntly.

'Tom!' I poked him in the ribs. 'Don't!'

'Well, sorry, but it's true. Also, it wouldn't make any difference if you did know why, would it? You can't change what happened.'

'I guess.' Hannah found a tissue and blew her nose. 'But if he hadn't—'

'But he did.' I gave the kitchen counter a pointless wipe. 'And that's one hundred per cent not your fault.'

'It was over between me and Nick really.' Hannah looked so sad, so lost and wan, it broke my heart. 'We'd already said we'd have a break till he got back from New York.'

The police had questioned her thoroughly at the time; the insurance people were cold, and none of it was helping her mental health, we could see.

'They kept saying someone had left the gas on,' she said. 'But it wasn't me, I'm sure. I didn't cook anything that day; I'd been at work at the print shop all day. Then we'd met in town before the party, to get drink from the cash and carry.'

'Just ignore it.' Jodie was prosaic. 'You know what insurers are like.'

'Not really.' Hannah sniffed into the cup of tea I'd made her.

The most likely and official scenario seemed to be that Nick had been smoking on the bed where his body had been found. He must have fallen asleep, dropping a burning cigarette. The bedspread had caught fire, then the rickety old boat, with its leaky gas canister left on. The fire spread, the gas caught and – boom!

'It's not your fault, mate.' Vicky was fierce, holding Hannah's hand tightly across the table. 'There's no way it's your fault.'

I tried not to look at Jodie. I had a nasty feeling in my belly, like a little mouse skipping around, though I couldn't say why exactly. Was it the very faint suspicion I had about why Nick might have left the party?

I thrust that thought as far away as possible as we all comforted Hannah as best we could, but it was hard when she seemed to feel so terribly guilty about it all.

It was why later on, I was always so pleased that Tom liked her so much.

It was a second chance.

SIXTY-FOUR

HANNAH

Isla del Diablo

'Wildfire?' I feel utter terror for a second, my hands immediately clammy, sweat breaking out beneath my armpits. 'Is it spreading?'

'No,' Simone says quickly. 'It's not, Han. It's OK.'

They don't know I dream of fire all the time – choking, suffocating fire – and when I wake, sweating and pounding the bed furiously with my fists or clutching my damp sheets in both hands until I'm calm enough to let them go, I don't dare sleep again.

I tried meditation; I tried hypnotherapy with a henna-haired woman who seemed sympathetic and also a little mad. Then, when I realised I couldn't get what I needed from my own doctor, I started to find the pills I needed online. I'm not proud of it, but I was desperate.

'Someone's lit a bonfire,' Jodie says with relief as a figure waves down at us. 'Up on the hill.'

Tom, I think. Unless it's Gary.

Anger floods me, leaving me breathless for a second.

'Probably trying to attract attention.' Vicky takes my hand. 'Like smoke signals?' The figure is fanning the flames. 'Sit back down, hon.'

I perch on the very edge of the bamboo chair, and I can feel myself trembling with emotion.

'What were you saying?' Jodie asks me. 'Or accusing me of?'

'What I wanted to know was' – I have to be braver, say what has bothered me all this time – 'didn't you have enough of him the first time?'

Jodie frowns. 'Who?'

'Tom, you fool.' Vicky is tart. 'Keep up!'

'All right, Vick.' Simone rolls her eyes. 'At least be polite, would you?'

'Tom? No way.' Jodie reaches out to touch me, but I pull away. 'I think you've got the wrong end of the stick – honest.'

'But I *saw* you.' I stare at her. 'With my very own eyes, an hour ago.'

'Saw what?' Jodie sounds frustrated. 'This is just not true, babe.'

'Don't *babe* me.' A tear falls from my eye and tracks down my cheek. But I don't move, don't brush it away. 'You always got away with everything; you charmed us all, all the time, strutting around with no clothes on, always so confident – but this is too much now.'

'Got away with what though?'

'You *know* what.'

Mae comes out of the villa, hovers nearby.

'Mae, baby, please,' Jodie says desperately, 'could you just go and see if your gran's OK?'

'She's in the jacuzzi *again*,' Mae grumbles, but she's a bit slurry, and I wonder if she's been drinking.

'Mae!' Daisy stands in the open doors of the villa in a pair of pink dungarees. 'Fancy a game of cards? And when Gary gets back, we can all play poker!'

'OK.' Mae wanders back inside. She definitely looks a bit vacant.

'Hannah.' Jodie turns to me now that Mae's safely gone. 'You *have* to believe me.'

'What, like I did about Nick?'

'What about Nick?' Jodie immediately looks wary.

'I know you were with him the night of the fire.' I gaze at the pathetic little bonfire that Tom has lit up there, and I think I'd happily never see fire again.

'How do you know that?'

'Oh, for God's sake,' Vicky expostulates, 'we all bloody know that.'

Jodie, for once in her life, is silent.

'I'm not even sure you didn't actually kill him,' I blurt out.

'What?' Now she jerks back to life. '*Kill* Nick? Don't be stupid!'

I remember – so vividly – when I saw the report they'd tried to hide from me. The photograph of her bag by the bed on the houseboat. My bed. Everything I'd feared but not allowed myself to know confirmed.

And I remember how I had to go to the police, and to the insurance company, and be grilled about the boat. All because of Jodie.

'I loved you both. You and Nick.' Jodie is grim. 'I'm not a killer, Hannah.'

'I mean, not necessarily on purpose,' I concede, 'but you got him wasted, and then you left him, and then...' But the words literally stick in my throat.

'He was wasted enough on his own,' Jodie mutters, and Simone strokes my hand on the table and I let her.

'Han, I know it was the worst thing, what happened, but he was absolutely off his head, wasn't he? And that's not Jodie's fault.'

Yes, of course I know Nick had the biggest appetite for

drink and drugs of anyone I'd ever met; he was the ultimate hedonist. And it was what drove us apart even before he said he was leaving for America, but I can't believe Jodie won't take some responsibility now.

After all these years, I'd just like her to say sorry.

I ignore Simone. 'You might even have set fire to the boat,' I say. 'And another thing.' I dash my tears away now. 'Another thing is – I don't even think anyone's trying to hurt you here. I think you're making it up.'

'What, am I throwing rocks at my own head?' Jodie lights her cigarette. 'Yeah, sure, Hannah. I love to plant snakes in my room, and write things on my mirror, and all the rest.'

I shrug. 'The writing – you could have done it. The rock – well, unfortunately, we only have your word for it.'

'If you say so.' Jodie's face is unreadable. She was always brilliant at hiding her emotions. 'But do tell me why I'd bother.'

'Well, you tell us what you were about to admit to, and then I can finish my theory.' I toy with the candle wax dripping down onto the table. I want to squeeze it, really hard.

'I was about to say...' Jodie drags on her cigarette. Exhales slowly, a dragon's plume in the dusky air. 'OK – here goes. I was about to admit that I *did* want you all to come. Because I've had an offer I couldn't refuse.'

'An offer?'

'Except then I changed my mind.'

'What offer?' Vicky demands.

'I said no.'

'To what?'

'I was going to write about you all.' Jodie says it very fast. 'My old editor offered me the gig.'

'Again?' Vicky raises her eyes to heaven.

'Yes. Again.'

'Didn't you do enough damage the first time?'

'Yes. No. Oh, I don't know.' Jodie inhales again. 'I'm sure I did.'

'And you stole Simone's job.'

'What? When?'

'Back then,' Vicky says angrily. 'Why pretend?'

'I didn't actually *steal* it.' Jodie sounds miserable.

'You did,' I say. 'I remember distinctly the week it happened.'

'Look, it's fine, girls,' Simone says. 'I was never going to write that kind of stuff myself, so...' She shrugs.

'What kind of stuff?'

'Putting it all out there,' she says. 'I didn't have it in me.'

'You mean you were too honourable,' Vicky says.

Tom has just appeared, looking sweaty, dirty marks on his white T-shirt. He stands there for a second – looking at me, I think, though it's so dim I can't really tell, and my stomach rolls round like a washing machine.

Then he goes inside.

'No, I just didn't want to share my innermost thoughts,' Simone is saying. 'And it's fine, really. I didn't want to be a journalist, I don't think. That's why I wasn't sure about that last job offer.'

'Don't let her off the hook.' I feel exasperated.

'I'm not. I've loved being a full-time mum. It was such a brilliant thing when I had Tiger. She meant everything to me, after...' Simone looks round at us and her eyes are really fierce. 'You know. So it's fine.'

'Is it though?' Vicky says.

'Yes. But...' Simone speaks slower now. 'Let me get this straight, Jodie – you asked us out here to write about us?'

'I had a brilliant offer. I turned it down.'

Vicky is frowning. 'But who would want—'

There's a shriek from the villa, and we all jump to our feet. 'What was that?'

'It's Mae!' Daisy appears from inside, white-faced. 'Please, she's acting really weird.'

'Where is she?' Jodie's on her feet, running to the door. 'What's happened?'

'I don't know.' Daisy follows her. 'But it's like she's really out of it.'

On the far side of the living room, Tom is trying to hold on to Mae, but the young woman is thrashing wildly against him, shouting something incoherent.

Then I realise that she's saying, 'You're not my dad!' crying it over and over, and Tom's got his arms round her, but she's raging desperately against him, pushing at him, and for a moment I think: what did he do?

Her eyes are scarily unfocused and she's running with sweat.

'She's having a hypo.' Jodie's voice is low and urgent as she takes over from Tom. 'Can someone run to her room and get her insulin? In a red leather case – looks like a kind of writing case.'

'I'll go.' Vicky's already on her way.

'Mae, baby, it's OK.' Jodie tries to calm her daughter. 'It's all going to be fine.' She speaks over the girl's head. 'She needs sugar please, someone, fast.'

Without being asked, Simone has already fetched a can of Coke from the fridge, and she cracks it open.

'Drink this, angel.' She holds it to Mae's lips as Jodie encircles her with her arms.

'Come on, baby,' Jodie coaxes. 'Drink it and you'll feel better.'

I stand uselessly next to Daisy, who's crying now, then I grab the broom from the cupboard to sweep up the shards of crockery from the floor. I'm guessing Mae knocked them off the counter, where they were being unloaded from the dishwasher.

Tom looks as helpless as I feel, running his hands back and forth through his hair.

'Han,' he says, but I stare down at the floor as I sweep.

'Not now.'

'But—'

'Tom.' I meet his eye. 'Leave it, please.'

He looks like he wants to be sick. 'We need to talk,' he mutters, but Vicky is returning now.

'I found it.' She's ashen-faced. 'But I'm not sure it's meant to look like this.'

She holds out the case to show Jodie, who flicks through the contents.

'For fuck's sake!' she mutters, chucking it aside. 'Keep giving her the Coke, yeah, Dilly? I'll just be a second.' She races to her own room.

I listen to Simone cooing banalities to Mae, who takes tiny sips of the drink, and I think what a natural mother Simone is, for all her own doubts; doubts she's voiced occasionally.

'I never go anywhere without spares.' Jodie's back with a smaller black pencil case. 'Thank God.'

Coolly but lovingly, she injects Mae. Her composure and her concentration is impressive, and slowly, slowly we watch Mae begin to calm down.

I pick up the other case, the red leather one, and open it.

All the little insulin vials have been emptied.

'Looks pretty deliberate to me,' Jodie murmurs, catching my eye. 'So what do you say now, Hannah? All in my mind?'

I have to admit I might have been wrong.

SIXTY-FIVE
VICKY

Jodie and Mae go to bed in Mae's room, because even though Tom says he's got rid of the snake, Jodie's not convinced.

'And I'll be locking the door,' she says loudly, but then two minutes later, she comes back. 'The bloody key's gone. Some-one's taking the absolute piss now.'

Simone checks her room, and Tom his – and we realise the keys have been removed from all the doors.

'Just put something against it if you're that paranoid,' I say, though it does seem really odd.

Jodie scowls. 'Paranoid?'

'Worried,' I correct myself. 'I meant if you're worried.'

'Wouldn't you be?'

I feel confused about everything that's going on. Do I feel scared though?

Not really. I'm sure Antonio will turn up tomorrow and this will be over. So I don't feel like I've got anything to feel scared about.

Someone's playing games though, and who knows who or why?

. . .

Everyone else disappears off to bed as I hug Hannah goodnight.

She's still shaken after the Mae incident, I can tell; upset about the conversation before that too.

'Sit up with me?' I say, but she murmurs that she's tired.

I take my vodka on the rocks outside; a pathetic measure, sadly, because the bottle's nearly finished.

We're running out of provisions faster and faster, so thank God tomorrow's nearly here.

Except – I don't really want to go home. Despite all the stress, the weirdness and the tension here, I don't want to face Dave.

On the terrace, the sky is huge and dark, Ibiza lit up like a fairyland in the distance, and I realise I feel sad. I haven't allowed myself to think since we got here, but it's not hard to understand why.

The whole Tom and Hannah thing has been incredibly tough to watch. It's brought up old hurts, scoring them out of me again painfully, like the deadly scalpel on the old lino prints Hannah used to make. It feels like actual pain.

'For God's sake, Victoria,' I mutter, furious that hot tears have sprung to my eyes.

I hear footsteps behind me.

She came back, I think, with the thrill of euphoria.

'Hey,' says a voice.

'Hey,' I say. 'Any sign of your best beloved?'

'Don't be a bitch, Vicky.'

Daisy sits on the swing seat beside me, sending it rocking.

I steady myself; sip my drink, listening to the ice cubes clinking against the side of the glass.

'That stupid note – what did it mean, hon?' I ask. 'I meant to ask you before.'

'What note?' She pushes the seat back and forth with a bare foot.

'The note in my purse.'

'Don't know what you're talking about.'

'You do, hon.' I know it was her.

But instead of replying, she leans over and tries to kiss me.

SIXTY-SIX
SIMONE

I sit in my room, thinking.

I think of my kids and my husband, and how desperately I miss them, and what the hell it's going to take to get off the bloody island.

If we're not collected, I can't swim it, I know that much. I'd try, but I doubt I could make it.

I think I'll check on Hannah before I go to sleep, make sure she's OK.

But something else is lurking in a corner of my mind, and I struggle to retrieve it – something I've seen in the past few hours, in the wrong place.

As I walk down the corridor, I spot movement through the window. A man is striding along the crest of the hill. Gary at last. Can't say I've missed him. I'd rather never see him again, all things considered: he's a reminder of the day my life changed course.

But Hannah's not in her room. I'm guessing she's gone to walk in the moonlight again. Or maybe she's somewhere with Tom. Second chances and all that.

Her case is on the bed, open. Maybe she's been packing, but

it's a mess, whatever she's been up to. I walk to the door, and then I pause in my tracks and turn back, struck by something I've half seen.

Something sticking out from beneath that salt-stained dress.

I pull it out: a big bag of pills, just like Vicky said. I didn't really believe it; I thought Vicky might have hallucinated it that night at Finca Maria.

I sift through them – Ambien, OxyContin, Xanax. Pills I'd associate with America, not England. I remember the customs officers at the airport.

Poor Hannah. Left to care for her parents while everyone else gets on with life. Broken-hearted about Nick, and then Tom.

But it's clear Tom still likes her, so at least now maybe she can start over. She certainly deserves that second chance. Or is it a third?

I put the pills back and slip into Mae's room, where Jodie's in the shower and Mae is sleeping curled up on her side, a bit of colour back in her cheeks.

It's very tidy in here. I noted it earlier when I came with Jodie to lie Mae down.

She must be the opposite of her mum. The polar opposite of my own whirlwind Tiger.

On the floor is a pile of folded discarded clothes; dirty washing probably, ready to repack.

And there's something sticking out of Mae's balled-up underwear. A black handle. I noted it absently earlier.

Now I nudge the clothes with my foot carefully, and I see the thing I half glimpsed before.

A knife.

The missing kitchen knife.

SIXTY-SEVEN
VICKY

Daisy leans across and tries to kiss me, and I think, oh no, I don't even fancy you any more.

'Not here, Dais.' I push her off gently. 'It's just not... appropriate.' But I wince at myself, knowing I sound like an old fogey. 'I'm sorry.'

'You're ashamed of me,' she mutters. 'I knew it.'

'No, mate, I'm not. I'm just...'

'You're not out to them, that's what you mean.' She sighs heavily.

'And you're Gary's girlfriend.'

'Well *you* didn't want me.' She glowers at the floor. 'And he did, so—'

'Daisy!' I look at her. 'That's not true, flower, and you know it. But this isn't healthy. Did you ever really want Gary?'

'Not at first,' she admits, tears in her eyes. 'I just wanted to hurt you.'

'I really am sorry.' I think maybe it's my fault, that I haven't apologised properly. 'I mean, it was amazing, you and me—'

'While it lasted, you mean.' Daisy is angry.

'But you always knew I was married.'

'To a man you don't love.'

'To a man I *do* love.' I finish my drink, savouring the heat of the vodka in the back of my throat.

I think about how miserable it's been with Dave this past six months; how we often sleep in separate bedrooms. I think about my dad, who, when he caught me in bed with my best female friend from school, aged seventeen, locked me in the draughty cellar for a day and a night, calling me revolting. Rationally I knew it wasn't, but I couldn't ever quite get the memory or his voice out of my head.

My relationship with him, already strained, never recovered. My shame eternally sealed in, the same sort of time I discovered vodka.

'I love Dave loads.' I ease myself off the seat. 'He's just the wrong sex. But you're right, Daisy. I'm fully to blame, and it's time I faced the music.'

On the way back to my room, I hear a voice coming from Jodie's.

Simone, I'm sure.

I'm about to knock when I hear her say, 'You can't tell her the truth – it'll break her heart.' A tiny pause. 'She'll know we lied.'

My clenched fist remains in the air, still poised to knock, as a tidal wave of shock crashes over me.

They've been in this together the whole time; pretending they didn't know why we were here. But they obviously set it up.

And on top of the ultimate betrayal, there's bloody Daisy.

I knew it was a mistake to sleep with my waitress when it started six months ago, but somehow I couldn't help myself.

But as it turned out, it was a far bigger mistake to let her meet Gary, when I asked him to visit me at the café.

I was always worried about the Gary thing, but it really came back to bite me.

I wanted to come out here to be with the one I loved, but instead...

What a mess.

SIXTY-EIGHT

JODIE

Isla del Diablo

I wake gasping from the most horrific nightmare, with such a bad feeling in my gut that I immediately prod Mae beside me.

Thank God, though, she mumbles something. I can see now she's sleeping soundly, colour in her cheeks again, her breathing regular and soft.

But something's not right.

At least it's the morning and we survived the night: that's a win, I suppose.

I did get up again briefly, very late, after Simone left, to get a drink from the kitchen – and I nearly broke my abstinence vow again, my hand lingering over the last of the cold wine.

But then I heard voices – Vicky outside, talking, or rather ranting, to someone, Hannah most likely, no doubt about me – and I slunk back to bed.

Now I pull the chair away from the door where I wedged it last night, and tiptoe down the hallway to Simone's room. How helpful that our names are all emblazoned on the doors. Simone has a picture of a club from a card deck beside her name. What the hell's that about?

I knock gently. 'Dilly?'

I think I hear movement inside the room, but my eye is caught by something outside on the edge of the sundeck.

An arm, protruding from the jacuzzi.

My heart stops in my chest; then, running down the hall-way, I scream for help.

'Mum?'

She's slumped in the bloody jacuzzi, her head just out of the water.

'Mum! Wake up.' I shake her, but her mouth is slack, her eyes shut. She's freezing to touch, though the water is still quite warm.

It's Simone who arrives first, thank God, with her nursing know-how.

She feels Mum's wrist. 'She's got a pulse, but it's incredibly faint. We need to get her out of the water, warm her up.'

The day is humid, cloudy for the first time, but my mum's skin feels icy.

How could I have not noticed she was out here all night?

'Mum?' I lean down, biting my fear back.

'I wonder if she might have had a stroke, Jodie,' Simone's saying as Tom arrives, pulling his T-shirt on. 'Looks like she's been sick.' There's vomit in the water, I realise.

Tom pulls my mother out of the jacuzzi as gently as he can, which isn't to say she doesn't still look like a sack of potatoes, and we wrap her in towels. And then I realise I have no clue what to do, whereas the other two seem much more efficient.

There's a glass and an empty wine bottle on the deck where her head was, I notice; the glass is covered in white powdery residue.

'Look!'

'Soluble pills, I'm guessing?' Simone sniffs it.

'Maybe she had a headache?' Tom suggests.

'Or maybe someone drugged her,' I say stiffly.

'Surely not,' Tom says. 'Who would do that?'

'Oh God, what's happened now?' A weepy-looking Daisy arrives in that prissy white nightie again, a pink satin sleep mask on top of her head. 'And Gary didn't come back last night.'

Half listening, I spot a tube of prescription pills in the ridge of the jacuzzi. It looks empty. Is Mum taking meds for a condition I don't know about?

'Try not to panic,' Tom tells Daisy, while I feel like shouting: *Stop being so bloody nice all the time.*

How little I know about my own mother; how badly we fell apart after my dad did what he did. She was never a maternal sort of woman, and I was busy.

I was very busy, running from my demons.

Tom grabs a cushion as I stand there stupidly. Carefully he slides it under my mum's head. I could kiss him, but I don't.

I won't ever go near Tom again.

I pick up the pill bottle instead.

'I *swore* I heard him come in last night.' Wide-eyed, Daisy twists her hands together miserably. 'But I took a sleeping pill.' She looks guilty. 'I hardly ever do, but you know, I was so tired from worrying about him.'

The label's been ripped off this pill bottle, I realise.

'I saw him,' Simone says. 'Gary. I'm sure. On the hill last night, when I went to bed.'

'And did you do that alone?' Now Vicky's here too, dark glasses on, hair on end. She looks like she's had a rough night. 'Go to bed?'

'Of course.' Simone frowns. 'What do you mean?'

'Oh, did you!' Daisy sounds pathetically grateful. 'Perhaps

he did come back then, but now I've overslept and...' Her voice breaks. 'Well, I still haven't seen him.'

Noises start to come from the living room. Music, or voices, I'm not sure – the television must have come on.

I look around. I know Mae's safely asleep in her bedroom, and everyone else is here, apart from Gary – and Hannah.

'Where's Hannah?' I ask, looking at the pills.

Hannah, whose fury with me was evident last night.

'I don't know.' Vicky shrugs. 'Not in her room though.'

SIXTY-NINE

THEN

DECEMBER 2003

The police didn't come that terrible morning, although I waited breathlessly for hours to be arrested.

The knock at the door was enough to terrify me.

'We've been tolerant.' The downstairs neighbour was lean and gleaming in expensive running gear, wrinkling her nose at the mess behind me. 'But if you carry on like this, we'll call the police immediately. Last night was the final straw.'

'OK,' I said politely. 'I'm very sorry. Really. Won't happen again.'

I was about to close the door when Jodie squeezed past me, face made up, collar turned up.

'People to see.' She winked at me and vanished down the emergency stairs.

As I walked back to my room, something out on the balcony caught my eye, and my stomach lurched savagely.

Robert Perry's cigar end.

I'd been praying that it had all been a terrible dream.

But the bruises on my arms, on my wrist and on my inner thighs, my sore knees where I'd fallen on them. The dull throbbing pain inside me.

They all said it was real.

Perhaps Perry had got up and walked away, and that's why the police hadn't come.

But then what if there was CCTV on this building? There was an intercom, though it wasn't a video one; there was a concierge office in the lobby, which was manned in the daytime.

A cold shudder went through me.

I washed myself thoroughly again and forced myself to get dressed. I slugged back some of Jodie's stashed bourbon, then took a mop and bucket onto the balcony, where, carefully, as if it would burn me, I picked up the soggy cigar end with a trembling hand.

'What the hell, mate?' Vicky knocked on the glass, making me jump badly. 'You washing the floor out there? It's not dirty, *and* it's raining.'

'Humour me.' I tried to smile, my hood up against the last of the day. I tucked the cigar end into my jeans pocket, and for a split second, as Vicky turned away, I contemplated climbing the railing and jumping.

The most terrible vertigo attacked me suddenly, the world spinning, and I clung on, my knuckles turning white. Imagine what it must be like to fall from here.

'Fancy a cuppa, mate?' Vicky knocked again, her face quizzical.

The world righted itself.

'Come in now. It's foul out there.'

Half an hour later, I limped down to the river, feeling like I'd been beaten up. Standing on the small bridge, I threw that cigar butt as far and hard as I could.

The grey water closed around it, and it was as if it had never been there. But I could remember every single second of last night's terrible events, and clutching the railing desperately, I contemplated jumping again.

An elderly woman with a shopping trolley stopped nearby. 'You all right there, ducky?'

'Not really,' I croaked, and I started to cry.

When I got back to the flat, bedraggled from the rain, someone was there, and for a moment, I panicked.

But it wasn't the police. It was the boy with the bright eyes, his feet up on a chair, reading Vicky's Jamie Oliver cookbook. Jodie's brother Mikey. He had a little anchor tattoo on his wrist too, I noticed absently.

'All right?' he said cheerfully. 'Have a good night?'

'What are you doing here?' I asked dully. I had no capacity to feel anything much.

'Little favour for my sister.' He grinned. Then he looked more closely. 'Or a bad night maybe? You look terrible.'

There was a video cassette on the table, I noticed idly. We didn't have a video player though.

'Thanks very much.'

'Still gorgeous,' he said. 'But terrible too. Sorry I had to dash off early.'

And I started to cry again.

He'd just got up to put an arm round me when Hannah walked in, followed closely by Jodie and Vicky. Vicky stared at Jodie with fury.

'You've got something to say, haven't you, Jodie?'

'I think we'd better all have a chat,' Jodie sighed.

Was this the moment when everything hidden was finally revealed?

SEVENTY

SIMONE

Isla del Diablo

The noise from the living room is distracting as Jodie and Vicky start arguing again.

Some things never change. Never a match made in heaven, for all the good times we had back in the day, they were both too alpha. Leaders, not followers, unlike Hannah and me. Or maybe just me. Hannah always trod her own path really, before her parents dragged her back home.

'You're trying to make out someone wants to kill you – well I think you're trying to throw us off,' Vicky tells Jodie flatly. 'You hate your mum, so this is the perfect opportunity.'

'So why are your pills here, if it was me?' Jodie flashes the bottle in her hand. 'And I don't hate my poor mum.' She glances at Sue, and honestly, her face does look stricken.

Vicky shrugs. 'Perfect set-up. You always hated Hannah too, for nicking Tom off you. And they're not my pills.'

'What? I don't hate Hannah either; I love her.' Jodie laughs incredulously. 'Pot, kettle, Vicky. It was *you* who wanted Tom.'

'No, I didn't. Tom really wasn't that special.'

'Um...' Tom coughs. 'I am here.'

'Sorry, mate. Just saying.'

'Are you saying someone's tried to kill Sue?' Daisy's gearing up for a panic attack. 'Oh God, this is just crazy now! You lot' – she looks around her wildly – 'you're *all* bloody mad.'

I think I'd have to agree.

Absently I watch the clouds gather over Ibiza. They're thick and dark, obscuring the sun, and it's incredibly humid now, the air sticky with wet heat.

The storm that's been threatening for days is arriving at last.

'And Mae?' Jodie rounds on Vicky. 'You seriously think I'd try to kill my own daughter? Piss off, Vicky.'

'But you hate Gary, don't you?' Daisy hisses at Jodie now. 'So what have you done to him?'

'Yeah.' Vicky grins at Jodie. 'What have you done to poor old Coops?'

'I'm going to get a blanket for Sue.' Tom looks rattled.

'Why don't you shut the fuck up, Vicky?' Jodie snaps.

'Frankly, *babe*' – Vicky pulls hard on her vape – 'given what I already know about you, I'd put nothing past you. Literally nothing.'

'Whereas you' – Jodie's face has drained of colour – 'you're lily-white, yeah, *babe*? God, I'd forgotten how annoying you are.'

'Not lily-white, that's true,' Vicky says, 'but I've got nothing on you.'

And I'm shot back twenty years again, to the arguments the day after Robert Perry fell from the balcony.

'You need to tell her the truth,' I could hear Vicky hissing at Jodie.

'Tell who what?' Hannah smiled, obviously just relieved to be back from her parents'. She put the kettle on. 'How was the party last night?'

'Awful,' I said dully.

The intercom buzzed and my heart nearly leapt into my mouth.

But it was only Tom.

'Tea?' Hannah rushed to hug him, but he was stiff, looking about as terrible as I felt.

'I need to talk to you,' he muttered to her.

Vicky looked smug. 'At least *someone's* got a conscience.'

'I'm gonna hit the road,' Mikey said. 'Bit tense here.'

He went into Jodie's room for a bit while I made some tea.

'See you later, gorgeous,' he said on his way out, slipping the video tape inside his leather jacket. 'Hope you're OK.'

Please don't go, I thought dumbly.

As if he read my mind, he paused at the front door. 'Fancy a drink on the square?'

The others were arguing now, Vicky and Jodie snarling at each other.

'Leave this lot to it? You look like you need cheering up.'

'Oh yes please,' I said, and I followed him out before anyone else could ask to come.

I heard Tom say to Hannah, desperately, 'But nothing actually happened,' as I closed the door behind me.

In the lift, I asked what favour Jodie had asked of him.

'She just said something bad happened.' Mikey looked at me intently, and I saw how dark his lashes were; I was such a sucker for nice eyes. 'A terrible thing. She asked me to get rid of something, just in case.'

The video tape. The CCTV.

SEVENTY-TWO

SIMONE

Isla del Diablo

'Sorry, girls.' I drag myself back to the present, feeling Sue's pulse, which is weaker still. 'But Sue *really* needs a hospital.'

'And how do you propose we get her there?' Vicky mocks. 'Build a raft? A rocket ship? We're totally stuck if that Antonio doesn't come back.'

'I'm a strong swimmer,' Daisy says, pacing up and down. 'If the worst comes to the worst—'

'Oh, do me a favour,' Vicky snaps.

'Why do you have to be nasty to me?' Daisy's sobbing now. 'I just want to get off this island.' She's tipping into hysteria. 'And where's Gary?'

'Calm down.' Vicky puts an arm round her in a way that surprises me. 'I'm sorry I snapped, hon.'

Tom rushes out with a blanket, looking even more shaken. 'I think you need to come and see this.'

We all hurry inside as he attends to Sue.

Footage is playing on the plasma screen: grainy, out-of-focus, shaky camerawork, but the people in the shots are unmistakable.

'Jeez,' I breathe as a clip of Gary and Jodie arguing plays. There's Hannah and Tom, talking in the orange grove; there's Mae, topless on the viewpoint. There's me carrying the cool box, looking over my shoulder; there's a badly lit Daisy and Vicky, Daisy leaning in for a kiss.

'Oh yeah?' Jodie looks at them both, and Daisy looks like she's going to melt into the ground.

'It's not what it looks like.'

'It is though, isn't it?' Vicky says wearily. 'It's time I came clean.'

'My God!' Tom has joined us now, standing open-mouthed. 'I saw a few security cameras around the place, but I didn't realise we were being filmed.'

Now Vicky's on the screen, looking furtive; she's fiddling around with her phone, setting it up on the mantelpiece above the fake fire.

'It was you!' Jodie turns to her, eyes blazing. 'You're trying to make out I'm the baddie here, but you're blatantly filming.'

'No, mate, you're not pinning this on me.' Vicky goes to the corner where velvet curtains cover the wine cellar doors. 'Look...' She points up at a camera. 'I saw this on Friday, when we got here, and I didn't trust it, so I did my own detective work.'

Mae comes out of her room, looking bleary. 'What's going on?'

'Good question,' Tom says. He's angry, I think.

'Anyone?' Vicky asks, glancing round. 'Anyone going to own up?'

'To what?' Hannah appears from the garden. She looks like she hasn't slept.

The clouds have moved in so quickly, it's alarming, the sky darkening rapidly.

'Where've you been, Han?' Vicky extends a hand to her, but Hannah pushes it away.

'I went to see if the boat was coming back for us. Own up to what—' But then she sees the screen, a shot of her and Tom, not quite kissing, but almost. 'Oh.'

In the distance, thunder sounds.

'What's going on?' Daisy furls and unfurls her hands. 'Who'd do this?'

Staring up at the footage of Hannah and Tom, Vicky looks mortified.

'Oh God.' Jodie slumps onto the sofa. 'I haven't got the energy to argue any more. I just want to go home.'

'Jodie?' I look at her.

'OK,' she says slowly. 'But I need a strong drink before I confess.'

'Mum!' Mae says. 'For God's sake!'

'Well, honestly.' Jodie pats her pockets – for her cigarettes, I guess.

'Go on then,' Vicky prompts. 'Confess. You tried to kill your own mum.' Her voice is full of something I can't quite put my finger on. 'Nice work.'

'No,' Jodie cries. 'I'd never do that.'

Mae frowns. 'What's wrong with Gran?'

'She's out there.' Vicky points at Sue on the sunlounger. 'But she can't tell you.'

'Vicky,' I say, as Mae rushes outside. 'Don't be so cruel.'

'Gran!' Mae is shaking her grandmother.

'We need to do something for Sue,' I say, but the others aren't listening, lost to their anger.

'You're a cow, Vicky. I'll confess if you do too, babe.' Jodie stares at her.

'To what?'

'You know what. It's time you told Hannah exactly how you feel.'

'Oh shut up, you bitch.' Vicky's eyes spark furiously. 'You blackmailed me with that once before, but not again.'

'*Hannah?*' I repeat. But of course; how utterly thick I've been.

Hannah sits on the armchair. 'What did you do, Jodie?' she asks quietly.

'I asked you to come here, OK?' Jodie spreads her arms wide, her laugh bitter. 'It was me. You knew it really, that I got you all here under false pretences. Happy now?'

'Why?' Hannah's voice is low.

'I didn't have a choice.' Jodie has found her cigarettes. 'I've lost everything. I've lost my lovely flat – we're back in assisted housing. My credit-card bills are astronomical; I've got so much debt.' She struggles to light one, her hand shaking. 'I got offered the chance to make a fast buck before I'm blacklisted forever, so...'

'Doing what?' Tom's voice is curiously level.

'A TV special.' Jodie inhales desperately. '*The Four Reunite – The Truth Teller Tells All, No Holds Barred.* It was a no-brainer, sorry to say.'

My stomach plunges. 'I knew it,' I mutter.

'Oh did you?' Vicky turns on me now. 'So you're in on it too!'

'Me?' I stare at her. 'What are you on about?'

'You and your BFF, soul sisters at heart.' Vicky glowers. 'Ever since you married Mikey, you've been in the wrong camp. I know his business is in trouble. You said so yourself.'

I stare back at her, speechless.

The truth is, if Mikey hadn't been around after what happened, I'm not sure I'd still be here.

'Could we take your bike and get out of the city?' I asked that afternoon after the party. 'Like... far from here?'

I wanted to be away from the fumes, the people, the concrete. I couldn't get to the sea, where I'd grown up, but maybe out in the fields I'd feel more like myself, less anguished, less terrified.

Because really, right then, I didn't know if I could ever feel free again.

But Vicky doesn't know any of this. I never shared it with her.

'Easy way to make a quick buck, yeah,' she says now, but she's looking less sure of herself. 'Shaft your mates.'

And suddenly, something inside me breaks. Something that's held me together all this time, since we first met, just snaps.

Blindly, I get up. I pass Sue's inert body, Mae snivelling beside her. 'You need to get your gran indoors,' I say, pointing at the gathering storm. 'Keep her warm.'

There's nothing else we can do for her, stuck here. And that's the truth.

We're stranded, and we can't get away from each other. From the harm that's unfolded over the past few days.

Over the past few decades.

We're bound together by silken ropes. By poison and disaster.

'Sorry, Mae,' I say with a sob. 'Oh, and I found the knife in your room last night. I put it back in the kitchen. Don't do anything stupid, for God's sake. You'll regret it for the rest of your life.'

I rush down the garden, away from the fury unfolding in the villa.

Somewhere far off, the distant roll of thunder is audible; moving closer, I'd bet.

I had some good years, some great years, after I left Royal Mews with Mikey. But I should have known.

It could only ever end in tragedy.

Tom was distraught when Hannah moved back to her parents'
soon after the party. 'She won't talk to me at all.'

'Do you really blame her?' Vicky, who was usually out with
Double Denim Dave these days, or old friends from her posh
school, was unsympathetic.

Jodie was still away a lot too; busy making money in whatever desperate dodgy way she'd decided on. I'd long since given
up asking.

I was dealing with my own horror. I'd buried the memory of
my assault as deep as I could; I didn't talk to anyone about it.
When it came up in my nightmares, I pushed it away violently.

Worse, I hadn't really dealt with the fact that there might be
consequences, until the morning I woke up in agony, a small
pool of blood spreading beneath me.

I hadn't thought it possible that I was pregnant, the act had
been over so fast, but the hospital confirmed it was true. *Had*
been true.

Sitting in a bed in a side room, dry-eyed, listening to the
consultant tell me there was a chance I'd never have children,

that was when I thought: perhaps Robert Perry *did* deserve what he got after all.

It was Jodie who came to be with me; the only other person who knew. I made her swear to keep it to herself.

How could I tell anyone else anyway? It was a secret that would have to die with me.

'I'm so sorry, babe.' She got into the narrow bed and hugged me.

'Please don't tell Mikey,' I muttered eventually through my sobs, and she looked down at me and said, 'Hmm, Mikey.'

Because Mikey and I had begun to hang out all the time. Since the day after the party, we'd become inseparable, talking about films and books, or not talking, just driving out to the country on his motorbike and walking in the hills. There was something infinitely safe about Mikey for me.

'Let's hope he takes after his mum's side of the family and not our dreadful dad's.' Jodie sniffed and kissed my cheek.

And I took that for her blessing if anything romantic happened between me and Mikey.

If my past didn't catch up with me first.

I arrived home one cold afternoon, when my fear about every buzz at the door had faded, to find the police in our living room, interviewing Vicky.

'Honestly, if he'd been here, I'd remember.' She pushed a photo back across the table. 'Sorry not to be more help.'

'What's happened?' Warily I unzipped my jacket.

'Some man's been found dead, and they think...' Vicky looked at the female officer. 'Sorry, what is it exactly you think?'

'And you are—?' The male officer ignored the question as he met my eye.

'Simone Dillane. I live here too.'

'Simone. Do you know him?' The woman nodded at me and then the picture.

My world became very tiny for a second, small enough to fit on the head of a pin.

I peered at the photo, pretending to think. 'Not sure, but is that Mr Perry? I met him once at Dizzy's.'

'Dizzy's?'

'The Bar of Life, in town. I work there. Is he...' I picked my words carefully. 'Is it *him* who's dead?'

'His body's been pulled from the canal, near the City Lock. Not that far' – she looked up – 'from these flats.'

'The *canal*?' Now my shock was real. 'How awful.'

'Quite.' She made a note. 'I believe he was your landlord.'

I registered Vicky's surprise from the corner of my eye.

'You'd have to ask Jodie.' I swallowed my fear as best I could. 'She dealt with the tenancy.'

'Jodie Austin?' The woman looked at her notebook. 'Is she in?'

'Rarely,' Vicky sighed. 'These days.'

When the police left, taking Jodie's mobile number, I went to get ready to meet Mikey.

'Mate.' Vicky stood in my doorway. 'What the fuck's going on?'

'What do you mean?' I pretended to study my tights for ladders.

'With you and Jodie. That bloke.' She gestured with her head at the front door.

'What bloke?' I stalled for time.

'In the photo. He *was* here the night of the party. I let him in.'

'Really?' I tried my hardest to act surprised.

'Oh, do me a favour! He was in some sad old Zorro mask

and a cloak and hat, but I'd recognise him anywhere. The size of him.'

My skin was cold to my own touch as I pulled my tights on. 'So why didn't you tell them?' My heart was beating very fast.

'Why indeed, mate?' Vicky looked at me intensely, and her eyes were burning fiercely. 'Why indeed?'

SEVENTY-FOUR

HANNAH

Isla del Diablo

I couldn't do it in the end.

I was so angry with Jodie last night, I got the pills out of their hiding place and sat looking at them. I stared at the bottles, all the pretty colours of the different drugs, and I debated taking a great handful of the tablets. Put all of this to rest now. But I found I wasn't done with life yet.

I might be angry, but I still have things to live for.

'One knife might have turned up – but another one's gone missing,' Vicky says as Simone disappears into the trees. 'The really sharp meat knife.'

'I *did* want to hurt you when we first came here,' I tell Jodie, and I turn the TV screen off. My voice has gone very low. I can feel everyone staring at me, and for a second, it's hard to continue, but I'm good at confessing.

I was born a Catholic after all.

'I was furious, Jodie.' I turn to face them. 'I felt you took my chance at happiness. Twice. But in the end, I could never harm you – though I did want to hurt myself.'

'I'm glad you didn't.' Jodie closes her eyes. She looks exhausted. Like I feel, in fact.

'What do you mean, your chance at happiness?' Vicky looks confused.

'I meant...' I take a really deep breath. 'Jodie knows what I meant. And now I mean Tom.'

I will never forget that day when I came back after the Royal Mews party. I was expecting to pick up where I'd left off: falling in love with Tom. But things had happened that night; what exactly was unclear, but everything had shifted.

And then my dad rang and said he needed me to come home, that my mother wasn't going to recover from the break in her bone easily. He said my place was there with them, as God would want it.

So I went.

'Hannah,' Tom says now, but I'm still trying to avoid his gaze when there's a screech from outside.

'Gran!' Mae is shrieking. 'I think Gran's dead.'

She's thrown herself on Sue's body.

'Mae. It's OK.' I pull the girl off her grandma as gently as I can as I try to locate a pulse. For a moment, I think I feel a flutter in Sue's skinny wrist, but that might just be my own racing heart.

'I'm not sure...' I say.

'CPR?' Tom meets my gaze, his eyes intensely blue in this strange light, and his expression is odd. 'It's worth a try, isn't it?'

'I guess,' I say.

'Come on, baby.' Jodie leads Mae away off. Her own jaw is very tense; I recognise that look. 'They know what they're doing.'

Is that true though? When have I ever really known that? I've dwelt in the shadows since I left Royal Mews. A life half lived.

Mae runs off, sobbing wildly, and I'm vaguely aware of

Jodie following her daughter down the steps into the trees as Tom and I begin chest compressions on the old lady.

'We can't always give up,' he's saying as I count. 'Like you did.'

I keep counting.

After the third round, Sue coughs, groans and splutters out water.

'Like I did *what*?' She's floppy as I roll her onto her side.

'Gave up.'

'What choice did I have?'

'I was helping Jodie, that's all. Didn't she tell you that?'

'Is that what you call it?' I feel Sue's pulse again. It's stronger. 'All right, Sue. You're going to be fine,' I murmur, though I don't know if she will be.

'After they killed that guy.'

'What?' I place Sue's arm down by her side. 'What are you on about?'

Tom stares at me. 'Hang on. Don't tell me you didn't know?'

'What guy?'

'After that party, I was just her alibi. And then later, Jodie told me you hated me, and I should keep away.'

'Oh,' I say slowly. 'Did she?' It's hard to compute, especially right now. 'So, wait – you're saying you didn't come back because she warned you not to?'

'Something like that,' Tom says, but he looks shifty, his eyes sliding away from mine. 'Have you got this?' He nods down at Sue.

I shrug. 'I guess.'

But before I can say anything else, Tom rushes off down the steps.

SEVENTY-FIVE

THEN

Moving in with Mikey eased the pain of the Royal Mews dream falling apart, as did landing my first job on the *Courier*, with Pat's help.

It went so well that I began to apply for junior jobs on national papers.

One morning in mid March, I caught the train to Manchester for an interview at the *Evening News*, on the entertainment section.

I waited in the lobby for what seemed like an age.

'I'm sorry, love.' The entertainment editor turned up eventually, a skinny guy with nicotine-stained fingers. 'Think there's been a mix-up.'

'What do you mean?' My stomach started the regular plunging that had begun with Perry's death.

'Thought you didn't want it. The job's gone, love.'

'But we had a meeting for... for now? Eleven a.m.'

He scratched his thinning hair with a pencil. 'Pretty sure we had a message saying you'd gone elsewhere.'

'Not from me. Definitely not.' Clutching the folder

containing my work, I felt a sense of clammy dread. 'Who told you that?'

'I'd have to ask my secretary, love. It's manic – we're launching a new-look paper next week. The point is, the column's gone, I'm afraid.' He was already backing away. 'Sorry you've had a wasted journey.'

'What column?' I felt a bitter kick of disappointment.

'BFF,' he said. 'Bit like that old classic the *Indy* used to run, you know. Birdy Jones, but with teeth.'

'*Bridget* Jones?' How could he work on a paper and not know her actual name? 'What do you mean, *teeth*?'

'Telling it how it is. No holds barred.' His smile was sickly, baring receding gums. 'Punters love that sort of thing. Sex, drugs and rock 'n' roll. The more honest, the better.'

'So you don't want me?'

'No space right now, I'm afraid, love. Leave your samples there.' He pointed at his secretary's desk. 'I'll get back to you if owt comes up, I promise.'

'Oh...' I turned back. 'And the journalist who got the job?'

But of course, I knew the name before he said it.

That was the real end of the dream.

A few days later, arriving back from a long shift at Dizzy's, I found a dark-haired youth in the living room.

He was pasty-faced and wearing a natty suit far too old and big for him, carrying a Mulberry Filofax and a briefcase I thought I recognised. In one hand he clutched a ragged copy of the *Courier*, the newspaper I still worked on.

Vicky stood at the kitchen counter, arms folded. I couldn't put my finger on the expression on her face.

'I've come to find out what happened to my dad.' The furious youth waved the newspaper.

'Sorry, who?' I murmured, but I had a very good idea. There was enough of a resemblance, despite his sinewy frame.

'My dad, Robert Perry.' He was trying valiantly not to crumple in front of us, and my heart twisted with guilt. 'The inquest said it's death by misadventure or some shit.'

'Inquest?'

He threw the paper on the table and jabbed a finger at a story on the third page.

Beneath the headline *LOCAL PROPERTY DEVELOPER DEATH INCONCLUSIVE* was a small, smudged photo: a family portrait of Perry and his wife and kids – two girls, this boy.

'Y-Your dad? Oh, I'm so sorry,' I stammered, fear clutching me. I felt like a klaxon was about to sound, a neon arrow pointing at my head: *It was her!*

Wouldn't it be a relief to confess though?

'I know he came here, and I know my dad.' The young man bit his lip and corrected himself. 'Knew him.' A short painful pause. 'And he'd never have killed himself.'

The front door opened, and Jodie walked in, accompanied, to my great surprise, by bloody Cooper.

'Jodie,' I said helplessly. I hadn't seen her since my failed Manchester trip. 'This is Robert Perry's son.'

'Ah, I'm so sorry, babe.' She took the young man's hand, didn't skip a beat. God, she was good. 'But Coops is gonna sort it, aren't you, babe?'

'Gary.' He puffed his chest out like a silly pigeon. 'I use Gary now.'

'Course you do, babe. You're gonna take care of the Perrys, aren't you?'

'Course.' Cooper put his arm round the young man's narrow shoulders, like a smug uncle at a wedding. 'You can rely on me.'

'Fabulous!' Jodie turned to us all with a glossy smile, and I wondered suddenly if she was high.

The boy sat down, shaky and verging on tears.

'Don't worry, babe,' she assured him. Then she caught my eye over his head.

What did I read in her look? So much, and absolutely nothing.

SEVENTY-SIX
VICKY
MONDAY, 13 JUNE

Isla del Diablo

Somewhere far off, the sun is shining, but on this little island, the blue sky has been obliterated by thick dark clouds.

The storm is truly on its way now: the surface of the pool is being whisked by an invisible hand, the palm trees bend as if they've given up, and the clouds race madly, chased by the angry wind.

'Look!' Daisy grabs my arm, pointing, and I resist the urge to slap her hand away. 'Thank God!'

There's a boat, just past the Devil's rocks.

'Thank God,' she repeats, clapping her hands, and I try to share her joy – but honestly, I feel so awful, I can't be nice right now.

'I'm going to get dressed.' She hurries inside as the wind tugs the cushions off chairs.

I stand there watching Hannah murmur to Sue after Tom has hurried away, and I think: it was always them, Hannah and Tom.

I just struggled to accept it.

The truth is, I knew Hannah didn't love me like I loved her, and I've let it ruin my life. I've never got over it; even though I should probably have stayed away from her, I couldn't. I've just wanted to protect her all this time.

As I watch, the boat – I think it's the *Scylla*, the one that dropped us off that first day – turns and starts to head away.

'No!' I shout. 'Come back!'

I *have* to get off this island today, before they realise.

Frantic, I run towards the stairs.

SEVENTY-SEVEN
SIMONE

I stumble down the path to the back steps, through the olive trees, emerging onto a beach I haven't seen before.

In the distance, on the curve in the bay, I see something – a little motorboat I don't recognise, bobbing gallantly in the gathering waves.

But I'm not interested in that boat now, or where it came from.

I have to get to where I'm going.

The first – and almost only – huge row I ever had with Jodie plays through my head like it's on an old reel-to-reel. It was just before she left Royal Mews, when I challenged her about my job at the paper.

'An eye for an eye.' She shrugged, but she was the least religious person I knew.

'But it isn't, is it? You've taken my eye, and now I can't see.'

'But I gave you mine.'

'How?' I was so angry. 'You took my bloody job! I worked so hard.'

'I needed it more than you. You'll be fine.'

'Why?'

'Because' – and her smile was fixed, glassy-eyed – 'I have to have something.'

'What do you mean?'

'Because, babe, I'm marrying Coops.'

'You're *what*? Are you mad?'

'Probably. But it's for you.'

'Hang on.' I didn't understand. 'How the hell is it for me?'

'Because I'm buying his silence.' She shut her suitcase briskly. 'And because...' She paused, then tried again. 'I'm pregnant. Obviously.'

'Pregnant?' I felt a massive jolt go through me.

'So. Anyway, you've got Mikey now – you'll be OK.' She smiled that glassy smile again. 'As long as he doesn't turn out like our bastard dad.'

'Are you going to...' I cleared my throat. 'Are you having the baby?'

Why did I feel so terribly, terribly sad?

'Not sure yet,' she said. 'I want a ring on my finger to protect me first.'

This was not the Jodie I thought I knew.

But then did I really know her at all? She was a consummate actress, that much I'd learnt, ever since she'd breezed into my life that first day in Dizzy's, defending me against bloody Coops.

A horrible thought occurred to me.

'Did you know him already?' I forced the words out.

She turned up the collar on her fake-fur jacket, the tiger-print one. 'Who?'

'Cooper. Bloody Gary.'

'Know him *when*?' She applied her red lipstick, and it looked like a slash of blood.

'That day in Dizzy's, when we first met. Did you already know him? Is that why he apologised?' Of course! How very stupid I'd been. 'Why were you even there?'

'For a drink, babe. And God, I'd murder a bourbon now.' She patted her stomach. 'But no, I didn't know him.' She met my eye. 'And you'll have to take my word for that.' She kissed the top of my head as I sat on her bed, her room still a tip, clothes discarded, even though she was leaving.

'I'm sorry though, babe.' She grinned at me from the doorway. 'The job thing was a bit shit, I agree. But' – she backed away, holding her suitcase – 'needs must, yeah, babe? Needs must.'

SEVENTY-EIGHT
HANNAH

'I don't know where everyone's gone,' I croon to Sue, lying her down on the sofa inside. 'But they'll be back soon.'

I fetch her a drink of water, then slump down on the nearest chair, feeling teary.

It's amazing that she's alive.

I hear a cough from somewhere nearby; a male cough, by the sounds of it.

A man walks out of the wood, and for a minute I think it's Gary, but I quickly realise it's not. This man is taller, with swept back grey hair, much stringier than Gary.

'Hi,' I say warily. Then I look again. *Oh, I know you...*

'Hello,' he says.

'What are *you* doing here?' I'm confused.

'I could ask you the same thing,' he says, and he doesn't look friendly.

He doesn't seem friendly at all.

SEVENTY-NINE
VICKY

As I race down the beach, shouting at the receding boat, the screaming begins.

On and on, carrying in on the wind.

It's bloodcurdling. I don't know which direction it's coming from, but I'm sure I recognise it, if that's possible.

I'm sure it's Jodie.

It's hard to work out which way to go, but I think I'm getting closer to it.

Suddenly the screaming stops abruptly, with a great choking sigh.

I scrabble up the rocks – and there it is. The stuff of nightmares.

A body, kind of pinioned on the sand, kind of floating in the sea.

The knife. I kept telling them knives were missing, but no one seemed to listen. It's one of the lacerating kitchen knives – high-end, expensive, razor-sharp – and it's protruding from the corpse's back.

I feel like vomiting as I try to think what to do.

I scramble away down the rocks again.

'Help!' I cry, as loudly as I can. 'I need help – now!'

EIGHTY
SIMONE

I realise there's another building on the far side of the rocks at the end of this beach – some kind of boat shed maybe, more basic than the one on the main beach that housed the rowing boat.

I head towards it.

Tom suddenly appears up on the rocks.

'Did you hear the screaming?' he calls, and I realise I've never seen him so angry.

He has blood on his leg, I notice, a big smear of it.

'Yes,' I say, and I point down the beach. 'It came from that direction.'

'Have you seen Jodie?' He's impatient.

'Oh no, 'fraid not,' I say innocently.

He jumps down onto the sand and looks at me.

'You know, I'll be glad when this is all over,' he mutters, and it strikes me that he looks quite possessed.

He was always so sure of himself really, so collected.

I relied on him when I worked for him. I looked up to him, even when he was at the centre of everyone's affections; even when he didn't behave impeccably.

It's been a shock to know that he messed up so badly.

'I'll bet.' I try to sound consolatory, but I wonder – what has he done?

He jogs off, and I wait until he disappears from sight.

Then I head to the building, and I realise I'm almost praying.

EIGHTY-ONE
VICKY

I meet her halfway across the next cove; she's dressed in boots, swimsuit and shorts.

'There's a body,' I splutter, pointing back to where I've just seen Gary, dead as fifty doornails, a knife through his back.

She frowns. 'A body?'

'Yeah, I mean, like a dead body.' Then I think, oh God, she's going to be devastated. 'I'm so sorry, mate.' I put my hand on her warm arm. 'It's Gary.'

'*Gary?*' Her eyes are unfocused for a second, or maybe I'm just delirious. 'He's here?'

'He's there.' I point again. 'And he's...' I clear my throat. 'He's dead.'

'Are you sure?' she asks, and I nod.

'I'm so sorry,' I say again, uselessly. What else can I say?

'Well,' Daisy says, and I sense her focus return as she looks up the hill towards the villa.

She's watching someone, and I turn to see a figure up there looking down, a figure who shouldn't be here at all.

'I'm not.'

'What?' I take my eyes off the man up there and try to concentrate.

'Gary.' Daisy's gaze is very intense. 'I'm not sorry he's dead. He was mean.'

I stand up uncertainly and walk towards Dave, Vicky's partner of all these years. 'This is a surprise. What are you doing here?'

'I could ask you the same thing.'

'Well...' I think about it for a minute. 'Ostensibly, I'm here celebrating Jodie's fictious birthday.'

'OK.' Dave sticks his hands in his pockets. 'And the truth?'

'I'm here to square up things that have ruined my life, I guess. Or...' I consider my words for a second. 'Well, things that have stopped me living my life, maybe, is a better way of putting it. I've come to put them to bed.'

'Well' – he steps very close to me – 'I guess that makes two of us.'

'I saw you, didn't I?' I realise suddenly. 'Running along the beach in Ibiza.'

'Yes. I wanted to tell Vicky not to go. I sat outside that old house all night in my rental car, debating whether to come in.' He looks sad. 'Oh, and I should say sorry about the airport.'

'The... That was you? You tipped them off about me?' It is bewildering. 'Why?'

'I'm sorry.' He shrugs. 'I just wanted to get at Vicky. It made sense to me at the time.'

'I don't understand.'

He shrugs again. 'Like I say, I'm sorry.'

But there's something in his eyes that's thoroughly disquieting.

EIGHTY-THREE
SIMONE

As we arranged, Jodie is waiting inside, the boat on the ramp behind her.

'So Tom didn't find you?' I ask. 'I was worried for a minute.'

'No, thank God.' She laughs shakily. 'And I want to get off this bloody island before he does.'

'But hang on – is that yours out there?' I point at the other little motorboat, bobbing on the increasingly angry waves.

'No.' She shakes her head and gestures behind her into the open shed. 'This boat was here all the time. I made sure of it. Thank God I did, given what's been happening.'

'Very wise.' I nod. It's a neat little motorboat called *The Daffodil*.

I look again. It's not *The Daffodil*, of course. It's called *The Lily Rider*.

But who does the other boat belong to then?

'And thank God for you, Dilly.' Jodie's gathering a bag she must have left here overnight.

'Hang on,' I say again. 'What about Mae?'

'Ah, she'll be fine.' She's getting ready to open the doors.

'She's so angry with me right now, it's best if we go our separate ways for a bit. And it's me they're after.'

'Angry?'

'About her dad.'

'Because?'

'Why do you think? Someone put a note with a DNA result under her door the other night, and... well, I thought she'd never speak to me again.'

'But what about her insulin?' I thought of last night. 'I mean, they had a go at her too, didn't they? Whoever it is—'

'I don't know,' Jodie says stoutly. 'I mean, it could have just been an oversight on Mae's part. She's a nightmare with keeping her meds topped up.'

'OK, if you're sure.' I look at her. 'Are you ready?'

'Once I'm off the island, I'll send reinforcements obviously...' But I can see the doubt on her face. 'Antonio is trying to get into the bay right now.'

I push the boat towards the doors. Then I straighten up.

'I mean, I have to say, Jodie, I *do* wonder if you should stay.'

But I can hear shouting, heading towards us.

'No!' She's clearly frightened. 'We have to go now! Before it's too late and I can't get away.'

I carry on pushing until the boat meets the water with a mighty splash.

'Hurry up and get in,' I call over my shoulder, jumping in myself.

'God,' Jodie groans, splashing out into the sea, waist-deep, 'it's not easy.'

'Don't be a wuss.' I extend my hand and manage to pull her in after me.

She lands with a big jolt, inelegantly.

'You make it look so simple.' She tries to laugh, struggling to right herself. 'I forgot what a water baby you are.'

As I engage the kill switch to start the engine, my mind's racing.

'I know you think I'm on your side,' I begin as it fires up and I steer away from the beach.

'Yeah, it's been amazing, Dilly.' She sits. 'Like old times.'

'Hardly.' And were the old times so good anyway? 'But I don't think it's all right, you know.' I won't look at her now.

'What do you mean?' Jodie holds her hair out of her face as it whips in the wind. 'I don't understand.'

'What you've done.' I start to ease the boat out of the tiny cove. 'Setting us up.'

'Hang on – I thought you got it?' She's frowning. 'How desperate I've been. Needing the money – it meant I was driven to do what I did.'

'No.' I'm picking my words carefully as we edge towards the first set of fangs, the grey rocks. 'What I understand is that you're still number one in your world, and your messed-up life is of your own making.'

'What?' She looks aghast. 'But you *have* to be on my side. You're family, after all.'

'Did you want me to be though?' I shrug. 'Family?'

'Of course!' she cries.

'I'm on my own side, angel. Mine and Mikey's and Tiger's and Mason's, and I'm not going to let you do anything to ruin that.' The spray flies in my face as I pray this is nearly over now. 'Nor will Mikey.'

'Ruin it *how*?'

'I know how selfish and mercenary you've always been.' We're heading towards the other little boat. 'And when I saw that photo you'd left in my room when I arrived—'

'What photo?'

'Oh come on.' I ignore her fake innocence. 'When I saw it, I knew exactly what I had to do.'

She stares at me. 'I knew it!' she says triumphantly. 'I knew it was you all the time.'

'*How* did you know?' I frown. 'How could you have possibly worked that out?'

EIGHTY-FOUR

VICKY

'I'm going to have some breakfast,' Daisy says, and I'm wondering whether she's actually lost her mind when I hear more shouting.

A boat appears round the bay, on this side of the toothy rocks, rocking unsteadily as the sea is whipped up by the wind.

It's not the *Scylla*; it's much smaller, and there are two figures in it.

Mae races down the beach. She's holding something up, yelling at the boat: a cool box by the looks of it.

'I'm so sorry, Mae,' I say, and I grab at her to head her off. 'Hon, please. I'm sorry, but it's your dad.'

'What is?'

'Gary.' I don't want her to see his bloated corpse, so I hang on to her.

'Gary? He's not my dad.' She shakes me off. 'I mean, I thought he was, but he's not.' Her eyes are brilliant in her small face, and she really reminds me of someone. Jodie, I suppose. 'And that's a bloody relief.'

'Oh.' I'm confused. 'Not your dad?'

'Look, Vicky, my mum's in danger out there' – she points at

the boat – 'and she can't hear me.' She waves the cool box. 'I found this in Simone's room just now.'

'So?' Even more confused.

'Look.' She tips it to show me something long, thin and papery that rattles in the wind. 'A snakeskin!'

I gape at her.

'That *snake*, the other night.' Mae's frustration is obvious. 'She must have planted it in my mum's room.'

'Who?'

'*Simone!*'

'No way.' But I look out at the little motorboat about to negotiate the Devil's teeth. 'Simone? There's no way,' I mutter again stupidly.

Simone and Jodie are sitting face to face, Simone steering. She was a natural on the water, Simone; took me sailing a few times near her parents' home down in Devon after we both left Royal Mews.

Daisy has walked away, but she heads back now.

'Is that Simone and Jodie?' She looks irritated for some reason. 'In that boat?'

'Yes,' Mae cries. 'I think Simone's going to hurt my mum, and we need to stop her – *now!*'

EIGHTY-FIVE
SIMONE

Jodie's still staring across the boat at me, eyes blazing, when I become aware that someone's running down the beach; sprinting towards us, waving frantically.

'I knew because I know you so well, Simone.' Her face is alight with her own cleverness. 'And that's why I wouldn't let you hurt Mae.'

I realise that it's Mae who's on the beach, screeching and waving her arms over her head, but she's competing with the rolling thunder now.

'Mum!' she's yelling. 'Mum, come back!'

'Oh God.' Jodie looks conflicted. 'It's OK, babe,' she yells. 'Help will be here soon.'

'You do actually love her then?' I say as I steer the boat towards the rocks.

'What? Of course I bloody love her, Simone.' She's annoyed, raising her voice over the racket of the engine. 'I love her desperately. Even if...' She clasps her hands tightly together for a moment. 'Even if I've not always been the best mother.'

'Do you want to go back for her then?'

'The worst thing is' – Jodie stares at Mae on the beach – 'she's so furious with me, I think she wants to kill me.'

Mae certainly looks hysterical, yelling and yelling, her voice carried away on the wind. She's holding up that cool box I used the other day, waving it frantically.

'I'll deal with you, then I'll come back for her.'

'Deal with me?' Jodie laughs unsteadily. 'You make me sound like a virus.'

'That's a matter of opinion.' I look for the lifejackets under the seat; I find mine and put it on, fastening it tightly. 'Better put yours on too,' I suggest.

But she can't find it. 'It's not here.'

'Oh dear.' I frown. 'Looks like there's only one.'

Lightning hits the water behind us, nearer Ibiza but close enough to be discomforting. But I don't have a choice.

'Dilly?' And now Jodie looks scared again. More than scared, in fact. Petrified. Like I was when her supposed friend and benefactor Robert Perry attacked me that night and almost ruined the rest of my life.

'I could give you mine, I guess.' I hold a hand over the clasps.

'You could...' she says slowly. 'But you're not going to, are you?'

'Well...' I gaze at her blankly. At this face I know so well, the face of the woman I trusted most in the world for a while. 'I mean, I would. Because I know what you gave me. But now' – I concentrate as I steer the boat carefully towards the gap between the first two rocks – 'now, I think you've changed your mind, haven't you? About our little arrangement.'

'No!' she cries. 'Of course not.'

'I don't believe you, Jodie. And I can't deal with that. I can't deal with that at all.'

'For fuck's sake,' Daisy swears loudly. 'Best-laid plans and all that.'

Mae is waving frantically at the departing boat.

'Daisy?' I can't keep up with events. '*What* plans?'

Standing behind Mae now, Daisy bends to pull something from her hiking boot.

Something long and thing: a very sharp stiletto blade.

I freeze.

In one swift move, she encircles Mae's neck with her arm and yanks the younger woman hard against her own body so she loses her balance, all before I can so much as open my mouth.

'What the hell!' Mae drops the cool box, grabbing the wrist that's pressed against her collarbone. 'What are you *doing*?'

'Daisy!' I shout.

'Don't move.' Daisy holds the knife to the girl's throat as the wind whisks the snakeskin down the beach. 'Either of you. Stay right there, Vicky.'

'Daisy, for fuck's sake!' I take a step towards her, but her smile has ice in it. 'Let her go.'

'Sorry, Mae' – Daisy's smile hardens – 'but let's see, shall we?'

'See *what*?' Mae frantically struggles to keep her throat away from the blade. 'Get *off* me, you bloody lunatic.'

'Don't move, Vicky. And you keep still, Mae, or you'll be sorry. Let's see if your mum really loves you.' Daisy looks out to sea. 'Like my dad loved me. Me and my siblings. Somehow, I doubt it.'

'Oh goddammit!' I swear. 'That's put the cat among the pigeons!'

'What?' Jodie turns to look at what I've seen. 'Oh God, Mae!'

'Do you want to go back now?'

'What the fuck's that mad cow doing?' Jodie stands in the boat, which sways dangerously. 'Daisy! Get *off* her! Let Mae go!'

'Sit down, Jodie!' I order through gritted teeth. 'Or we'll both be in the water.'

For all my confidence at sea, I'm feeling increasingly unsure now. The weather is worsening so fast, the dark clouds gathering over the tiny island, the wind picking up so much that the sea is getting rougher almost by the second, the waves growing in height.

All I want is Jodie's assurance, that's all, and then I can go home to my family. I may not have had the starry career she's had, or any career to speak of really, but I have had love. And I don't want to die in this boat now, before I can see my family again.

'Promise me!' I yell at her. 'Sit down and promise me you won't tell Tiger. Then we can go back.'

'Tell her what?' Jodie looks baffled. 'Take me back to Mae – now!'

'Don't play games, Jodie!' Salt flies up from the sea, stinging my eyes. 'You put that photo of us all in my bedroom drawer in the villa. Of me and my kids.'

'To let you know I had your back.'

'For God's sake, don't lie.'

'I'd never take Tiger from you, you nutter,' she cries, as suddenly the heavens open above us. 'Is that what this is about?'

'Of course.' I feel calm suddenly descend on me along with the rain. 'Because you know that mother love is the strongest bond.'

'You're Tiger's mum, not me. Just get me back to Mae!' Jodie is waving desperately at the beach. 'Mae!'

I turn back towards shore, steering the little boat as best I can, but the sea's so turbulent now, and the warm rain lashes down, blinding me, and I feel the fear rising in me because I can't keep the boat steady enough to—

We hit something with a mighty thump, sending us rocking madly.

'Oh shit!' It must be a rock beneath us, although I can barely see. I open up the throttle, but the engine's at full capacity already and I can't seem to find any more power.

'Dilly.' Jodie grabs my arm, water streaming down her face. 'Please. If you ever loved me, get me back to her now, before it's too late!'

EIGHTY-EIGHT

THEN
AUTUMN 2006

I was lugging my groceries up the fire escape of the little block of flats by the sea when someone called out to me.

'Dilly!'

Even hearing her voice felt lacerating.

I hadn't seen Jodie since she left Royal Mews, at the same time as I'd left the city with Mikey.

I'd seen photos of her baby, because she'd written about it in her starry newspaper column – THE TRUTH-TELLER'S BABY – but I hadn't seen either of them in person.

She looked the same really, maybe a bit more tired, maybe a bit plumper than the last awful time we'd met.

She was famous now. She'd made an absolute fortune from her writing, as far as I could see, from the moment she'd stolen that job from me. Every time I turned the TV on, there she was, the chat shows' darling; on everything from Jonathan Ross to Graham Norton, about to smash it in the States.

They all lapped her up.

But the day she wrote about Vicky's love for Hannah was the day she went too far. She changed their names, but anyone who knew us all would have known immediately. I didn't believe it, to be honest. Vicky seemed happy with Dave, and I thought Jodie was just settling old scores with Vicky – couldn't help feeling she was still smarting over Tom preferring either and both of them to her. But it was spiteful and cruel, true or not.

That column came out a few weeks after I found out I'd fallen pregnant by mistake.

Mikey and I were nothing if not excited; overjoyed, in fact.

I'd secretly contacted Jodie when I did the test, because she was the one person I wanted to tell. I sent her a text, feeling divided loyalties. Hannah and Vicky would have been mad with me; so would Mikey.

She rang and congratulated me.

The next week, I lost the baby.

The following month, Mikey and I got the same treatment in the newspaper at her hands, about family and friends not being a good mix, and after that, Mikey wouldn't talk about her at all any more.

I texted her again, to tell her how hurt and angry I was.

I heard nothing back.

And now here she was, looking as cool as rain on a summer's day, getting out of a car – a sporty red BMW, suitably flashy – outside my flat.

'Simone.' She caught me up. 'Let me help you carry those bags.'

'You can't come up.' I glanced up the stairs. 'Mikey's in.'

'He won't answer my calls,' she replied, and I looked at her, surprised.

'I didn't know you *had* called him.'

'Regularly,' she said. 'Since Dad died.'

It had been a horrible death, quick but painful, and Mikey's feelings had conflicted him.

Finding out I was pregnant, well, it was the only thing that had cheered Mikey up since, given him new hope for a fresh start.

But it was over too soon.

Now we were stuck, walking hand in hand along the beach in the evening after our tedious day jobs were through. Feeling a deep loss; feeling something enormous, something like fear for what the rest of our lives might bring now.

'Can we go somewhere?' Jodie asked. 'I just want to talk.'

I looked up the stairs again furtively.

'Oh, come on.' Her irritation was blatant. 'You're your own woman, aren't you, Dilly?'

'I don't know.' I was hesitant. 'I mean, yes, of course but...'

Didn't trouble always follow in her wake?

'I have a proposition for you.' She smiled, but it didn't reach her eyes.

In the end, she drove us to the promenade at the far edge of our road.

'I'm so sorry about the baby.' She turned the engine off. 'Really.'

My eyes immediately filled with tears. 'Thanks,' I muttered.

The sea was a great grey swell that day, a blanket that promised nothing as we sat side by side, gazing at the colourless expanse.

'So, the thing is, I've left Gary, not before time, and...' She pulled back her coat, a more sober affair than the old days: expensive, dark red wool. She held her belly for a moment. 'And this.'

'You're not?' I felt it like a physical wound. 'You're pregnant *again*?'

Life was nothing if never a level playing field. Where was *my* piece of luck? I thought bitterly.

'Yep.' Jodie took my hand, and I nearly pulled it back, but she was stronger. She placed it on her belly. 'And the thing is—'

'What?'

'I want you to have her.'

'What the hell?' Now I did pull my hand back, like I'd been burnt. 'Don't be so stupid.'

'I'm not. I can't take care of another baby. One's hard enough on your own. And I've got the chance to go to the States. Make it really big. But *you* could.' Her own eyes were suspiciously bright. 'You and Mikey. I can't think of better people.'

'But what about Gary?'

'It's not Gary's,' she said quietly. 'He's history, babe.'

'I can't,' I choked out. 'I can't just look after your baby till you want her back. And Mikey'll go mad.'

'I won't want her back.' My old friend looked ahead now, at the desolate sky above the grey English sea. 'You can adopt her. I'll relinquish all my rights, straight away. I've checked it all out. It's quite straightforward.'

'But why?' I whispered.

'Because,' she said, and now she looked back at me, and met my eye. 'I owe you, Simone. I know that. You were the best mate I ever had, and I totally ruined it. I ballsed everything up.' Fiercely she wiped away a tear that had escaped. 'I always bloody do.'

We sat in silence, watching the gulls wheeling above, watching ordinary people on the promenade, with dogs and prams and toddlers and ice creams, despite the bleak day, going about their everyday business, searching, maybe, for that little bit of joy.

And so once Mikey was on board, my darling Tiger came into our lives.

EIGHTY-NINE

SIMONE

Isla del Diablo

'Just get us back to shore!' Jodie is shrieking into the wind. 'Let her go, Daisy, you monster!'

'Believe me, I'm trying,' I mutter through gritted teeth, but the boat's still rocking perilously, and I don't know what damage was done just now by the rocks as I try my hardest to steer against the crazy currents.

'Oh God, Mae!' Jodie's moaning, about to jump overboard and swim.

'Don't!' I cry, because she won't make it.

'Take me instead!' she's yelling, but now I see someone else on the beach.

Tom.

He's sprinting from the trees towards the two girls, and as he reaches them, Daisy turns, Mae still in front of her like a shield.

He's pleading with her, gesticulating furiously – it's impossible to hear his words from here – and eventually, somehow, as if by magic, Daisy lowers the knife.

She drops it on the sand. Vicky picks it up quickly and backs away, holding Mae's hand, while Tom remains between them.

'Who the hell is she?' I wrestle some control back over the boat. 'That nutter?'

'I don't know.' Jodie looks green, as if she might be about to throw up. 'But please, Dilly, just get me off this boat and back to my daughter.'

NINETY
VICKY

Tom is pleading with Daisy to take him instead of Mae.

'I'm so sorry, darling,' he tells Mae, 'but I'm here now. I'm sorry it took so long.'

Gary's bloated body floats through my mind.

'You lot are disgusting,' Daisy sneers. 'I'm surprised you can keep up with who's fucked who.'

'But who are *you*?' I ask. This is a woman I've slept with. How could I have got it so terribly wrong?

And oh God, poor Dave – I'll have to confess it all now.

'Don't you know?' Daisy's eyes are furious black whirlpools in her manic face. '"Vengeance is mine; I will repay, saith the Lord."'

'What?' Tom shakes his head. 'What vengeance?'

'My dad went out one night to meet your slag of a mother' – she cocks her head at Mae – 'and he was never seen alive again.'

'But who's your dad?' I can't keep up.

'Who d'you think?' Daisy's almost frothing at the mouth now; there is actual spittle on her chin. 'My dad died 'cos he gave that bitch Jodie a job.'

'Gary?' My mind boggles. 'You were shagging your own dad?'

'No, you stupid cow.' Daisy laughs hysterically. 'Robert Perry. My lovely dad Bob.'

NINETY-ONE
SIMONE

By the time we get to the beach, Jodie jumping out and half swimming, half wading back to shore, both of us drenched from the rain and the crashing waves, Daisy seems to have given up the fight.

I drop the anchor that's stowed beneath the seat and jump into the water to follow Jodie, battling to keep my balance as a mighty flash of lightning lights up the whole beach.

Everything feels perilous indeed.

Up ahead of me, Jodie has grabbed Mae and, holding her tight, leads her away up the beach, away from Daisy. The latter stands, head down, one arm held firmly by Tom.

She is a lost and broken woman by the looks of it.

'I'm sorry.' We can all hear Jodie sobbing. 'I'm sorry this happened. I'm sorry for being so awful.'

'What the hell's going on?' I ask as I reach them all.

'This is Robert Perry's daughter.' Vicky looks like she's been shaken hard by the collar, knife in her limp hand. 'And I brought her here by mistake.'

'What do you mean?' Jodie turns back from Mae. '*Perry's* daughter? How did *you* bring her here?'

'Not on purpose,' Vicky mutters. 'I mean, I must have led her here. We were... we've been sleeping together.'

'What? When?' I'm astounded. 'Here?'

'No.' Vicky looks mortified. 'She worked in the café with me. I thought she actually liked me.'

'You were OK.' Daisy shrugs. 'The sex wasn't bad, if you like that sort of thing. Personally, I'm not fussed.'

Vicky flushes. Poor Vicky. Tom rolls his eyes.

Where are the leaders when you need them? I wonder wearily.

'Thank God this is done.' Jodie wipes her face. 'We can get off this bloody island now.'

But the thunder crashes above our heads as though the wrathful gods have arrived, and I can feel my heart thumping in my chest.

'I wouldn't be too sure,' Daisy says calmly. 'About going anywhere.'

It's eerie how calm she is now.

'Gary's dead,' Vicky announces, pushing her dripping hair out of her eyes. 'Did you know that?'

'Gary?' Jodie looks stupefied. '*Dead?* Are you sure?'

'Yep.' Vicky looks at Daisy. 'Someone knifed him in the back.'

'Christ,' I say. Poor Gary, too. What an unholy mess.

'I mean, he's actually been dead since yesterday.' Daisy grimaces, rain streaming off her face. 'You're just all too stupid to have noticed. Or no one cared.'

'And she only met Gary because I invited him to the café.' Vicky is mournful.

'Yeah, that's right.' Daisy grins now, her top lip baring her teeth like a rabid dog. "Cos you're such a good person, hey, Vick?'

'No,' Vicky mutters.

'What the fuck was Gary doing at your café?' Jodie asks.

'I'm not proud of this.' She pauses. 'I was... I kind of black-mailed him.'

'Blackmail?' I'm lost.

'I saw how much money he'd made from that Nine Elms development, and I asked him to lend me money for my outstanding loans. The bank wouldn't give me any more and I was desperate not to lose the café. But Gary said no, so then I said...' She clears her throat. It's obviously a huge effort for her to admit this. 'I said I'd shop him if not, tell the police about Royal Mews. I'm sorry now...'

'Oh, Vick!' I say, and I'm about to assure her it's not her fault, because all things considered, it can't be, can it, but I'm distracted by Hannah, who suddenly appears in the trees, followed by a man.

'Jeez!' I say. 'Isn't that—'

'*Dave?*' Vicky starts to cry. She runs towards him. 'What are you doing here?'

'I was worried.' He holds his arms out to her. 'I was really worried about you.'

'Not without reason,' Jodie says levelly. 'She's been shagging a psychopath, it appears.'

'Oh, do shut up, Jodie!' Hannah fires, and everyone looks at her. 'Well, honestly. It's hardly the time, is it?'

'And Sue?' I look at Daisy. 'Why poor Sue?' We can imagine why Jodie, sort of, but... what about me? Does she know about me?

'The pills were for Jodie, but her mum's as greedy as she is, so...' Daisy shrugs again. 'It was just bad luck Sue drank that last wine.'

Like so much is bad luck, I think. Such very, very bad luck.

Daisy will never know how awful her father truly was unless someone tells her. She'll never know the monstrous things he did when she was a small child.

She revered his memory – and look what's happened because of it. She's killed a man who, feckless and annoying as he was, didn't deserve to die. She nearly killed Jodie too, and Mae.

'She's so messed up.' Vicky's still rigid with shock as we watch Tom and Dave march Daisy up the beach. 'I'm just...' She trails off.

'Stunned?' Jodie suggests. 'She couldn't get over her dad's death, I guess.'

I have a horrible feeling though, deep down, that it's all my fault.

But then I think about Mikey, about when we began to fall in love just after Perry attacked me. I remember the night we rode out to the moors.

'I want to say,' Mikey spoke slowly, looking out at the star-spilled night, choosing his words with care, 'I know something happened, and it was bad. There's no pressure from me.' He leant over and fastened my jacket to the top: it was freezing that night. 'But I am here. I'm here when you're ready.'

I've always held those words in my head and heart some-where, like a precious object, remembering them when things have felt overwhelming – or worse.

And now, if I can keep Tiger safe and by my side, I'll live with that. She is my priority in all of this. I still have her, and Mason, and my beloved Mikey, who is enough like Jodie to remind me of her from time to time.

I have all I need; I did get my luck.

And so I'm not going to be the one to tell Daisy what her father did to me. Let her live, wherever she might end up – in prison, no doubt – with her good memories of him.

'But the thing is' – Jodie smiles brilliantly, as if she's read my mind, and it seems she's regaining her confidence again, Mae's hand in hers, 'the thing is, everyone's got a lot of crap, don't they? It's not really an excuse for anything.'

The rain is dropping away now as she heads towards the villa.

'Certainly not for murder.'

There's no arguing with that really.

NINETY-TWO
JODIE

Ibiza

After I switched the Wi-Fi modem back on, hidden in my room; after the storm abated, and we called for help, the *Scylla* managed to get into the bay.

Finally we were able to get back to the mainland. What a blessed relief.

The others headed straight to the airport, while Daisy was removed in a police car, looking nothing less than dazed.

Who knows what will happen to her, poor damaged girl.

I have to hand it to her though; she pulled off quite a feat convincing me she was a TV producer; convincing me that it would be worth shooting this TV reunion; that it would be a first, a piece of television history, earning me a massive wedge of cash. And there was the chance that the reunion might actually be good for us old mates.

Ha! She sniffed out both my financial desperation and my final weakness: a craving not to be forgotten. Fame and kudos: once you've tasted them, well, they're hungry beasts that demand to keep being fed.

. . .

My mum's in the hospital for the night.

She might be skinny, but she's tough as the proverbial old boots, and I wasn't surprised when they said they thought she'd be fine.

I've booked Mae and me into the best hotel in Ibiza Town I could afford, on the final credit card I haven't maxed out.

'I'm going for a bubble bath,' Mae said after we dumped our bags.

So I sit out on the balcony alone, watching the turquoise sea, which is calm again, the storm having passed. Stupid mocktail in hand, watching the beautiful people below in all their glory, glossy bodies sliced by tiny thongs and high-cut swimwear, flipping away in their Havaianas and their high heels, I mull over the past few days.

Few months.

Few decades.

'Don't be a stranger.' I hugged Simone tightly before she got into her cab to the airport. 'I'm sorry for it all. Can we start over?'

'Hmm.' She raised an eyebrow. 'Let me talk to Mikey.'

God, I miss Mikey. Always my favourite brother. And Tiger...

But I can't think of Tiger. Mae's half-sister. Wilder than my Mae apparently, who I named after the queen of naughtiness herself, Mae West.

But perhaps there will be a way they can be in each other's lives now.

I really hope so.

I've never had a sister of my own; Simone's the nearest I've come, the other two not all that far behind.

But Hannah could barely look at me as she left with Tom, Vicky and Dave. She's the one I still feel bad about. Vicky and

Dave won't make it, that's clear. Vicky needs to be true to herself now. But she'll be OK.

Sisters don't always like each other, I've come to understand; still, wouldn't it be true to say that usually they have each other's backs?

And that makes me think about poor old Coops, aka Gary Dixon, my erstwhile ex. Dead as a dodo, with a knife in his back, removed by police boat to some desolate mortuary, likely unmourned.

Wincing, I shift in my chair. I swig the mocktail, wishing it was bourbon. Even with a maraschino cherry, it's not cutting it.

Coops, the man who started it all; the man who became collateral damage. Daisy tried to get to me and mine, but she didn't mind who else she took down on the way.

Simone almost sussed me that day years ago when I left Royal Mews to marry him.

'Did you know him already?' she asked, narrowing her eyes, and I could reply honestly that no, I didn't. But I *had* seen that gold Amex card he'd waved at her that first evening in Dizzy's when he'd been so rude. It was chance: I'd only gone in for one drink after walking out from a job in yet another crappy 'gentlemen's club'.

Gentlemen my arse.

I had my eye on the main chance back then; I had to.

Robert Perry preyed on that.

I didn't have the secure family home Simone came from, or Vicky's money, or even Hannah's (mad) parents and their religious conviction.

I only had my wits and my face to rely on.

I finish my mocktail and light a cigarette. I try not to crave a real drink. When I get home, I need to go to a meeting; it's been a while, but in the end, attending AA saved me, along with my love for Mae.

The great sun has turned the ocean gold and bronze as it

sets above it, the sky flaming, alive with apricot and fizzy pink smears, and I wonder idly about poor old Gary, Coops that was. Did he ever get round to changing his will after we divorced? I chuck my cigarette away.

'Mae,' I call. 'Come on, baby. Let's get some dinner.'

If we're lucky... well. Perhaps we'll be quids in after all.

And after everything we've been through, wouldn't that be a turn-up for the books.

EPILOGUE

HANNAH

Life has been disappointing ultimately.

Funny how there isn't a word for breaking up with your best female friends. Funny how short forever can suddenly become.

Not funny how much it hurts when it ends in betrayal.

When the person you trusted most sells you down the river – for less than a song. When you realise you were expendable instead of loved.

I can't lie, not really, never been good at it. Life's not turned out at all the way I thought it might.

The way I prayed it would.

And Lord knows, I was good at praying: I'd been taught by the best. My mother had me incanting with my head bowed, my knees bare and freezing by the uncomfortable old bed, before I could so much as read.

After all the hard times with my parents, leaving home was the best thing I ever did, and my friends were the thing that really kept me sane: them and my art.

Meeting Nick at sixth-form college had helped me escape my dull and sober home, and when I lost him, it was Jodie, Vicky and Simone who kept me going.

So I trusted them. Implicitly at first.

But I was wrong to do that.

It certainly wasn't meant to turn out this way, but in the end, I suppose the whole stupid trip to Ibiza became a test of their loyalty.

I had never planned to avenge that dreadful time in my life, but when Tom started to contact me again last year, it sparked things off in me.

I thought he wanted to start afresh, and I felt such a burst of joy.

But it turned out he just wanted to make amends.

It didn't take much to set it up. They thought I didn't know back then in Royal Mews that they had done something to that man.

I knew the police had come, wondering what had happened to our landlord. I saw the article in the *Courier*. I saw their faces, Simone's pallor; I heard her crying in the night before I moved out.

And I heard Tom talking in his sleep that last time we spent the night together, after I came back from my parents.

It was a terrible mistake to go to bed with him again. I already loved him too much. I'd ignored Vicky's distress at my blossoming relationship with him; I'd followed my heart – and in the end, I guess I paid the price for love.

I had my principles, but it was more than that. Jodie had tarnished him for me, just like she took Nick too.

Although there are things people will never know about what happened on *The Daffodil* that night. Things that I'll take to the grave.

A year after I left Royal Mews, I went to find Tom again.

Life at home with my parents was so miserable. So bloody miserable in that stale and loveless confessional they inhabited.

I missed Tom so much; I wanted to see if we had a proper chance. I knew Vicky loved me – even before Jodie wrote about it for everyone to read – and I appreciated it. I know she still loves me today, but she was never the one for me. Vicky, the Queen of Spades in the card pack – 'a spade's a spade', she'd say, and tell it how it was. I was the soft one, the Queen of Hearts.

And look how that panned out for me.

No, the difficult thing was, I still loved Tom. I dreamt of him all the time, when I wasn't dreaming of fire, and so I went back.

I followed him on and off for a month, sitting in my dad's old Ford Fiesta, watching his movements, trying to pluck up the courage to approach him again.

I saw him meet Jodie; I followed them to that hotel.

I sat outside in the Fiesta for an hour or two, freezing because the heater was broken, and when they didn't come out again, I knew the worst. They must have been in bed the whole time I waited.

I knew then I couldn't do it. I couldn't be with Tom. It was too late.

I knew then he must have lied about not sleeping with her that first night too; the night of the party, when I went back home to look after my mother.

And things began to add up, and I thought I'd die from the pain.

Something ignited in me though, when Tom Facebooked me last year.

It confused me.

I wanted to know if my friends were for me or for themselves.

And then, out of the blue, Daisy contacted me. I was the first, and that was either her good or bad luck. That's for others to decide.

She knew we'd been her father's tenants: she'd gone through his old paperwork, our tenancy agreement that Jodie had signed on behalf of us all. She was on a mission to discover the truth about his death.

She wanted contact details for the others, though she'd already found Vicky by then, and her determination gave me an idea.

Robert Perry's death wasn't even a cold case: there was no proof of foul play, and it had been long forgotten by the police.

Via email, anonymously, as a 'friend', I persuaded Daisy to pose as a TV producer as a way in for her. It was easy. With Jodie's own fame on the decline, I knew my old friend would bite. I instigated the whole reunion idea, and Daisy acted it out for me, contacting Jodie, suggesting the invites to a belated birthday do as a cover for a way of bringing us back together.

Daisy never knew it was me; she didn't see my face when we discussed it.

Initially, I just wanted to find out if they would go to meet Jodie or be loyal to me.

How tragic.

At the same time, it wasn't hard to prove that Mae was Tom's, once I'd met her in that club she sang in; once I'd seen Tom again for a drink in town, after he started sending me all those messages saying sorry.

It was easy to get their DNA, and I had it tested.

It sealed their fate.

'Vengeance is mine; I will repay, saith the Lord' is a favourite Bible line of my mother's. So is 'Do that which is good, and no harm shall come to thee', but I didn't bother with that one. I'd followed it all my life, and look what happened.

I fed the idea of revenge to Daisy.

I didn't realise she'd get sexually involved with Vicky.

I didn't know she'd meet Gary that way too.

The morning we flew out to Ibiza, in a stroke of bizarre serendipity, that article came online about Mae and her silly boyfriend. I suggested Daisy print it and take it with her.

That was Gary's downfall in the end. He found the article in Daisy's bag, and it was curtains for him, it seemed.

I felt bad about that. Poor man.

Did I want anyone to die? Not really.

For me, it was all about the test.

I just wanted to know if my best friends would betray me.

Would they meet Jodie again, after we had sworn never to? Who was more important – me or her?

I would have done anything for them once.

I could never have known how mad Daisy was, or how it would play out.

But you know now, the little voice says. *Now you'll have to live with what she did.*

Yes, but! I shush the voice. Be quiet, I say.

And so, in the end, will they.

A LETTER FROM CLAIRE

Dear reader,

Firstly, a huge thank you for choosing *The Birthday Reunion*. If you enjoyed it and want to keep up to date with all my latest releases, just sign up at the following link. Your email address will never be shared and you can unsubscribe at any time.

www.bookouture.com/claire-seeber

I think – I certainly hope! – that most of us are lucky know what it's like to have good female friends. Like the four friends (or enemies?!) in *The Birthday Reunion*, I'm imagining most of us have had our share of friendship breakdowns. We might still be in touch with school or college mates, or for the slightly older amongst us (ahem, like me!), those we met in our first jobs, when still working the world out (I think I still am), deciding on career paths or whether to have families or to stay footloose and fancy-free. But, however we met, it's always sad to lose touch over the years, and always good to hear from old friends.

Writing *The Birthday Reunion* made me think that it's funny how there's no word for splitting up with our BFFs – but it causes lots of heartache, especially if we're 'dumped' by a friend and don't know why. Or if a friend is as much fun as Jodie in the book *can* be – but behaves badly, or is just plain unreliable.

I'm also a therapist, and I listened to some podcasts about

friends when writing. Often friendships seem to be ruined by how hard we find it to tell each other when one does something that upsets the other. It seems all too often we might just avoid our friend instead. And yet, if we did find the courage to bring tricky subjects up, of course it might cause some bumps in the road, but it might also actually save the relationship in the end.

At the end of the day, I don't know where I'd be without my good female friends.

On that note, I'm also sincerely hoping that none of them think they're the inspiration for this book: Simone, Hannah, Jodie and Vicky are all made up, I promise! Though to divulge a secret: when I was about 18 (so just the other day – ha ha!), my mate and I met a handsome young man in a nightclub who tried to guess our names. He said I looked American, which I'm not, and like a Jodie... So I've always thought that a Jodie might be my naughty alter-ego!

Anyway, as ever I'm genuinely delighted when someone gets in touch to say they've enjoyed a book of mine. Being a writer can be lonely, so it's great to hear from readers. If you feel like leaving a nice review on Amazon of *The Birthday Reunion*, thank you in advance. I really do try to write the absolutely best book I can.

Most of all, a massive thank you for choosing *The Birthday Reunion* out of all the other books out there vying for your attention. I'm sending you all the best energy and happy times with mates, unlike this catastrophic lot!

Love,

Claire

www.claireseeber.com

ACKNOWLEDGEMENTS

As usual, my first thanks go to all at Bookouture, in particular to my very dedicated editor and fellow-*Happy-Valley*-lover (bereft!) Laura Deacon; I've really appreciated the process, thank you! Thanks to Jane Selley's and Laura Kincaid's copy editing and proofreading eagle eyes; to Alexandra Holmes; to Jess Readett and the PR team; to Peta Nightingale; and to the whole gang behind the scenes who help send our books flying into the world with the best wills in the world. Thank you so much.

And to my first readers, my sister Tiggy Whitham for reading fast as I wrote, and for the feedback (especially about landlines!). As ever, to the hugely patient Nicola Smyth, also my very dear friend, and to Veronica Braviter-Roman for the Spanish.

As always, all the hard-working bloggers, reviewers and TikTokers using their own time to support our books are invaluable. Thanks too, to The Shut Up & Write Group, set up by the inimitable Katherine Black, which I was introduced to by my good friend Rachael Critchley. Sharing coffee and quiet writing time at the fantastic Halcyon book/coffee shop on Lee High Road has been fun! Thanks also to the crime writing crew, and to Tracy Buchanan and the Savvies, always on hand with advice or support.

This is a story about friendship and once again, and because of the Ibizan and party setting, it reminds me of old friends, lost but never forgotten: Louisa Haswell Coles and Liam Gilsenan, honorary female friend. The Lily Rider's for you, lovely Liam. Onwards, the Rave Slag gang.

Finally, big thanks to Verl, Fenn and Raffi (not forgetting Colin and Freddie, of course). As the saying goes, we can pick our friends, but not our family, so I'm ever so glad I've got you.